The First Mile

Over vale and heath the Stukas flew, over farmhouses and barns, over the banks of a brook where villagers with hunting rifles rushed out to loose wild shots into the sky. On the horizon the redbrick terraces of Leeds sprawled. There were no lights alive in the city tonight, but surely it still sat there, waiting for another storm. Down there, the railways ran, the clock towers chimed, old men ran drills as if they were still soldiers at war. Down there, the munitions factories hummed, the mills turned – and, in the shadows of a looming viaduct, Captain Abraham Matthews warmed his hands in the crooks of his arms and chewed the dog-end of a rolled cigarette.

He had been waiting an interminable time, but tonight the wait was almost at an end. A fire truck rolled along the empty thoroughfare of Kirkstall Road and, when it passed, he saw a figure appear in the window of one of the houses behind. Lean and angular, the thief pushed open the blackout blinds and clambered out. Poised on the ledge like some runaway from a circus, he took his time to breathe in the night – and then shimmied down a drainpipe to disappear into the terrace.

Abraham drew his collar high and followed.

The boy was fleet of foot, loping over the carriageway to cross the yards of a workingman's club silent since the outbreak of war. At the yard's head he entered an alley where wild brambles had risen through wire mesh to make malicious walls of thorn. Abraham trailed him at a distance, making certain that the shadow did not snake out of sight.

THREE MILES

Robert Dinsdale

faber and faber

First published in 2011
by Faber and Faber Ltd
Bloomsbury House
74–77 Great Russell Street
London WC1B 3DA
This paperback edition published in 2012

Typeset by RefineCatch Limited, Bungay, Suffolk
Printed in England by CPI Group (UK) Ltd, Croydon CR0 4YY

The right of Robert Dinsdale to be identified as author of this work
has been asserted in accordance with Section 77 of the Copyright,
Designs and Patents Act 1988

A CIP record for this book
is available from the British Library

ISBN 978–0–571–26026–3

2 4 6 8 10 9 7 5 3 1

They emerged, one after another, into timber yards where logs were roped and piled high. A rusted truck sat in tall grasses at the gates, and the boy slipped behind to squeeze through railings to the road below.

Before he too had scrambled through the opening, Abraham heard the sirens starting to sound.

At first, the song came from somewhere behind, wardens on the other side of the viaduct rushing to crank up their contraption. Then, one after another, the alarm began to sing in ports across the city, spreading from station to station like wolves sending up a howl. Abraham paused, searching the skies – but there was only starlight above. The Stukas were not here yet, and he pushed through the railings; if all that remained of his life was to be wrought tonight, he did not mean to get distracted.

The boy turned into the eastern terraces, following roads that Abraham knew well. Hundreds of families had already fled to the hills, like men banished by their king, but the few that remained emerged from their houses as he passed, hurrying to reach their shelters. A mother with a baby in her arms scurried past, a teddy bear dropping to the ground as she ran. Abraham stooped to toss it back to her, and cut between houses to head off the boy.

Somewhere, in the distance: dull thunder. The planes were already here.

A deep rumble moved in the earth, rooting Abraham to the ground. Over his shoulder, he saw a spire of dark smoke spiralling upwards. Fire lapped along the alleyways between buildings.

From a garden, a young woman appeared, two bawling children scrabbling in tow.

'Captain!' she cried. 'You can't go that way. They hit the infirmary!'

'I have to,' he said, shouldering past. 'Just get those children to a damn shelter!'

Further on, up the road, the boy was slowing under his burden. Abraham began to run. A tan alley-cat streaked out of the rubbish bins, mewling as it shot between his legs. The boy looked back – but if he had seen the night-watchman nearing, he did not betray a thing. Abraham was almost upon him when he turned and scrabbled over a wall.

'I'm getting too old for this,' Abraham murmured, and heaved himself up.

He landed in the rubble of a bricklayer's yard and flailed his way to the street. Along the redbrick row, the boy was climbing toward Woodhouse Moor. The myriad townships of Leeds had once huddled sullenly in the shadow of that heath – but, since the days of Abraham's youth, they had sprawled together, encroaching upon the slopes. No doubt there were thickets over the Moor where the boy might lose him. Fountains of fire broke over the roofs through which he had come, and he forced himself to rush on.

There were men drinking their way into sweet oblivion in the Royal Park. It was one way to see out the night, thought Abraham as he came to the taproom doors. Up ahead, the surging trees of Woodhouse Moor were lit in the reds and yellows of fires burning in the terraces beyond. Abraham hurried to the peak of the road and saw the boy, laden with his bulging knapsack, skirting the edge of a stagnant pond. The yards across the city were littered with Anderson shelters – but on the fringes of the Moor, deep brick sanctuaries had arisen. The boy stopped before the first of them, lifting his head as if to sniff the air.

Too late, Abraham heard the familiar thunder. The rooftops quaked and, somewhere back along the terrace, a column of fire roared upwards. Smoke and dust rampaged in great waves up hill, swallowing the houses and taproom and lanes along which Abraham had tracked the boy.

The Stuka tore above them, climbing steeply into the darknesses over the Moor.

In the shadow of the trees, the boy shouldered his bag, and dove toward the shelters. As he ran he lost his footing, righting himself against one of the towering oaks. Then, with a final glance back, he disappeared into an open door.

Abraham felt the smoke flurrying at his back, but allowed himself a momentary respite. After long months of plotting, Albie Crowe was his.

When he was certain that the Stukas had flown over, he strode across the road and descended to the dell where the shelter sat. Rapping squarely on the wood, he waited for the speak-hole to slide open.

'Night watch,' he uttered when a face appeared.

The door drew back, and Abraham ducked within.

It was the smallest of the shelters, set half into the ground and with a thick pitched roof above. In alcoves, families from the terraces were gathered. As his eyes grew accustomed to the light, Abraham peered into each in turn. In the first, a mother sang lullabies to her baby; in the second, two brothers hunkered over a game of chess; in the third, an old warrior kneaded his hands in silent entreaty.

In the final nook, the boy reclined against the bare brick wall, his plunder spilling out of the knapsack at his feet.

'Captain Matthews,' the boy began, mock-doffing his cap.

'Sit down, Albie. There's nowhere else to run.'

Albie Crowe did as he was bid, but Abraham did not for a second believe that the boy had learnt obedience. Theirs had been a long, though largely distant association, and Abraham knew, at least, that the boy was not taken yet.

'Am I to understand that this is an arrest, Captain?' Albie grinned.

'Albie,' Abraham began, returning and raising the smile, 'you can't sing your way out of this one. I've been meaning to catch up with you for a very long time.'

There were a hundred charges that could have been levelled at Albie Crowe and his gang; Abraham had spent months painstakingly recording each crime, piecing together scraps of evidence, conversations overheard and secrets spilled by boys on the street. Variously, they had called themselves the Knives, the Desperate Ones, the Fences. The name by which they were now known had risen among the younger boys of the terraces, those not old enough to know any better who had found, in Albie Crowe and his cohorts, an adventure thrilling in their own streets. The Young Bloods, the gang had been dubbed – and the name had stuck.

Before the deluge began, they had been petty thieves, the scourge of shopkeepers and brewers – but little else. Once the bombs had started falling, however, the world changed. There were new bounties for thieves, in those first days – and Albie, the shrewdest boy never to have attended school, had seen himself dealt a five-ace hand. From that point on it had been a short ride from petty thief to professional fence. Families along the length and breadth of Leeds had suffered from the nocturnal forays of the Young Bloods; the tendrils of their enterprise reached as far as Manchester and Sale.

'Let's not pretend you're here because of a little plunder. You and I, we've come past all that.' Albie paused. 'How is your wife, Captain Matthews?'

Abraham shifted back along the shelter to squint out of the speak-hole.

'You can't bait me like that, Albie. Ada is gone. I won't deny it.'

'Somewhere in the country, no doubt. She ran from the bombs, I presume?'

Abraham dared a smile. No, the boy could not bait him in this way either.

'She didn't run from the bombs, Albie. My wife ran away from me, couldn't stand the sight of me any more – and all because of you. I got home one night and there was nothing there, just a picture of my daughter ripped from its frame. Remember her, Albie?'

'I remember well enough.'

'Ada said she saw you the day we put her in the ground. Hovering on the edge of the churchyard, dressed up in your Sunday best.'

At first, Albie did not respond. Then, slowly – as if having rehearsed each word – he spoke. 'Your dear wife must have been mistaken. I'm not a man who cares for dressing up.'

'We came back from the churchyard. Sandwiches with their crusts cut off and cold sausages on a plate. And the people of the terrace milled around our home – and Ada spoke to every last one of them, but she couldn't speak to me. And I knew, Albie, why she hated me so. Because I could have stopped you, couldn't I? I thought I could be a decent man, I kept turning my cheek – but I could have put you away long before Elsa was dead.'

'I didn't kill your daughter, Captain.'

There was silence in the alcoves now, a dozen different ears listening to the story. Though the sirens droned outside, they were not loud enough to drown out Abraham's fable.

'Everyone has to sign their ledgerbook in the end, Albie, account for the things that they've done. You and me, we'll both scrawl our name on that line. You'll answer for everything before this night is through – for fucking with my city, for fucking with my daughter. And then – well, perhaps I'll answer for my own crimes as well, for ever letting my Elsa walk with you.' He paused. 'But before my wife can speak to me again, I'm going to unpick this little mystery of yours.'

Fists rapped at the wooden door. As men shifted to peer around, the light of lanterns spilled serrated shadows onto the wall. The figure closest to the speak-hole slid back the shutter and peered out. Somewhere, reds and yellows blossomed from one of the factories, a cascade of fire pouring over some part of the city. There were whispered words, a cry for common sense, and then three boys – fourteen or fifteen years old – were admitted to the shelter.

'What's happening out there?' asked one of the women in the shadows.

The boys huddled under the collective glare of the shelter. Abraham had seen the lead boy before, a gangly youth who, at the age of fourteen, had tried to sign up and fight. His dark hair was slicked back, and he wore a ribbon of tiny birthmarks at his collar.

'What do you reckon?' the boy began. 'There's blazes running up the hill at Clarendon Road. Bastards hit the infirmary. And there's men coming up the Kirkstall Road like torched ants, carrying all their packs on their backs.'

'A night to be treasured.'

The boy's eyes widened when they saw Albie step into the halo of light. Abraham had witnessed the drama before, like a stone skimmed across a pond and setting the water to ripples. He did not claim to understand it, though he had made a study of it and documented its effects. Just as some people were able to raise the hackles of another, some could inspire a strange kind of awe in even the pettiest of acts.

'Albie Crowe!' one of the boys declared, as if receiving into his arms some relative long thought buried in the ruin.

'Boys,' Albie grinned. 'I trust you've been keeping well?'

Abraham watched their eyes track from Albie, to the alcoves, to Abraham himself. As if they didn't already know who he was, his overcoat screamed out his profession; he wore the garb of the Leeds City Night Watch.

'It's true, then, Albie?'

Albie arched an eyebrow, as if to invite further news.

'There's word in the taprooms that that ol' bastard caught up with you, at last. What's it to be?'

Abraham might have considered them a threat, had he not seen the nervous glances of the other men gathered in the shelter. For the first time, he was glad he was not alone.

'Who knows?' Albie ventured.

'It was Shepherd that saw. He was headed here himself when he watched that old fox follow you in. After that, he couldn't come near, not even with the roads on fire.' The boy stopped, peered into the gloom to see if Albie was welcoming the news. 'He sent feelers out. The rest of the gang were drinking in the Packhorse taproom, just before the bombs dropped. Then, there they were, just drinking on the pavement outside, watching the fire, deciding what ought to be done . . .'

'Did you hear that, Abraham?' Albie crowed, crossing his legs at the ankles as he rested his back against the wall. 'My brave Young Bloods – they're coming to get me.'

For the first time, Abraham turned his back against Albie. He saw the jagged shadows cast upon the brick before him, picked out the angular form that was Albie, shifted himself so that his shadow dominated the boy's. There were a dozen and more regulars in Albie's gang and many more who had adopted the name – boys who had grown up dreaming of cutthroats and brigands, instead of soldiers and knights. If the Night Watch were assembled, perhaps there would be a skirmish, perhaps half a dozen boys would be cuffed and tried and convicted, enough to bring down the Young Bloods and reclaim the streets. But, tonight, Abraham stood alone – as, long ago, he had ordained.

The long years of his life had been leading to this night; of that, Abraham was certain. He heard the muffled song of the sirens, the roar of an engine as some gang of volunteers rushed out to staunch the blaze of a distant building. The city, then, hunched under the worst barrage in these long months of assault – and, yet, Abraham did not mean to sit here until Albie's cohorts came to spirit him away. Only three miles away, at the city end of Meanwood Road, there stood a station of the constabulary: a sprawling building that, in times past, had housed city archives and courts of law. It would be a strange night – but Abraham had prepared for nothing less.

From his belt he unhooked his handcuffs.

'You worn these before?'

'Manacles . . .' Albie mouthed.

'Consider them bracelets, son.'

Albie submitted to his chains, and Abraham locked the other around his own wrist.

'It doesn't have to be difficult,' Abraham began, a warning trembling on his tongue.

'They're dropping bombs out there.'

'If they fall on us, we won't feel a thing.'

He moved to the speak-hole and drew back the shutter. Perhaps, he began to believe, a bomb would make things easier. One bomb spiralling out of the sky, and the night would be finished, the story spun at last. And yet, that kind of a punishment was not fit for Albie Crowe: one night on the rack and that boy would be back on his feet by breakfast the following day. Abraham Matthews had taken an oath that he would see this through to its end. That oath was all that he had to cling to now: his daughter, cold in the ground; his darling wife Ada, gone to the hills. Tonight the streets were his alone.

Abraham pushed open the door, peered tentatively out to see the roiling sky. In the city tonight, the prophets were risen and drunk as hell. They flung back their heads and moaned wild, lupine howls. They danced without clothes in the rubble and spires of flame.

'Albie,' Captain Abraham Matthews began. 'We picked one hell of a night for this.'

The darkness of the scrub welcomed them; there were no gaslights here to draw in the Stukas wheeling above, no need for blackout curtains to mask the townsfolk cowering within. Through the trees, men were following a trail to the highest pastures, where it was said stargazers gathered to watch the trailing comets of dogfights above – but Abraham steered Albie Crowe along one of the lesser trails, silent until the men had passed on. The boy did not strain at his side but hobbled on instead, barely breathing a word in protest.

They ploughed into impenetrable night, but Abraham was a watchman of many years' standing, and like all good men who pounded the beat, his feet knew the way. The soles of his boots were thin from endless months marching, and he could sense the changing textures of the ground beneath him. A good watchman knew it all: cobbles and paving and grass and bare earth. The trail that they followed was banked with ashes and oaks, and the track beneath their feet was trampled by centuries of wanderers.

'Captain,' the boy in chains began. 'I'll call you Captain, if I may?'

'You've always called me Abraham before. You don't need to dignify me tonight.'

'Do you want to talk about her, Captain?'

'Elsa?' Abraham replied.

'There are things I could tell you. What she was really like. A parent doesn't often know their child.'

Albie Crowe had decided, at a young age, that he would rather be winsome than handsome: beauty, he was certain, was something that came from the beholder, an attitude or a pose over which he had no bearing; charm, he could control. People responded to Albie Crowe. A flashed smile or an arched eyebrow – these were the tools of Albie's trade.

'You think you know a lot about me, don't you, Captain?'

Abraham had ledgerbooks filled with the story. Albie Crowe was nineteen years old, born on an April day in the spring of '21. His mother was a waif, his father some travelling salesman whose roaming had brought him to the Kirkstall streets when he came back from shirking his duties in France. There were others in the family, a shapeless brood as had once been seen up and down these terraces, but they were only step- and half-siblings to Albie; family history told that his mother had thought nothing of the past nor the future, living only for the day.

'I know you were afraid of the dark when you were twelve years old,' Abraham countered. 'I know your mother had a man who liked to taunt you with snuffed candles.'

Abraham had learnt a hundred other things about Albie Crowe since the day his daughter died. When the boy had been eight years old, he had developed persistent stomach cramps that plagued him night after night. At first, he had prayed each time the cramps came, sitting in a backyard waterhouse with his head craned to the sky; only when he had learnt to direct those prayers to the caverns below had the cramps subsided. It was a lesson the boy had once been fond of quoting.

Abraham might have said more, then, but sudden voices in the darkness quelled him. They climbed, together, to a ridge between the trees, and found themselves on one of the highest trails, an old drover's road that cut from one side of the Moor to the other. Along each side of the trail, between oaks that had seen the rise and fall of countless other wars, great steel cables were tethered to the ground. High above, the vast barrage balloons floated. Abraham drew Albie into the shadow of the first, heard the creaking of the cable as the balloon shifted overhead.

Along the trail, men were working at one of the tethers, roaring as they strained to anchor it down. Abraham scurried across the path, keeping Albie Crowe in his shadow, and descended to the other side, so that he might follow the road on its lowest bank. Past one of the great cables they came; then, fifty yards further on, past another. On the other side of the trail, the men reared back from the concrete anchor and lifted torches to check their work.

The barrage balloons had been flying since the onset of summer, before the first of the bombs set the city aflame. They marked routes across the city's skyscape now, aerial pathways along every major thoroughfare and railway, forcing the German boys to fly so high that they might not hit their targets crouching below. The men who worked them were those rescued from service across the water, too old or invalided to wield a gun – but not yet so spent that they would sit back and let the barbarians march in. One of them lifted his torch, to a chorus of warnings from his companions. When the beam swept across the trail, it chanced across Abraham's face as he pushed through the scrub.

'Who's down there?' one of the men bellowed.

Abraham wrapped a hand around Albie's mouth. 'Don't breathe a word,' he whispered.

'These are your men, not mine,' Albie retorted, twisting each word into a mock smile.

'Men you've plundered,' Abraham warned. He turned, and Albie could see the peaks of his features emerge from the shroud of night: his large Roman nose, the ridges of his brow. 'I swore to take you to the end of Meanwood Road,' he said, 'not throw you to the wolves.'

They pushed along the trail but, before they had reached the next of the groaning cables, Abraham could hear footsteps pounding on the drover's road above, men with picks and tools slung over their backs. Reaching the shelter of the great concrete mound into which the cable was set, Abraham sunk to his knees and waited for the footsteps to pass. A winch contraption dug into his back, gears grinding as the cable swayed.

'No doubt they'll think you're a saboteur, Captain, parachuted in to play with their balloons.'

Abraham looked up. The great balloon could barely be seen against the blackness of night. Then, suddenly, a fountain of fire rose from some corner of the heath – and, for an instant, the balloon was illuminated, stark black against oranges and reds. Beneath it, there hung the small gondola into which the steel cable fed.

'Who is it?' somebody thundered.

'It'll be one of those boys . . .'

'What do they call them?'

'Young Bloods,' a third voice interjected. 'My brother's boy runs with them. Thinks he's a Roundhead, going to change the world . . .'

'He's old enough to fight, isn't he? Your brother's boy?'

'Six months,' the first workman replied, 'and we'll be shot of him. The infantry'll knock some sense into him. Whoever heard of petty thieves thinking they were heroes?'

Abraham pushed down the bank, Albie Crowe in tow. Plunging into scrub that reached his waist, he heard the workmen scrabbling behind. A cry went up, one of the men slipping – and suddenly the cable started to creak. Abraham looked back, saw one of the workmen scrambling back to his feet with his hands clasped around the winch. The other men – mere sketches in the darkness – hurried to right the cable before the balloon strayed out of its path.

'You'd better start running,' said Abraham.

'It wouldn't be the first time I've run away from those men,' Albie Crowe returned. 'The question is – can you keep up?'

They bolted into the darkness, leaving every trail behind. Though it was awkward at first, soon they found a rhythm, running three-legged as if they were schoolboys engaged in a race. Stuttering down an escarpment where reeds gave way to shale, they came to one of the Moor's lowest tracks. The trees that banked the path were sprawling hawthorns and, in their shadows, workmen's huts cowered, their windows taped and blacked out like in every terrace across the city.

Abraham stalled. He could hear no other footsteps flailing through the scrub, but that did not mean the workmen had given up; the song of the sirens still drowned out all other sound. He squinted into the sky that he might get his bearings, and then hauled Albie Crowe around. They had come further over the Moor than he intended, but he did not mean to let that stop him.

They made haste along the trail. On one shoulder, the highest rises of the heath; on the other, the low pastures and the stretches of the city beyond. Through the trees, fire dotted the horizon, the infirmary and college buildings ablaze.

At a conflux of trails, where the heather had been burned back, there sat the anchor of some barrage balloon long since abandoned – a boulder of concrete with the stub of a cable still jutting out. In its shelter, heaped with cardboard and blankets, lay a man, a pint of whisky in a bottle at his side. As they skirted past, he turned, grumbling in his stupor.

'Albie!' the vagabond bawled. 'Albie!' he yelled, scrambling from his sacks to lurch along the trail.

Abraham heaved Albie forward – but, for the first time, the boy was resisting.

'Throw him some pennies, Captain,' Albie crowed. 'These aren't good times to be sleeping under the stars.'

Abraham heaved, but the boy was dead weight. Already, he could hear the slap of the vagabond's feet on the earth, his breathless cries as he tried to catch up.

'One of your associates?' Abraham began.

'Why not? It's never mattered to me where a man comes from, who his family are, where he sleeps at night,' Albie responded. 'That's what the Young Bloods are, Captain. That's what they stand for.'

Abraham knew well the sort of boy who had flocked to run with Albie Crowe's gang. Some had been strays, boys without families, or whose brothers had gone to fight over the water and never returned. Others were those whose fathers were crippled in the campaigns of the last war, half-men who filled their days in factories and promised nothing better for their sons. The only boy who had come to loot houses with the Young Bloods and been turned away had committed no other sin than being a cousin of Albie Crowe himself; the Young Bloods were a new beginning, for anyone who cared to sign up.

The vagabond scampering to catch up was certainly not one of those boys who saw such romance in petty theft – but perhaps he was one of those others, drifters who traded gossip with the Young Bloods. Albie Crowe called them his Whisperers. There had been little room for them in the long pages of Abraham's ledgers, but they were as much a part of Albie Crowe's story as the boys in the Bloods.

There were craters in the earth on the low escarpments, carved by bombs that had not found their targets. On one stretch, a grey hulk still sat, cordoned off by twine wrapped around branches and hammered into the ground. Abraham paused on the cusp of another, reining Albie to a halt. Trinket hunters had spirited the mangled wreckage of the bomb's casing away, but in the crater scraps still remained.

He turned. The vagabond, arms outstretched, loomed in the darkness.

Suddenly, the air snarled. It was as if the sky itself was being sundered, some ancient magic finding its way, at last, back into the world. Abraham froze, his feet rooted to the earth. Above, one of the Stukas tore a hole in the night, banking sharply to the right. From somewhere beyond the Moor, a bright searchlight arced up, tracking the plane as it disappeared over the city's heart.

Abraham turned. The vagabond, almost on top of them, was nowhere to be seen, spooked by the Stuka and sent sprawling into the scrub. The German boys, it seemed, were good for something.

'Captain,' Albie began, 'you don't know what you're doing. You've never walked the streets in it. Don't you understand what's going to happen if we just plough on?'

Abraham steeled himself, pulling Albie to the cusp of the crater.

'Don't fight me, Albie,' he began, rising from his reverie at last. 'The more you resist, the longer this will take. I don't want to be out here any more than you.'

'You're the same as the rest,' Albie answered. 'But I've walked in it, Abraham. I've walked it every night since it began. It doesn't touch me. I don't let it! But chain me to you? Chain me to you and it'll rain on me as well! Damn it, Abraham, hasn't this bombardment taught you a thing?' He stopped. 'It's the patterns they fly, you stupid old fool. Patterns of eight, round and around! They'll fly back this way!'

Abraham descended into the crater and clambered to the other side. Through oaks stripped of their boughs, the furthest climes of the city rose, Meanwood sitting on the northern hillsides with Sheepscar glowering in the east. And there, over the thoroughfare, it lay: the fiery hell through which they would walk.

'Three miles, Albie,' he began. 'We can do it the easy way, or we can do it the hard way. Work together and live – or fight and die. It's all the same to me.'

'You still have a wife, Captain . . .'

'Not if I don't get you to Meanwood Road.'

They dropped from the Moor. In the middle of the thoroughfare, Abraham cast glances back and forth, saw a motor car lying on its end against an outcrop of trees – and, beyond that, a trap whose horse strained at the ropes binding it to its carriage. In one direction lay the heart of the city: empty now, but for the families hiding far underground. In the other, lay Otley and Poole and the other outlying towns to which the people of Leeds had fled. There were more fleeing every day. If he made it through the night, perhaps he would join them. Ada would be waiting, happy that the score was settled at last – and life could begin, all over again.

They passed the first line of houses, and then the Moor was all but gone, only the dark shape of the mount sitting on their shoulder to remind them from where they had come. A charred sign hung above the street, creaking in an acrid wind. In faded black letters the words 'Meanwood Road' could vaguely be read. Further down the vale, planes wheeled and danced.

'How well do you know these streets, Albie?'

'One street is much the same as the next,' the boy answered. 'More often than not, it's the people you have to look out for.'

They came a little further, and now the sky was alive with sound. It was not only the clouds that shifted up there; the sky seemed suddenly to be made of vast plates, each grinding against the next. There was a shriek on their shoulder, and another plane ripped over, appearing from the skies over the Moor.

'Abraham?' Albie hissed.

'What?'

17

'Abraham! Why do you care what's happening down the vale?' He sung the next words, some twisted melody dredged from the earliest days of his childhood. 'They're behind us, Captain ...'

Abraham craned back. Over the Moor, great searchlights arced from three corners of the city. When they converged, the light exploded – and into the conflagration soared one of the Stukas. For an instant it seemed trapped by the light, an insect frozen in amber. Then, as it thundered on, the searchlights followed. As it tore over Abraham's head, the rooftops shuddered, slates and shingles clattering into the alleys. Further down the terraces, new searchlights swung to follow the plane, passing it on to a third station on the other side of the city.

Forcing his way ahead, Albie pulled at the handcuffs – but Abraham was a pillar of stone.

'Stupid old man!' Albie roared. 'You'll get us both killed ...'

It was Albie that led Abraham then, each man straining at the ties that bound him to the other. Into the shadows of abandoned houses they thundered. In the snicket between two buildings, a stray dog scrabbled out of its hiding, beseeching Abraham to come to its aid. There were other planes screaming past now, fighters banking sharply left and right on the tail of the Stukas.

From high above: the sound of toppling bricks. Abraham squinted skywards, saw chimney stacks crumbling. Instinctively, he cowered. At his side, Albie tried to run.

Something shifted deep in the heart of the street. There was a lull – and then, on the other side of the houses, the noise rose high into the air. They could see nothing in the alley where they were hidden, but still the explosion moved in them. Bricks screamed at mortar. Mortar screamed at slate.

'There's a shelter,' Albie hissed. 'An Anderson shelter at the bottom of the Woodhouse lanes. We could make it there, Abraham. If we're clever, we could do it ...'

Abraham pushed down the snicket, emerging into some parallel road, seemingly untouched by any bomb. For a second, he felt like some long-lost wanderer stumbling upon an oasis in the desert.

'It's abandoned, Captain. There hasn't been a family in that stretch of the terrace since the spring. They all took to the hills. We can get there, sit it out – and then, come the morning, well, you can have your little crusade then, put me in a cell and be damned . . .'

Abraham was not to be swayed. 'I'd walk into that shelter to find a dozen of your boys sitting there with plunder,' he said. 'Shepherd and the Brownings and Drew and the rest – all those sorry bastards who'd squabble to be the first to kiss your feet. I won't be ambushed, son.'

'You'd rather get killed.'

'You've lied to me before,' Abraham said. 'Remember?'

They followed the road, listening to fires on the other side of the terrace. Over the rooftops, the searchlights came together again, picking out a plane as it rose sharply, another on its tail. When the planes had climbed out of sight, the searchlights swung back, illuminating the Spitfires scrambling to the defence of the city's centre.

'When I was a boy,' Abraham began, 'and there were thunderstorms, I used to get together with my brothers, put on our boots and rush into the street. Not even our old mother could stop us, shrieking from the doorstep as we splashed and kicked in those puddles.'

'Happy memories, Captain,' Albie sighed, craning at the sky. 'What's your point?'

'No point, Albie. I just enjoy singing in the rain.'

From somewhere on the other side of the townships, there came the stutter of anti-aircraft fire. Abraham had visited the installations once, before his daughter was dead, before his head was filled with Albie Crowe and Young Bloods and nothing else. The great towers were gathered in three ports of the city – in the east, from where the Germans flew; the south, where the factories cowered; and the west, into which the planes disappeared. Tall pillars of iron and concrete, with turrets where the great barrels could revolve and flay the sky, they were surrounded by Anderson shelters and banks of razor wire. No doubt the boys out there were scrambling now, slinging their own shells along the lines of the searchlights.

The turrets sputtered out fire, tonight. Abraham stopped, cocking his head that he might judge in which direction the guns were blazing.

'It's the St James blockhouse, Abraham,' Albie said, keeping his head low against the terrace.

'How do you know?'

'It's the sounds they make, you old fool. There's a lag between each round. There must be battle on the south of the city.'

Begrudgingly, Abraham nodded. It was just like Albie Crowe to know the intimate details of such matters. A boy did not lead his acolytes out to loot and pillage during the storm without knowing which way the wind was blowing.

'They'll stay south?'

'They'll fly patterns over the city,' Albie replied. 'If they're being harried they'll cut trails west. They never fly out the way they flew in. But there'll be another wave, Captain. It isn't midnight yet.'

They rounded a crescent that swung back toward the broad thoroughfare of Meanwood Road. In a great cleft in the earth one of the village buses had been upended, as if some great demonic hand had clawed up to drag it into the caverns below. Beyond the crater, a figure emerged from one of the buildings and, a knapsack over his shoulder, struck out along the ravaged road. Albie started as if to cry out, but Abraham hauled him into the shadow of the bus and waited for the figure to pass. Above their heads, the front wheels spun slowly in the wind.

'Your boys are running raids tonight . . .'

'I didn't know it,' said Albie. 'There are more boys than I care to mention now, Abraham. It isn't like it was, when your daughter used to keep house for us. I can't keep my eye on every last Young Blood.'

'There'll be more, between us and the end of the road?'

For the first time since the last planes roared over, Albie Crowe smiled. 'They'll be on our tail as well, Captain. As soon as word gets back to the taproom, they'll be smoking out to find us . . .'

They were caught beneath the creaking bus when the searchlights went up again, vast conical beams scouring the sky over the Moor, bursting over the rooftops like geysers of oil. Over the slates on the other side of the thoroughfare, a great cloud of grey drifted. It took Abraham a moment to understand that it was one of the barrage balloons, torn from its mooring. Still trailing its cable, it turned slowly in the wind, dropping out of view in a surge of smoke, before riding over the southernmost stacks.

A plane appeared, whipped along Meanwood Road by the searchlights, and picked up by a convergence of beams somewhere far along the road. From this distance, it seemed strangled there, arrested in the light. It was only when the next plane roared on its tail that Abraham understood it was being harried. Two shapes appeared on either flank, climbing sharply. Stuttering fire broke the night and the first plane rolled.

A dark shape fell from the rising craft – but, with smoke curling from its undercarriage, it did not stop climbing. As the fighters banked on either side, giving chase, a column of grey rose from the ground beneath.

Suddenly, the searchlights swung away. Abraham turned to Albie Crowe.

'You've seen it before?' he asked.

'It wasn't an incendiary,' Albie replied. 'You'd know if it had been a bomb.'

'If not a bomb, what else?'

Albie Crowe sighed gravely. If the Captain really knew so little about the night, he ought to have been at home, wrapped up in his bedclothes and waiting for dawn.

'We'll find out soon enough,' he said. 'We're heading straight for it.'

For a second: silence. The world seemed to slow. Abraham emerged from the shelter of the upturned bus, peering up and down the street. Even the sirens seemed softer, now. No doubt one of the stations had been carved apart by the bombs.

'You see the shop-front?' Abraham began. Across the thoroughfare, a hundred yards on, a grocer's had been boarded up – but the doorway, set back from the road, was still shelter of a sort. 'On my count, we run . . .'

'What if I don't care for running, Captain?'

'Then we both end up smeared across the ruin.'

Abraham dragged Albie from their shelter and bolted into the middle of the street. Seconds later, a roar went up somewhere through the houses, and instinctively he froze. When, at last, he came to, it was Albie who was wrenching at the handcuffs. Together, they loped to the furthest side of the street and scuttled along the pavement, pressed close to every boarded house and shop-front they passed.

When they fell into the alcove, Abraham saw that the door hung limply from its hinges. Cautiously, he pushed through, sending Albie over the threshold first. Bombs had carved away the back half of the terrace and, through a portal of crumbled bricks, he could see the parallel road. Empty shelves sat disrupted, the till on the counter upended and empty.

The shop must have been abandoned days or weeks ago, for already it had been pillaged. No doubt it was the work of the Young Bloods. As they pushed on, Abraham felt wind whipping through the hallways and knew, then, that he would find no indignant inhabitants lying in wait. He kicked at a storeroom door and, making certain that nobody lurked beyond, sent Albie sprawling into the rubble. They were exposed to the fiery vaults here, half of the wall toppled by a gas lamp uprooted and sent skittering over the street, but that did not matter to Abraham; it meant only that he would not be cornered if the Young Bloods moved in. Peering out, he saw the loose barrage balloon still moving slowly over the terrace, kicking up clods of stone and earth where its cable trailed.

He turned. Albie Crowe looked small to him, tonight.

'You say there'll be a lull', he began, 'between the first and second waves?'

Albie strangled his first response, unwilling to share his secrets with the Captain. Then, picking out the song of the sirens, he began, 'If I'm right about which blockhouse it is, they're shepherding the fighting further south. But they'll wheel back this way, Captain – *our* boys won't pin them down for long.' Albie paused. Surely the Captain was beginning to see sense. 'How far have we even come, Abraham?'

'One mile down,' Abraham replied.

'And you really think you can walk into it – for another two miles?'

'Look, son,' said Abraham, softening at last. 'I know how it goes. I was a coward once, too. But, when I was your age, we used to brave worse storms than this to cross a lousy fifty yards of ground. We'll get to the end of Meanwood Road. You don't have to worry about that.'

They slumped together, onto piles of bricks. In the roads outside, a sudden engine reared and then disappeared again – fire trucks moving through the terrace to stem the tide.

'Tell me,' Albie ventured, 'what do you think she's doing now? Your wife, up there in the hills. Is she really praying that you catch up with me?' Abraham hauled at the chains that tied them, and his captive lurched forward. 'Or is she wishing you were there with her, hunkered down where the bombs can't touch you, holding each other now like you used to back then? You've never been a hero for her. You've never had it in you. Ever since the first night you met. I know how the story goes.'

All men had stories, Abraham knew; the trajectory of a life was simply a man's slow discovery of how his own story went. If Albie had not come to the realisation yet, he would reach it before the night was through.

'You want to know the difference between you and me, son?' he asked.

'I've been waiting for an explanation all night!' Albie declared.

Abraham pitched forward, a thin smile creeping onto his face. 'We both know how this story began,' he grinned. 'But there's only one of us knows how this night's going to end.'

* * *

It had been 1921 before Abraham returned from his years of war. It was true that he had been discharged from his battalion – an invalid, or so a kind nurse proclaimed – in the first months of 1919, but it was a long road home, and Abraham did not have a family to go back to; there had been brothers once, but they had been felled in the deeps of Flanders – and though his mother grieved on their account, she too had succumbed before the final days of the fighting. Abraham, then, had not joined the columns of men tramping back to their home towns to see what had become of them. He had turned his shoulder on his fellows instead, taken up a knapsack and laid down his gun, and roamed.

There were stories he would tell, in later years, about his roaming; there were other tales over which his lips would be forever sealed, as if there was embarrassment in the anonymous acts of kindness he had performed while struggling to shake off the memories of what he had seen and done at war. But, all along, Abraham had resolved that life would begin again on the day he set foot back upon English soil. For a week he stayed in a Southwark boarding house, reacquainting himself with tea and toast and slate-grey skies; on the seventh day, he travelled north.

On his first night in the old town, he sat in a taproom by the canal, drinking an ale he did not recollect, searching for faces he recognised in the shifting throng. He had nowhere to go, no old house to go back to, and though he saw faces that cried out to him, they were not really people that he could claim to know. So he drank alone, slowly and deliberately bewitching himself, allowing himself to believe that this warm giddiness was the real feeling of coming home.

When the time came for the shutters to be drawn and the all-nighters to be locked in, Abraham rose from his stool at the bar and, reeling now, lifted his collar to go back into the night. There were men here with whom he had shared brief conversations. They goaded him to stay as he teetered toward the doors, but he rebuffed their good-natured demands with promises and lies. Outside, it was cold; a chart of January stars was plastered across the skies, and frost was already forming in the grass that banked the canal.

There were few people moving in the streets as he came along, but occasional drifters shuffled on, collars high and hoods drawn tight. In the halo of one of the gas lamps, a girl younger than he was waiting. Abraham stalled as he approached. Perhaps it was only the drink clouding his vision, but she appeared lost; she peered into the night as if unknowing of what she might find. On either side of her, towers of red brick loomed.

'Are you well?' he asked.

She hesitated before she replied. Though her face was in shadow, Abraham could tell that she was pretty. She had brown hair and thin lips, and it struck him, oddly, that he had not seen teeth as straight or as small.

'I'm well,' she answered, guarded.

'And you know which way you're going?'

It seemed to Abraham, then, that she feigned her smile.

'I've been living here all my life,' she replied.

He nodded to her as he moved on, looking over his shoulder only once as he rounded a bend in the street, and left her to the looming warehouses.

They picked her out of the canal later the same night. She was blue, but she was not dead. In the days that followed, rumour was rife on the streets. Abraham had slept in a hedgerow that first night, but at the flophouse where at last he found a bed the stories were told and embellished. There had been a man, bent upon taking everything she owned; there had been blows; there had been midnight walkers leaping into the water to drag her out. There were snatches of it in the newspapers, but rumour had always been a greater weapon than the printed word – and soon, or so it seemed, Abraham had learnt every lurid detail, heard stories so varied that they might as well have been separate girls.

The man – or men, for speculation abounded that there was more than one assailant – had struck twice before. Each time, the girl had been stalked for whatever petty treasures she carried. Each time, the girl had been left for dead.

She was called Ada. It was a name dear to Abraham, for he had once had a sister with the same name; polio had taken her to *a better place when she was barely seven years old, but Abraham could still vividly remember every inflection of her voice. The investigations continued – but crime on these streets was rife, the years of war leaving the city unguarded – and there was word that the man might already have struck again, along the back roads at Wakefield.*

Perhaps it began with thoughts of her, but it was not only Ada that made Abraham drift down to the station of the local constabulary seven days after his return. There were few jobs that returning soldiers found they were equipped for – war was a trade like any other, but the talents of a soldier did not match those of a carpenter or welder – but police work, at least, felt right. Abraham was not the sort of man to retire to a life of tilling and harvesting, like so many men from his battalion; the city was in him just as he was in it, and he yearned to find a way to serve.

There were others like him at the station, boys who had drifted back from the carnage over the water, and Abraham was readily accepted into the fold. He was told that a man with a service record such as his might even rise through the ranks one day – but, though Abraham was thankful of the sentiment, it was not a thought that gave him particular joy; Abraham had no desire to be an officer again, nor any great lust to be a leader of men. Instead, he learnt his trade like any carpenter or welder might: he listened to his superiors and adopted their techniques, and dutifully did as he was told. There had been boys in his battalion who resented every order flung their way, but Abraham had never been one of those; he understood that the world turned slowly, and that young men might one day be old.

It did not take long to work himself into a routine. After the years of his roaming, he found the day-to-day merry-go-round a strange sort of comfort; it felt, in its rigours, as if he was a soldier again – and he drew, from that, the strength of structure and routine. He would rise early, at the break of day, and eat his breakfast with the boarding-house landlady, while studying texts the constabulary had provided, and versing himself as best he could in Common Law. Mornings would be spent in pounding the beats, growing to know this city that had once been his; afternoons with his head in paperwork and quiet rumination; evenings in following the beats again and learning how different a terrace appeared beneath the shroud of night.

It was a scant few weeks before Abraham's captains congratulated him on how thoroughly he was applying himself to his apprenticeship and welcomed him formally to the constabulary. There was a certain pride in that moment, and he shook the hand of each of the officers with a sense of increasing warmth.

'You'll go far, son,' one of the elder watchmen whispered, as if divining in Abraham's eyes the real reason he had come to the watch house that first day. 'You'll put a thousand bad men in their mausoleums before you're through.'

They left him with that thought, drifting away, one after another, to smoke contentedly in the afternoon sunlight. As ever, Abraham remained behind. He resolved, then, that, on the next day he did not work, he would go to his mother's graveside and, though not a shred of him believed she could hear, he would tell her how his life now looked.

When he turned to leave, he saw that there were maps stretched across the walls, sketches of the city streets with coloured pins pressed into them – and, along with that, scraps of paper and scraps of stories. He froze. His eyes were drawn to the spiralling streets at the city's heart, where the canal ran with the railway and the bridges rose above. He traced a path with the tips of his fingers.

And there she was, pinned to the wall: a portrait of the girl he had left for the killers in the murk, grinning into the camera with an arm around a friend, unknowing of any cruelty in the world. She was captured there for ever like an insect in amber, thinking nothing, never to be changed. Abraham lifted a hand to pluck the picture from its pin; then, slowly, he dropped his hand at his side.

That night, when he donned his greatcoat and changed his boots, some of the other constables were going to a taproom beneath the railway bridge. As always, they urged Abraham to join them; as always, they riled him for being boring and mean-spirited when he claimed he could not come. One of the constables looked over his shoulder as he left, threw Abraham a commiserating smile and then disappeared. Abraham waited to give the boys a head start, and then he too set out into the dusk.

It had not been hard to find out where she worked. That was what boxes and files were for. He had been to the Violets tearoom once before, when he was a boy, and it was a strange comfort to think that the place still existed. It sat on the corner of Woodhouse, along the thoroughfare that took traders to Otley and the outlying towns. He took the small road, skirting the edge of the Moor, and ventured quietly along that path.

They would not catch the killer, nor recover any of the trinkets he had taken before rolling her into the canal's inky depths; that was the talk of the station, and Abraham had no real reason to rail against it. He had long ago abandoned the fiery belief of his youth: that bad things happened to bad people, and good to the good. Abraham had killed too many times to believe a sorry thing like that. He came down the Otley Road, the clouds of night massing at his shoulder, and he gazed over the city in which he had become a stranger: the stacks and slates of Woodhouse on his right; the glowering moorland on his left. The man who had stalked Ada from the shadows was out there somewhere, toasting a celebration with his friends, sharing the bed of his wife, leading a black dog on its leash through the lanes. There were men like that in every terrace; you did not have to hold a bayonet to be a bastard.

He came, at last, to a meeting of roads, where a cluster of buildings sat at the corner of the scrub. There was a taproom here, and beyond that a string of little shops: a grocer's and a butcher's and a man who made his living winding clocks. The Violets tearoom was the last of that crooked row, and more than once, as he approached, Abraham stalled, as if he might turn and retreat – back over the parapets, back into the earth, back into those grateful holes in the ground. There were still lanterns lit within, and through net curtains he could see figures come and go. When he grew close, he stalled for the final time. Through the weave he could see her bowed above one of the tables, laying new cloths. She looked over her shoulder, as if somebody called her name.

Abraham had seen countless men die: friends and brothers and enemies and the nothing men in between. That the good died just as easily as the bad had been one of his first lessons as a soldier. He wondered, now, if he was wishing for a man's death for the very first time.

'Ada,' he said, pushing through the doors. 'My name is Abraham Matthews. You won't know me. I'm working for the constabulary, stationed out of Burley Park.'

'I remember. You want to talk to me about that night?'

'No,' said Abraham. 'But I would like coffee. Strong and black.'

He found reasons to see her. The coffee was not reason enough, for there was still little in the country, and the beans that tearooms such as hers could find were invariably salvaged from the cellars of some obliterated warehouse. It tasted like gravy – but, in his time at war, Abraham had tasted worse.

There were days when he sat there and didn't venture to speak to her; there were others when she came, tentative, to his table, and shared his scones and read aloud to him headlines from the newspaper. They talked of all manner of nothings, and both took *pleasure in that. With no deliberate effort, Abraham came to know the timings of her shifts in the tearoom, the hour she arrived each day and departed each evening. He was there, often, when she donned her overcoat for the night and her mother arrived to take her back to their terrace – but not once did he leave the tearoom with her, or suggest that he be the one who walked her home. There was something in that that did not seem right, or felt too bold; this was his entire universe with her: cups of tea.*

On the day that Ada did not appear in the tearoom, there was a gentle dusting of snow across the city. Abraham drank his coffee and read his papers as he always did, and though the other waitresses looked on him sadly, they did not venture an explanation for Ada's disappearance. The day after, it was the same – and the day after, and the day after that. On the fourth day, Abraham resolved not to visit the Violets tearoom – but, by dusk, he was there again, nursing a pot of coffee as the evening regulars came and went.

He was the last to leave that evening. The night was deep, and as he looked up from the dregs of his coffee, he understood that the last of the waitresses had been waiting politely for him to be done. As he scattered coins onto the counter, she gestured to him and he came close.

'She's not well,' the waitress whispered. 'Some of the girls went to see her last night. She said you weren't to know, but she woke up one morning and she didn't want a part in it any more.'

'A part in what?' Abraham asked, nervous of the answer.

'We didn't ask,' the girl answered. 'It didn't seem a thing she wanted to say.'

Abraham wandered the terrace. He tried to return to the boarding house where he had found lodgings, but he knew he would rather talk to the wind than that lonely bedroom. He roamed from Woodhouse Moor to Burley Park, and when he found himself back outside the Violets tearoom, staring through shutters at the darkened room beyond, he understood, at last, that there was only one place left to go.

He had a simple image of how the future would be. There was no drama in it, no grand romance. It was morning, and sunlight broke through the curtains to reveal their clothes lying entangled together on the bedroom floor. That was all.

He reached her road. He had plucked flowers from the verges along the way and realised, now, that he had been holding them so tightly that the stalks had crumpled and the heads fallen. He laid the bouquet quietly in one of the yards and approached her house.

Her mother was at the door. At first, she was reluctant to admit him, furrowed her brow as if to menace him away, but he did not give up. He had an armful of books for her. He said he wanted nothing but to sit with her, to waste her time – and, finally, she permitted him within.

It was like the house he had grown up in, small and dusty and filled with the clutter of a dozen lives. As he climbed the stairs, he got to wishing that the last ten years of his life could be undone, that he might begin again; he was happier, then, with no real memories or thought, before he even considered what being happy might mean. He and his brothers would spend their days in idleness and not think their days wasted; would berate a mother they loved and not think it cruelty; would taunt and mock and fight each other and not think it unfair.

He knocked twice at her door before slowly pushing within. It was bigger than he imagined, and the light of gas lamps spilled in from the prominent bay. In cross-stitch above the mantel, there hung a framed embroidery of the Lord, hands folded in his lap. At the foot of the bed, wrapped up in crocheted blankets, Ada sat with her eyes closed, bowed at that icon. No matter what he had witnessed in the fields outside Mons, Abraham did not begrudge

Ada her prayers. In his blackest hours, even Abraham had folded his hands together and asked for some spirit to descend from on high.

'Most of us are sad,' he said, lowering himself at her side.

Slowly, she lifted her eyes to his. 'Is that so?' she chided him. For a moment, he was tricked into believing that she was genuine in her scold. Then, he opened his eyes.

Abraham held Ada. He was not given to wild claims of affection, but he held her tightly and breathed the soft, sweet air from deep in her throat.

'I hate what happened to you,' he said. 'I hate it to the distraction of everything else. And – I believe I am in love, for the first time in my life.'

* * *

The Second Mile

Deep in the terraces, the clock tower tolled.

'You hear that?' said Albie. 'Midnight, Captain. The witching hour.'

Abraham knew what the boy meant. There were boys across the terraces who were learning the tongue of the Young Bloods, and many had been eager to show off. The witching hour. The hour for pillaging and looting, when not a man would condescend to catch a crook.

They lingered on the fringes of Meanwood Road, watching as the fire trucks and their hordes of blitz scouts rolled, at last, into the streets. 'You people can't stay here!' one of the scouts roared as they passed. 'Don't you know what's happening tonight?'

Straying from the main thoroughfare, they advanced through the grounds of a redbrick church whose belfry stood silent and still. The graves were low mounds here, weathered crosses of stone sitting above each. Abraham led Albie across the yard, taking care to trample as many of the graves as he could. With a simple pleasure, he noted the tread of Albie's feet, the way he recoiled when his feet lit upon the mounds. Abraham thought back to the ledgerbooks he had filled these last months as he pieced together the fable of Albie Crowe; it seemed that the stern Sunday lessons that Albie's mother and countless stepfathers had beaten into him still left their mark.

'This isn't the way to the station,' Albie breathed, straining for the first time at his cuffs.

'There's a stop we have to make first,' said Abraham, hauling his captive through an archway to follow a lower run of the terrace.

The land was steep and, when they reached the bottom of a street cut like ancient farmers' terraces into the hill, they passed into one of the thin yards. The flowerbeds here were meticulously tended, and baskets hung from the eaves of an overhanging porch.

Abraham rapped at the door. Up and down the terrace, blackout curtains cocooned each house, so that it might have been the whole town that had been abandoned – but Abraham knew that life lingered here tonight. He did not have to wait long. The door drew back and, in the darkness of the passage beyond, his old friend Wilbur was waiting.

'Did you get my message?'

'The bird came at dusk, Abraham. I was beginning to doubt you would show.'

Abraham gestured his thanks. 'I followed him into one of the air-raid shelters,' he said. 'But word's already out. His boys will be moving on me quick, but if I get him to the station, they won't be able to do a thing.'

'I just hope you know what you're doing.'

Wilbur was older than Abraham, ten years or more his senior. He had been a proud man in his day, but he walked, now, with a stoop, so that passers-by might think he had spent his life in a library instead of walking the beat. His hair, once blond, was a shock of white, and he wore a flannel gown of burgundy and gold. Following him into the hall, Abraham was aware, for the first time, how his friend had shrunk with the years. There had been a time the two of them staked out the dens of thieves together; in recent years, there had been tea and games of chess, and endless talk of their younger days.

Abraham hesitated as he came along the passageway. The door fell shut behind them, and his eyes flickered into every corner, head cocked as he listened out for words in the walls.

'It's all right,' said Wilbur. 'There's no one else here.'

At the end of the hall, Wilbur stooped to light a candle.

'And Kate?' asked Abraham. 'She's safe?'

'She went to Ada,' Wilbur began, thinking of his wife. His words were wary at first, as if he was uncertain how Abraham would shoulder the news. 'Into the north country.'

'Fresh air and hills and fishing on the lake,' murmured Abraham. 'That's good news, Wilbur. I'd have asked for it, if it was my place any more. Ada deserves someone by her side.'

'Have you heard from her?'

'No,' Abraham conceded. 'But she hasn't forgotten me yet. Given up on me, perhaps . . .'

Wilbur paused. For the first time, his eyes fell fully upon Albie Crowe.

'Bring him into the light,' he breathed.

They moved into a living room, piled high with the clutter of two entangled lifetimes. Wedding portraits lined the walls: Wilbur and Kate frozen in a perfect moment of the past, and among them – mere ghosts hovering in the background – Abraham and Ada, younger and bolder, in the days before Elsa and Albie Crowe.

Wilbur paused before the boy.

'What is it?' asked Abraham.

'I was expecting him to be . . . *different*,' his old friend responded. The word would not do, but it was the only one that came to mind. 'They speak his name with such reverence – but he's hardly a man at all.'

'We were younger than him when they told us we were men.'

'A pleasure to meet you, sir,' offered Albie.

They thrust Albie into a threadbare seat and snapped the cuffs around its arm. Behind a grate, the embers of a fire still glowed.

'Look into the glow, son,' said Abraham as they moved past, shifting the crooked chair so that he could see the fiery stones. 'You can watch the fire demons dancing there.' He scoffed the last words; a boy like Albie Crowe would surely hear those false demons whispering to him.

Back in the hall, they bolted the door and took to the stairs. Wilbur went first, Abraham following in the puddles of light his candle spilled.

'Don't say things like that in front of him,' Abraham cautioned. 'An inch of pity and that boy's in your head. I've seen how this works, remember?'

'You forget me, Abraham. I wouldn't have been in on this if I wasn't made of sterner stuff.'

It was a small house, only two rooms upstairs and an attic above that. Wilbur led Abraham along the landing, stopped to unfurl a rope ladder from the trap in the roof; then, one after the other, they ascended into the rafters.

Abraham was poised, half way up the ladder. He hung there, suspended in the darkness – but when he reached for Wilbur, his old friend's hand paused.

'Abraham, before we go on, there's something else. I can't keep it from you.'

'Is it of consequence tonight?'

A warning growled at the back of Abraham's throat; there were certain things, he seemed to be saying, a man did not need to know.

'There's a man at the lake with Ada,' he breathed, 'from one of the local 'steads. I'm sorry, Abraham. I thought you should hear it.' He stopped, willed himself to go on. 'She hasn't been unfaithful.'

'That's because there's no faith to keep,' said Abraham, clawing into the attic at last. There were no blackouts in the windows up here, and orange light spilled in from the fires without. 'Ada and I aren't together. Elsa's dead on account of him, and I stood back and let it happen. How could she love a man like that?'

'It was my impression the two of you had an understanding, that you might end your days with her yet . . .'

Abraham allowed himself to look back, through the trap door. Down there, in the darkness, Albie Crowe sat between him and everything he had known and loved. 'That may fall apart too, if I don't wrong a few rights before sun-up . . .'

The latch dropped, and Albie Crowe was alone. There was a story he had been fond of, one of the few things he treasured from his youth, and it came back to him now. In his head, it was Elsa's voice that did the telling. It was only a Christmas ago that she had presented him with the tome of those ancient tales. She had read to him aloud every night until the New Year came in – and then, when Albie could take her condescension no longer, he had tossed the book into a fire. Words on a page had never meant a thing to Albie Crowe, and if she was to run with him, neither would they mean a thing to Elsa.

Like the spurned prince of that story, Albie Crowe was in his own dungeon tonight. The gods had imprisoned him here, deep underground, for there lay dormant within him the seed that might destroy them all. That was the seed the spurned prince had treasured since the nights he lay in his crib, the thing that devoured and set him apart from the rest. He nurtured that seed, and the seed grew, and now a creature of thistles found succour inside him.

'Don't fall asleep,' Albie murmured, over and again, three words tumbling upon each other like a nursery rhyme. 'Don't fall asleep. Don't let them catch you.'

He jerked against the chair, discovered that he could move it by an inch with each thrust. In that way, he turned and surveyed the room. That a family might have spent their every night sitting in this chamber, while they talked about their days and dreamt their little dreams, was a sacrilege to Albie Crowe. It still seemed, in his most honest moments, as if he was the only person in these terraces to dream of something beyond. Not for Albie Crowe, the nights in front of the fire while the wireless played some trite declaration of love. Not for Albie Crowe, the Sunday roast and bread and honey. Not for Albie Crowe, the girl and the child and the clothes entangled on a bedroom floor.

'Honey,' he mouthed, aping the words of a song his mother had been known to warble, 'you have such *pretty little lives.*'

He kicked his way to the hearth, where more portraits sat on the mantel. Wilbur and Kate had borne a child, once. Like Elsa, she was gone, preserved only as a grinning toddler in these frames, never to grow older than her eighteen months. He came closer to the dying fire, felt at last the warmth of the coals. The hearth was flanked by two pillars of stone, and finally Albie understood what manner of magic might free him from this cell. He kicked again at the chair, turned so that he could rock back against the pillar. The warmth rose at his back, and each time he kicked back to smash the slats of the chair against the stone, he felt a flurry of fire.

On the mantel, the portraits began to tremble. Each time they rattled, he dealt another blow to the chair. Proud of the petty destruction, he caught his reflection in a mirror hanging from the opposite wall. There was scant light in the chamber, but there was enough to glory in that image. He smashed the chair a final time, felt the wood give – and heard the shatter of the portraits as they tumbled to the hearth.

At his feet, a picture lay in its broken frame. Soft orange light fell upon the figures, and out of instinct he pitched forward that he might see them more clearly. Among the wild flowers of Woodhouse Moor, four old friends held their newborn babies between them: Wilbur and Kate, with the child that would not last; Abraham and Ada, with the girl he would one day take from them.

'Elsa.' He breathed the word oddly. If any man had been there to hear, they would not have thought it sadness, they would not have thought it regret – though perhaps both those things were singing in that single word. An attentive man might have caught the way Albie inhaled as he spoke, recognised it as a gasp of sorts. But the attentive man would have been wrong. When Albie Crowe breathed the word, it was an accusation.

'Elsa Matthews,' he began, gazing into the photograph through shards of shattered glass. 'I should never have let you waltz into my life.'

The chest stood against the attic wall. Wilbur lifted the bundle from within and unwrapped the service revolver, oiled and cleaned but not used since the days he crouched in a hole in the ground.

'I tested the barrel last night. It's still a good shot.'

Abraham nodded. He pressed the weapon into a loop of his belt, and fastened his greatcoat around it. There were daggers in the chest too. Wilbur offered up one of the blades, but Abraham refused; he had known knife fights before, and was too old to face it again. Instead, Wilbur sheathed the dagger at his side.

'When you hear the bells tolling in the old clock tower,' said Abraham, 'you'll know I got him to the station. Send the bird straight away. If I'm fortunate, Ada could have it by morning. There could be a bird back by dusk. I could be with her again before sun-up next day.' Abraham paused. 'Thirty-six hours, Wilbur. It could all be right.'

Wilbur was still. He had not doubted Abraham before – but the city was on fire tonight.

'Did you tell anybody where you were taking him? He might have his Whisperers listening . . .'

'There were boys poured into the air-raid shelters. And a vagabond sleeping wild on the Moor. Not Young Bloods themselves, but it might have been they were whispering secrets . . .'

Whisperer. Abraham lingered over the word. He had heard it often in the days after Elsa passed on, when Ada could not bear to look at him and he heard his daughter's name on the tongue of every stranger in the street. He had drifted from taproom to taproom that week, but not once had he taken a draught of the drinks for which he lay down his coins. Already, the name of the Young Bloods was being breathed – in curiosity by the tongues of the old, in reverence by their children – but it was not a name that Abraham could stomach to hear. People said they had seen the Young Bloods crowing to crowds on the blasted stretches at the top of the Moor; others that boys were downing their tools and deciding instead to run with Albie Crowe. And Albie knew and saw all; he had Whisperers on every street corner, professional gossips on his payroll, ready to pass on even the secrets of their friends for the promise of glory with the Bloods.

'Listen to them, Wilbur,' Abraham sighed. He pressed his hands against the window-pane, spectred himself there. 'They make stories up, and then they act them out as if the fables were real, draw portals in the air and then just step into the fantasy. These things shouldn't exist. They didn't, two years ago. Whisperers and Young Bloods and that boy down there, styling himself as some Overlord of the Streets, as if it was anything more than lying and stealing like any old thief from the old times . . .'

'At least there was honour in thieving back then. Honesty too.'

It was worse than that, thought Abraham. It was the youngsters, too young even for Albie's gang, who were listening, growing up knowing precisely what Whisperers and Young Bloods were, like another generation might have known of Roundheads and Cavaliers. And, in that way, the things Albie Crowe plucked from his imagination were made real. Boyish fantasies sprang into life and started jostling with the old ways of the world. They would last without Albie Crowe, if this thing was not stopped soon.

'We're part of it too,' said Wilbur, crouching at the chest and rifling within. 'The moment we called them "Young Bloods", we were taken into their myth. And now, look at us – the real world has us down as two old fools who should just go to ground – but the fantasy . . .'

'A demigod stalking the backstreets of Leeds with a wild daemon on a leash,' said Abraham, grinning at the absurdity of the image.

'A warrior who has nothing left, looking to end the story in the only way he can,' corrected Wilbur, sterner now. 'Refusing even the company of his friends . . .'

Abraham put a hand on his shoulder.

'This is my war, old friend. I could have stopped this, long ago.' He paused, weighing the gun at his side. 'I've been trying to be a decent man all these years, ever since we put down our guns – and, somehow, I thought I could be decent with the boy. But Elsa's dead now. Ada's gone. And, with every day that passes, there are more boys out there who think Albie Crowe is a hero. A master thief. A tender murderer.' They moved, side by side, along the rails at the top of the stairs. 'Now,' Abraham went on, 'you promised me your dogs?'

When his captors returned, Albie Crowe was waiting. His back was to the fire, and the flames leapt higher, dancing softly where there had been only embers.

Instantly, Abraham understood where the fuel for that fire had come from; the chair was in pieces, and new logs smoked in the grate. He did not flinch as Albie Crowe rose to his feet, hauling shackled hands in front of him. He was taller than he had seemed only hours before, when he tracked him into the air-raid shelter. Perhaps it was only the way he was holding himself, triumphant and free – but Abraham did not care.

He stepped aside and, in the hallway, the hackles of Wilbur's dogs rose.

They were good hounds, mongrels of decent stock with low snouts and legs muscled by miles of hunting over dale and heath. There were three, and though they stayed at Abraham's command, they were neither leashed nor tethered. He opened his palm, and one after another the dogs advanced.

Albie Crowe strained at his cuffs, sank back into the remnants of that splintered seat.

'You clever bastard, Abraham,' he breathed. There might have been some twisted compliment in that, but Abraham did not acknowledge it. Instead, he gestured again, and each of the dogs took up its station in the room. Abraham had handled hounds looking for men left living after the eruptions outside Ypres, and had always had a way with the beasts.

Albie Crowe shrank.

'I've never seen a man like it,' Wilbur marvelled.

'One of his stepfathers used to run the dogfights off the Kirkstall Road,' Abraham explained. 'It's all in my ledger. His mother decided that there was a profession here, something the boy might grow into. But there was a cellar that stank of their shit, wasn't there, Albie? And mongrels bred to tear chunks out of each other.' Abraham ushered the dogs on, commanded them to heel. 'He hasn't been able to pet a pup since.'

Albie kicked against the remnants of the chair. 'I've always preferred cats myself.'

'Don't worry, Albie. They're just here to accompany us to the station. I couldn't do it alone.'

He advanced on Albie. He was certain, now, that the boy would not lash out in one of the wild frenzies that had coloured his boyhood.

Abraham reached down. His fingers hovered in the air for just a moment, as if to taunt his captive, and then he tore back the folds of Albie's shirt, exposing his breast. The boy had not washed in days, the odour that rose was thick, but Abraham saw, for the first time, the scars that were spoken of in the back rooms of alehouses across Leeds. They coloured most of his breast, and below them there sat a greater mark, etched there in celebration of some greater crime: perhaps, Abraham allowed himself to believe, his own daughter's death.

'What are they?' asked Wilbur.

'The marks of the Young Bloods,' explained Abraham. 'They carve a bloody notch for every night of crime they commit. The deeper, the better.' He paused, flickered his eyes between Albie and Wilbur. 'Pass me your knife.'

Wilbur had the blade in the loop of his belt. Abraham took it by the hilt, turned it neatly between the fingers of his right hand and tore back the buttons of his own shirt with the left.

'This', he said, pressing the point into his chest, 'is for the boys I killed when I soldiered in France.' He gouged at the flesh above his heart, and the blood began to well. 'And this', he went on, 'is for turning the other cheek when Elsa told me which boy it was she loved.' A new notch, just underneath and deeper than the last, sprang scarlet to join the torrent. 'And this', he beamed, 'is for the night Ada cried and cried and I couldn't console her.' He carved again, quicker this time, as if he was growing used to the sensation. 'There, Albie – all of my crimes accounted for, my initiation complete.'

Before he turned the knife to hand it back to Wilbur, he carved again, a thin slash unlike the others. It blanched white for only a second, and then the ribbon was red.

'What's the last mark for?' Albie asked.

'The last mark?' Abraham said, fastening his shirt and watching the scarlet stain spread. 'That, Albie, is for tonight.'

The boy named Drew was tending to his ravens when his grandmother halloed from the end of the yard. The sky was aflame tonight, and there was a strange kind of terror came upon his birds when fire fell on the roads. On nights such as this, Drew spurned the Anderson shelters, and came out here to be with his flock. His grandmother fretted for him, he knew, but the ravens fretted too. He would not let them go through it alone.

There were three lofts at the end of the garden, two of them the ill-hewn remnants of runs where his grandfather once kept his own birds, the third a construction of canes and wire mesh that Drew himself had crafted for his hatchery. The final enclosure had been built around a stunted elm, and the ravens sheltered in the skeletal boughs tonight, turning circles whenever one of the great silver birds thundered above.

When he heard the call, Drew ventured to the edge of the wire. He was a boy too big for his body, as if something in him carried on growing long after his skin had stopped. He pressed his face to the farthest stretch of wire and watched as the silhouette became a man.

'Shepherd!' Drew exclaimed. He gestured for the ravens to leave his shoulders, and palmed along the wire mesh to reach the aviary doors. Once there, he admitted Shepherd and embraced him awkwardly. 'Is it true what the Whisperers are spreadin'? That Captain Matthews found Albie at last?'

'Albie wandered into one of the old fox's snares,' explained Shepherd. He rested against a pillar, saw the mordant black eyes watching him. 'Yeah,' he sighed, 'it's true enough.' He stopped again, reached into the folds of his overcoat. 'But that isn't why I'm here, Drew.'

Shepherd had a kind face. It was scarred now, in a way it had not been scarred when they were boys, but something underneath the hairless pale tissue retained its former warmth. He reached between the folds of his woollen cowl – a gift, Drew remembered, from his own grandmother – and produced a bundle of black feathers. When Drew lifted the bloody raven, he knew it had not been dead long.

'Where did it come from?' Drew asked. He raised the cadaver and marvelled at it in the orange light.

'Shot out of a tree over the Moor,' Shepherd answered. 'We haven't had any trading this week. There weren't supposed to be ravens flying tonight.'

Drew cupped the bird to his breast.

'I don't understand.'

'We thought it might have been a message coming in from Sale,' Shepherd went on. He rested against the twisted elm, but when he saw Drew's face contort – as if in horror for the poor malformed shrub – he rocked back onto his heels. 'But the bird wouldn't land, so we took her down. There was a message, Drew. I didn't know Albie had ordered messages tonight.'

The Young Bloods had ferried messages by raven since long before the bombardments began. There were some messages you could not trust to wires. Far better, in this age, to trust in the selfishness of birds. People said that pigeons were the best at ferrying messages, but people were wrong. Trusting a secret to a pigeon instead of a raven or a rook was like asking a rodent to fetch you a newspaper instead of a dog.

'Did he ask you to send the message himself?'

Drew understood, now, that Shepherd was accusing him of acting without Albie Crowe's consent. Involuntarily, his fists clenched. It was a lesson hard won, but he managed to keep himself from lashing out. It had been after he lashed out as a boy that he first met Shepherd, cooped up together in the back room of some watchman's station. Drew had been big for his age, even then, and had not understood why the other boy's face had crumpled so easily. Shepherd, chained up there for a habit with matches, had been the one to teach him what it meant to be strong.

'I didn't see no message,' he stammered.

Shepherd drew a tiny roll of paper from a fold in his coat. Drew was not a reader – but he had often seen Shepherd read to Albie and the rest. He shifted back into the shadows at the rear of the lofts, as if shying from the words.

' "Stalwarts – the siege is tonight," ' Shepherd read. 'What's a Stalwart, Drew?'

'I don't know, Shepherd.' His voice broke. 'I didn't send a single message tonight. I haven't seen Albie. I haven't seen any of the gang.'

Shepherd snatched at the dead raven in Drew's grasp, but the ogre curled his arms around it, as if even a dead thing deserved some protection.

'You mean to say this isn't your raven?' Shepherd began.

Drew seemed to be wrestling inside his own skin.

'I'd've known,' he mumbled, 'if one o' the girls just didn't come back. And this'n, this jus' isn't the same as the rest. I didn't hatch this raven here.'

'How can you be so sure?' Shepherd went on. His hands were tearing at the carcass, now. Black feathers flew, but still

Drew's huge fingers held it tight. 'One bird's much the same as the rest, right?'

Drew grinned.

'You've gotta learn to pick a raven right,' he slurred. 'And this, Shepherd – this is a cock bird! I never tie messages to a cock bird. My flights are full o' hens! Hens think faster. They got it bred in 'em, on account of their chicks. And they're quicker, more vicious, know more about hawks and how to outfly them. I only ever keep cocks for breeding. I pluck the rest out of the brood, toss 'em to the cats.'

Beyond the wire of the rookery, Shepherd saw one of the sinewy felines shadowed in the trees. There were dozens of vagabonds like this roaming these streets; they lived in prides along roof slates and gutters.

'If it wasn't your bird, Drew,' breathed Shepherd, 'who else?'

Drew did not answer. Slowly, he placed the cadaver on a ledge at his side. The ravens thereabouts, scenting death, skittered apart.

'They's not another gang, is there, Shepherd?'

There had not been other gangs since the beginning, when there was only Albie Crowe and Shepherd, holing up together in one of the abandoned terraces, and the words 'Young' and 'Blood' had not yet been thrown so gleefully together. Those had been the months of runs in the depths of the night, of stopping trucks on their way to the taproom and convincing the driver that his wares were best sold elsewhere. The whole endeavour had changed when the bombing began. Albie Crowe was not the first to plunder evacuated houses – but he was, at least, the first to see how the maps of the city might be recast. He had gone among the other gangs, then, yoking them to the Young Bloods.

'If it's another gang,' said Shepherd, 'they're telling us something. They know the raven's our mark. They're trying to rankle Albie.'

'They wouldn't fool with Albie,' breathed Drew. He came forward, into the faint glow of light, and his eyes were wide. 'Everyone knows what he did to Monmouth the night he tried to leave.'

It was a story the Whisperers had not needed to embellish. Not a man would see the orphan boy Monmouth walking these streets again. He had been running with the Young Bloods since long before Elsa Matthews died – but Albie had followed him into the dusk, barely a week ago, and only one of them had walked back. Albie himself had been a different man, after that night was finished.

'Where is Albie, Shepherd?' Drew said, trembling as he drew breath.

Shepherd put an arm around his old friend. 'The old fox is taking him to the station at the city side of Meanwood Road,' he said. 'All the Young Bloods are headed that way now. You should make haste.'

Drew retreated from his friend, startling the birds at his shoulder.

'What about you, Shepherd?' he asked.

Shepherd turned, fumbling with a wire clasp as he sloped out of the aviary.

'I'm going after the Captain,' he breathed.

Through the terraces of Woodhouse, the prisoner shuffled. Shackled by his wrists to the frame of a pram not used in fifteen long years, the black dogs were tethered at his sides, two to blaze a trail through the ruin, one to snarl a warning behind.

From a shaft wired to the front of the old pram, a birdcage dangled. The raven caged there did not shriek. Wilbur had trained the bird well.

'You know why you have to do this alone?' Albie asked.

'I wouldn't hazard a guess, if I were you.'

'You've seen the things the boys of these streets think about me. You'd think it yourself, if things had gone differently this year.' He shuffled on, bound in by the dogs, refusing to look down. 'Don't you get it yet, Abraham? This city likes me. The people out there, they look out and see what's happening in the world, and they *need* somebody like me. For hundreds of years, people like you talked about honour and justice – and still the bombs fall. Your age of lances and jousting is over.'

They came again to the broad thoroughfare of Meanwood Road, but could follow for only a hundred yards before the ruin grew so deep that they had to leave, plunging back through abandoned gardens where weeds grew tall and foxes made their dens. The windows here had each been shattered in the bottom right-hand corner. Albie smiled at the sight; he remembered every one of his marks.

Two great boarding houses squatted at an intersection of alleys, and as the dogs dragged Albie into their shadows, he saw suddenly through which streets Abraham was dragging him. No doubt the wily bastard had taken pleasure in devising this route. A memory rose suddenly: Albie Crowe, twelve years old, doffing a cap to a man who had once been his half-brother and a girl who had once been his stepsister, who bedded together in the flophouses of this part of town. If they had not fled with the sacking of the city, perhaps they cowered together behind the blackouts tonight. Whatever had become of them, Albie did not know nor care. They had long since ceased to be his family.

'Don't be scared, Albie. It's only a street.'

The way between the boarding houses was narrow, but they came at last to a broader street that ran parallel to Meanwood Road, and Abraham drove them on. After a little way, Albie found that he was free of thoughts of his brothers and sisters.

He pushed on, the wheels of the pram squealing as they turned, and gloried that those images were gone. In its rocking cage, the raven leapt from bar to bar.

'This raven won't fly right, Abraham. You didn't clip its tail.'

'That's the secret, is it?' muttered Abraham, scaling a mound of bricks that had been flung into the road like some crude workers' barricade.

'They have to be taught obedience. If you'd only asked, I could have sent you to see Drew.'

There was no message tied to the raven's leg. Albie supposed the Captain kept it concealed somewhere on his person, ready to let the bird take flight when the hour was nigh. It occurred to him, as the dogs drew him toward the ridge of bricks across the road, that Abraham must have been waiting for this night an inordinate length of time; he would have needed to decide upon the raven's destination when it was only a chick, taught it which roosts were its home, so that he could have faith it would not disappear. Drew and the other raven-keepers, the ones stationed in Sale and the outlying towns, were like priests when it came to their birds; if Abraham's messenger were to be trusted, he would have had to have switched to that vocation as well. There was something unsettling in that.

At a snarl in the streets, where a water tower once stood, the buildings were fallen. Albie did not know how recently the bombs had rained, but he knew it had not been part of tonight's devastation; no fires roared in the wreckage, and some of these buildings had already been plundered.

The dogs drew to a halt, unable to drag the pram and its cargo into the rubble. Atop the barricade, Abraham stood tall to survey the land.

'I'll find a way through,' he said, dropping onto a lower ledge of stone. 'I trust you won't be going anywhere?'

'You have my promise,' winked Albie.

Abraham pushed on, stumbling when he took to a fallen chimney stack. He did not drift from Albie's sight, but in the darkness he became only a silhouette, framed against low-lying fires on the other side of the ridge. Albie dared to glance at the dogs – and knew he would have no better chance than this.

He threw himself at the pram and pitched it forward.

For the first time, the raven cried out. It was enough to rouse Abraham's attention, but he did not turn to rush back. Where the pram hit the first line of bricks, the two dogs in front smashed against the stone. The smallest one whimpered, rising back to a hobbled paw, while the larger twisted around, strangling itself on its leash. Once, Albie might have hesitated. Once, he might have heard the pain in that whimpering and stayed his hand. Tonight, he sang with them.

He forced the pram forward again, throwing himself again and again at the bars until the wheels lodged in shattered brick. Behind him, the lone hound still standing sent up a howl. There was a story in this, Albie decided, one of the dozens Elsa had read to him in their long nights together: a runaway prince, rampaging through heather high on the moor, the hound pack in full cry as they hunted him down. In the corner of his eye, the Captain clawed back through the brick.

Albie leapt high. The shackles chaining him to the pram dug deep into his wrists, but somehow he found that he could scramble on top of the contraption. Below him, the black dog, already half-choked by its tether, looked up lamely. Its eyes had not met Albie's for more than a second before the boy knew what he must do.

He wrapped his hand around the leash and drew the dog high. For an instant it resisted; then it dangled there, little legs scrabbling. At last, it was still. Albie slumped back for only a second, before he rounded on the next of the mutts.

The dog closest recoiled – but it was only a feint. The creature weaved before thrusting itself forth.

'Stop!'

Barking out the command, Abraham thundered through the bricks, raising his hands to the dogs with a wild look on his face. Throwing himself over the last mound of rock, he snatched at Albie's shirt to drag him out of the way. On either side of him, the two remaining dogs relented. Stillness descended upon the little group, with only the raven's cry to pierce the silence. Where the pram had smashed through the wall of bricks, the cage dangling at its front lay crumpled. Albie watched with glee as the panicked bird emerged and rose, black wings spreading, into the night.

'Albie,' Captain Abraham Matthews sighed. 'Haven't you had enough fun for one night?'

'Captain,' Albie began, breathless as he fell into the bricks. 'We can do this the easy way or the hard way.'

'Isn't that what I said to you?'

Albie's shoulders rose, as if in despair. 'I'm just giving you even odds, Abraham . . .'

Abraham dragged the dead dog into the mound and raised a cairn of bricks there, tall enough that, come the dawn, he might tell Wilbur where his hound lay buried. It did not take him long, but he lingered over the grave so that he might say his thanks. Once he was done, he turned back to Albie Crowe.

The boy opened his palms in mute apology.

'You'd have done the same thing,' he began, as if expecting Abraham's fatherly advice.

'Don't look at me like that,' Abraham began. The pram lay mangled in the bricks, and he unlatched Albie from the bars to lock him again to his own wrist. The two dogs at the boy's side lurched to move on. 'I'm not shocked. I'm not sickened. I'm not surprised. I have it written down, the first thing you ever killed, a dog your father brought home, strung up there in the garden . . . It's in my ledgerbook.'

There was a shadow stalking them. Albie had noticed it three streets before, but he was not yet certain whether Abraham had seen it as well. If he had, the Captain was hiding it well – and even Albie would grant him a modicum of respect for that. Up ahead, the shadow crossed an alley, framed momentarily in the firelight, and then disappeared once more.

'Abraham,' Albie began, as if to lure him from the scent. 'One of your dogs has kindly pissed all up my leg.'

'It's a cold night. He probably wanted to keep you warm.'

The shadow moved again, closer this time, prowling one of the lanes that ran into this. This time, Abraham gave himself away: his head dropped low, he tracked the man as he moved, slowed slightly as if to allow the figure to disappear.

'Who is it?'

Albie's eyes widened, fractionally, in what the Captain might have read as delight. It was not often that Albie betrayed himself so freely, but he allowed himself some leeway tonight; these circumstances were certainly unique.

'Some night walker,' Albie returned. 'Captain, you don't honestly believe he'd be one of *mine*, would you?'

Abraham opened his palm, and the dogs drew to a halt. Between them, Albie too froze.

'Any boy stupid enough to be walking the streets in this has to be one of yours, Albie. What's his name? Shepherd? Browning? Drew?' He walked forward, leaving Albie in the shadows behind. Further on, up the road, an alleyway opened onto the street, half-hidden by hawthorn and scrub. 'Monmouth?'

'Captain, don't play games, surely you know that Monmouth doesn't run with us any longer?'

Albie watched as Abraham's eyes narrowed. The Captain, it seemed, did not know about the boy named Monmouth. And if he did not know about him, well, he barely knew a thing about Albie Crowe at all. It was all just bluster. The Young Bloods still had their secrets. There would be a way out of this, if he bided his time.

'He's been with us since we set out. Didn't you know?'

Abraham hissed some indecipherable command, and the dogs began to move again, drawing their prisoner further on. Unable to resist, Albie Crowe fell into the march, pursing his lips together to trill out some ditty he had once known. Not even Abraham's glower could silence him, then.

At an outcrop of hawthorn, they turned from the thoroughfare and pushed through tin cans overflowing with refuse. On one side, there loomed the terrace; on the other, a brick wall, taller by far than the Captain or Crowe, separating them from the yards on the other side. There were scuff marks half way up the brick where boys had scrambled over, and a shallow trench of ditch water lying at their feet.

It was two or three hundred yards until the alley opened up. There, at the end, cauldrons of fire flickered, so that it looked to Albie as if they were bound for some otherworld at the end of the lane. At intervals, Abraham drew them to a halt, crouched low and cocked his head.

There were footsteps on the other side of the wall.

'Is it him?'

'I don't know, Abraham. I haven't studied the sounds of all my associates' footfalls.'

They went on, but the footsteps continued, rising and falling whenever Abraham stalled or set off. Albie watched the Captain's jig with growing glee. The old man moved with a dancer's regularity, and Albie – a boy who had rehearsed studiously for all the greatest moments in his life – got to thinking that the routine had been choreographed some time before.

'Albie!' a shrill voice cried.

In the narrow alley, Abraham spun on Albie Crowe. The boy was pleased to see the stern set of the watchman's jaw.

'Don't say a word . . .' Abraham whispered.

'I'm here!' Albie called out. There was no urgency in his tone – or, if there was, he had conquered himself so completely that not a crack showed. Abraham lifted a hand as if he might strike him, but Albie refused to flinch. 'Are the rest on their way?'

'Is he with you? Can you talk?'

Albie lifted the shackles at his wrists to Abraham, but the Captain did not smile at the jest.

'Say what you have to say. There are no secrets between Captain Matthews and me.'

Albie saw that Abraham had drawn his revolver. He commanded the dogs silently, and they turned to lead Albie back the way they had come. For a moment, the footsteps on the other side of the wall were silent. Then, Albie cried out.

'Captain!' he announced. 'These dogs of yours are testing my patience!'

The footsteps quickened through the brick as they turned and hurried to catch up.

'You breathe another word, Crowe, and I'll make one of them mount you.'

They switched direction again, clattering through fallen corrugated cans. The noise was enough to summon the stranger on the other side of the brick all over again.

'Listen,' Albie began, turning his head to judge the pattern of footsteps over the wall. 'If I don't come out of this alley, there's something I want of you . . .'

'Oh, you'll come out of this alley, Crowe.' Abraham growled out the promise. 'I swear it on Elsa's life, you're coming out of this lane . . .'

'What is it?' the unseen stranger called.

'I want you to go after his son.'

'Edmund?'

Abraham heaved Albie forward, but Albie would not be put off. If tonight was about Elsa lying in her grave, well, Abraham had a son who still walked. Edmund had first come to the Young Bloods when his sister was still alive, keeping house for Albie and his gang down in the terrace. That he had stayed even after Elsa passed on had been a delight to Albie Crowe. Even the son of a watchman had seen there was a world on the other side.

'You know where he is,' Albie began.

'If the boy has any guts, he'll be bound for Meanwood Road with the rest of the Young Bloods.'

'If I don't come out of this alley,' Albie repeated, eyeing Abraham, 'go for him. Tell him he has to answer for his father's crimes. Make sure you list Elsa among them. He'll understand that, well enough.'

At last, they neared the end of the alley. The fires rising in the thoroughfare beyond danced wildly, but Abraham did not breathe a word of his son, nor of Albie's command. He only hovered there, listening out for the tread of the Young Blood's steps, fingering his old revolver. The footsteps were gone – but he was certain the boy remained.

At the maw of the alley, he crouched with the dogs at his heel.

'Who is he?' he finally hissed.

'You know the name,' Albie answered. 'In all honesty, I'm surprised he came for me himself. It never has been Shepherd's style to do the dirty work. That's where he and I have always differed. Shepherd – he has no style.'

Abraham thought he saw a shadow, imagined that Shepherd had his back pressed against the very corner in which they hunkered down. Albie saw him inch forward, fought the temptation to launch himself at the old man and go tumbling, together, into the thoroughfare.

'You've got a gun, Abraham. Shoot the boy down – *if* you've got it in you . . .'

Abraham would not acknowledge the taunt. This was not the right place for a stand. He loosed a shot into the air, felt the kick of the old revolver in his fist, wondered if perhaps he might feel the thrill tonight, just as all those boys in the battalion had felt the thrill when they were young. He did not know if he had the guts to level the weapon at a stranger's face any longer. He supposed he would find out soon enough.

'Are all your Young Bloods petrified of little dogs?' Abraham asked.

'I make certain to tutor them in it the moment they sign up,' Albie returned.

Abraham stooped. When he untethered the first hound, it did not run. It stood there instead, turned its snout toward him, sniffed tentatively at the other still tied to the boy. Abraham drew a hand around its muzzle. Albie recognised a goodbye in that gesture. He opened his mouth, as if to cry out to Shepherd, but Abraham commanded the bitch at his side to lunge – and, hating himself for his fear, Albie shrank against the brick.

The untethered dog bolted into the street. In seconds, a gun rang out.

In the middle of the street, the dog seemed to lift from the stone, freeze there, suspended by some invisible thread, and then silently collapse. Even in this darkness, Abraham could see the wound in its side.

He turned to Albie Crowe.

'Your boys have guns?' he asked.

A strange look ghosted across Albie's face. 'Of course my boys have guns,' he replied. 'Isn't it in your ledger?'

Abraham turned back to the mouth of the alley. Out there, black blood pooled around the fallen dog. His ledgerbooks had been meticulously crafted, stories carefully researched and stitched together. He had thought that he understood every little thing about the Young Bloods' lives – but not once had he pictured them with revolvers or shotguns thrown across their backs.

At his side, Albie Crowe smirked. 'That's two down, one to go . . .' he began. 'Your friend's going to be awfully upset about his dogs.'

Abraham did not hear. He pictured, again, the way the dog had spasmed and fallen, remembered his days in the battalion, and how they had come to know the spots in which a sniper dwelled by the way his victims had fallen.

'Come on,' he said. 'There isn't a mile to go before . . .'

Quickly, before he lost his nerve, Abraham dragged Albie out of the jaws of the alley. In the road, the dog lifted its head to look at him, tongue lolling to the stone. Its tail lifted when it saw him staring, beat sadly against the ground. Abraham drew Albie around and started to run, blotting out the death throes of the dog. You could not rush over the wire to draw back a fallen comrade, not with the guns wailing down, not with the skies on fire.

Abraham froze. Shepherd was not against the wall where he had pictured him.

He turned in the direction of Meanwood Road, searched in vain for faces lurking in the windows of the bombed-out buildings around. The thoroughfare seemed deserted, only the dying dog to tell him that somewhere, out there, an enemy lurked.

Against Abraham's back, Albie Crowe squirmed. Across the road: the shell of an old schoolhouse. No windows were left in the building's face, but shadowmen moved in the gutted windows. He squinted through smoke, saw a figure turn, hoisting a rifle onto its back.

'Abraham!' Albie Crowe yelled. 'There!'

Another shot rang out, and Abraham wheeled. Dragging Albie back between two buildings, he threw himself against a wall, the boy sprawling at his feet. A sharp pain hummed and then exploded in his arm. It was not the first time in his life he had taken a bullet, and he breathed deeply. Focusing on the last dog at his side, he looked into the face of Albie Crowe. Even the boy seemed frightened.

'Who were they?' Albie asked.

Abraham did not understand. He had not seen a single man in the street.

'Your Young Bloods, surely?'

Albie Crowe's eyes were wide. 'Young Bloods?' he laughed. 'They were old men! Home Guard or ARP or . . .'

Abraham ripped at his shirt to see how ugly the wound was. Dark blood drenched his arm. The bullet had torn flesh from his shoulder, but that was all; he raised his arm and the bone was not gone.

'Step down, Abraham,' came an old, feathery voice. 'We'll take him from here.'

Abraham reared back. Lurching back into the alley, he found shelter in an alcove of brick and stopped to check his wound. It was clean, he supposed – and, fashioning a crude tourniquet with his shirt, he staunched the bleeding. Then, making sure that he and Albie were shackled by the other arm, he pushed back into the street. The air was acrid with a smell that visited old horrors upon Abraham. Smoke lounged low over the rooftops – and, although the vague sketches of men moved slowly through that haze, not a sign of Shepherd remained.

'Abraham!' a voice cried from the dirty veil. 'Is it bad?'

Abraham knew that voice. He tried to turn, head for the cover of the buildings, but the voice called out again, as if reining him in.

'Son, you're bleeding badly – you're leaving yourself a trail . . .'

Abraham thrust Albie forward, back into the shelter of a ruined building. The rafters of the floor above had been exposed, and only half a staircase remained. For now, it was enough.

They set off, taking the crumbled steps two at a time. On one side, the wall was fallen, but Abraham reined Albie close and did not let him fall. There were rents in the outer walls here, like murder holes looking out – and, half-way up, Abraham stopped to peer through. A gang of men surrounded the house in a wide circle, a strict formation drilled into them many years before. At first count, Abraham sighted five; a step further, and he saw the sixth, lurking in an alley that snaked away from the main thoroughfare.

Three of the men bore torches of fallen rails bound in rags and plunged into fire. In the alley behind, the shadowman grasped a small flashlight, whose dim beam roamed the alleys on the other side of the street.

They were all old men, two decades and more older than Abraham, and yet they had come armed. Old hunting guns were slung over shoulders, more than one wore a service revolver at his waist and one bore a butcher's blade. The man who seemed eldest held to the reins of a horse, whispering words of encouragement in some lost equine tongue. Perhaps the men had ridden in tandem, for other than the horse, only two others had mounts: crippled motorcycles, one bolted to a sidecar and spluttering thick black fumes.

'The Home Guard,' uttered Albie Crowe. 'It's an army of old men, Abraham. We can outrun them – if you let me out of these *silly* chains . . .'

'It's Ada's father, you sorry bastard.'

In the shadows, Albie's head craned. Abraham bundled him through an archway of fallen brick, into the rubble of a room where some family once gathered.

'Elsa's grandfather?' Albie mouthed.

'I know you're not a family man, Albie, but that is how it works,' Abraham explained. 'And make no mistake about this: Ezra isn't here to make his peace with you. The young boys had a name for him, back when we were fighting. The Lord, they called him.' There had been variations on that name, though Abraham had not heard them all. He had not served under Ada's father, but stories spread like rats through the trenches in which they campaigned. 'If he's brought his wolves out here, it isn't so they can suckle you, son. They were soldiers long before me. It's deeper in them, all the things we did.'

He turned, forcing Albie further up the stairs, into the demolished bedrooms above. There was no roof here, the slates piled in heaps against the walls, and through a hole in the brick, he saw the chambers of the house next door. He risked a glance through one of the fallen blackouts, and saw that only three of the men remained in the street below. Heaving Albie to his side, he stopped dead.

'What would happen if I cried out now?' ventured Albie Crowe.

'Hung, drawn and quartered,' answered Abraham.

He hung on to Albie until he was certain: Ada's father and the others in his troop moved, now, in the hollow chambers beneath. He heard the grating of stone against stone, the clatter as they kicked their way through obliterated tables and chairs. Abraham knew old Ezra's voice well, but the others he could not name; only in the earliest days of his courtship with Ada had he accompanied Ezra on his taproom rounds, been introduced to his father-in-law's friends.

He stopped at a tear in the floor, looked through to see a man with a farmer's overcoat tramping with Ezra through the wreckage.

'We don't want any trouble with the Night Watch!' the scarecrow called out.

'Well, you found it . . .' Abraham seethed to himself, sensing them shift below.

'We just came for the boy! Go home, Abraham . . .'

Abraham thrust Albie through the portal of brick, emerging behind him in the hallway of the house next door. This house had been further from whichever blast shook the building at its side, and the devastation was not as deep. Squares of faded colour marked the places on the wall where portraits had once hung; mattresses lay bare, bookshelves empty. This was not the work of the Young Bloods, he decided – what use had they for poetry and plays? – but of the family itself. No doubt they were somewhere in the hills.

Above the mattresses piled in the master bedroom, an attic trap door had been shaken from its hinges.

'Up there . . .' Abraham whispered.

'With these still on our hands?' Albie asked, lifting his shackled arm.

'I'll admit,' said Abraham, 'it might be a squeeze.'

Together, they scrambled through the opening. The attic was pitched, with steep sloping walls and thin cracks between the slates that let in slivers of firelight. Thick beams ran along the ridge of the roof, reaching a joint only inches above their heads. Against the walls, packing crates had been stacked.

The sounds of Ezra and his followers were distant, and for that Abraham was thankful. They had not yet found the crumbled wall.

'Take off your shirt . . .' hissed Abraham.

'What?'

'Take off that lovely shirt.' Abraham paused. 'What's wrong, Albie?'

'Nothing, Captain,' Albie Crowe groaned. 'I look good without a shirt.'

So slow was Albie Crowe in the disrobing that, in the end, Abraham ripped it from his shoulder. The few buttons that were left skittered across the barren floorboards. And there, in the dull light, he saw again the lattice of marks carved into the boy's breast. Beneath the other notches, the deeper scar stretched.

'For my daughter?' he asked, tracing the wound with a finger, pressing it sharply as if to see the boy recoil.

'There wasn't any crime in what I did to your daughter. She seemed to enjoy it, as I remember.'

Abraham enjoyed forcing the shirt down Albie Crowe's throat. He had seen some of the boys in his battalion perform the same ritual on a German boy who strayed into their trenches. He took the sleeves, dangling from Albie's jaws, and tied them tightly around the boy's head, so that the gag would not slip. Then, wrenching the boy around, he brought his arms behind one of the attic's sloping beams and shackled him there, hanging forward.

'You're right, Albie,' he said, turning around. 'You do look good without a shirt.' He stopped. 'Breathe through your nose until I'm back. You'll be fine.'

It was a difficult thing to raise his fist and bring it back against his eye, but it was a trick he had known men in the constabulary play before, and he supposed it might even have been some distraction from the burning pain in his arm. When it was done, he plunged back through the trap door. Wilbur's hound was thankful to see him. It turned in frenzied circles, but Abraham lifted a hand and commanded its silence. Then, the pain in his eye beginning to blossom, he lifted the mongrel to the trap door and helped it scramble through. Perhaps he was imagining it, but he thought he heard Albie Crowe's silent screams, all his infantile terror muffled by the shirt crammed into his craw.

He scrambled back through the crumbled wall and into the building where Ezra and his followers moved. When he heard them in the chambers beside his, he knew they were already too close. Back through the brickwork he climbed, down an unknown staircase into the empty halls beneath. In a living room shorn of all life, he pulled back thick burgundy curtains to see the other men still parading the terrace.

Atop the mantelpiece, there remained a small jet paperweight. Abraham measured it in his hand, tossed it from palm to palm. In the scullery at the back of the house, he lifted his good arm back and pitched the rock at the glass.

The shattering was loud enough to be heard in the houses around. He lifted a boot, kicked the remaining shards into the yard outside, then turned back into the house. The front door was bolted, but the bolt was not strong. He did not have the time nor the finesse of any Young Blood thief, but his method was just as successful: he tore the bolt from the wood, and tumbled into the street.

Three faces, showered in the fire of their torches, turned to him. One man stood on each of his flanks while the third rose from his alleyway across the road.

Abraham's eye throbbed. He strode into the thoroughfare, and turned back at the house in which Albie Crowe was cocooned.

'Ezra!' Abraham cried. He cupped his good hand to his mouth, and bawled again. 'Ezra, quick!'

The old man appeared in one of the windows, tearing back the blackout and pushing the glass open wide. Marked in shadow, he looked older than he was, and older than any man had the right to be. A moustache, thick and black, dominated his face.

'He ran out back!' Abraham thundered. 'West!' he cried. 'Back toward the Moor!'

'What in hell are you waiting for, boy?' Ezra thundered.

Abraham looked fervently from side to side. 'I'll need to take your bike . . .' he said.

Framed by the window slats, Ezra nodded his consent.

'We'll be on your tail,' he said. 'Don't let the bastard get away.'

Nursing his arm, Abraham shouldered past Ezra's watchmen and swung onto the motorcycle without sidecar. It had been a long time since he rode. In those days he too had been young, a runner ferrying messages up and down the line. He kicked until the motor started roaring – and then the wind was in his hair.

He rode low over the motorcycle, his head close to the handlebars, listening to the engine as the redbricks flickered by. He had not reached the end of the long, snaking road before he heard the other bike screeching in his wake. Behind them, no doubt, rode the scarecrow on his nag, the remaining members of the gang thundering on foot. Abraham risked a look over his shoulder, and was heartened to see the dust trails Ezra's own motorcycle carved. He allowed himself a moment of respite; they had taken his bait.

He kicked hard at the pedal.

The distance between the riders and the Moor was shortening fast. Perhaps he did not have time to outdistance them – but there were backstreets he could use, alleys he might lose himself in if he made enough ground. He forced the bike over a rise in the road and then, kicking hard at the brake, swung into a lane that ran parallel to the edge of the Moor. High on his right-hand shoulder, the heaths glowered down. He kicked again, coming from the shelter of the terrace to the broad thoroughfare of Otley Road – and then he heard the first plane tear holes in the sky.

The stuka flew so low that, instinctively, he cowered. Beneath him, the bike started to slide – but he righted himself, riding until he could drop back between the buildings. Through the redbricks, he heard the roar of Ezra's motorcycle. He skidded to a halt, tore the bike round in the middle of the road. Then, he took flight again, doubling back through alleyways strewn with trash.

Looking up, he saw the second plane tear overhead. It was just as Albie had told him: they were turning their figures-of-eight over the city, returning to deliver another devastating load.

In the mirror there was movement: a motorcycle and sidecar appearing from a meeting of roads. Ezra and the man who rode with him were gaining fast.

He had led them in circles too long. The fantasy was finished. If they stopped him now, it was not words that would get him out of their grasp and back to the attic where Albie Crowe still choked. He lifted a hand from the handlebars, checked that the revolver still hung in the holster at his side. Through an archway of brick he came, the bike weakening with every turn.

A hand on his shoulder. He lurched forward, reined the bike back in, looked up to see the scarecrow who rode at Ezra's side grappling toward him. Abraham kicked out, smashed his foot against the man's shoulder – but the man held fast to Abraham's boot, drawing the two bikes together. Locked in that preposterous embrace, they hurtled on, diverging only when one of the unlit gas lamps reared from the road.

'Abraham!' Ezra thundered, voice muffled by engines. 'Abraham, stop!'

From a side street ahead, the horse and its riders appeared. There were two of Ezra's men atop the poor brute, and when they saw the motorcycles, they reined the beast in. In his mirror, Abraham saw Ezra throw his hands wildly at them – and then they lurched into the road.

The wheel slid from beneath him, and he could not kick out in time. He plunged to the street, the bike whipped away from him, its wheels still turning viciously as it spun into a low brick wall.

Abraham stood. In one direction, Ezra and his bike; in the other, the horsemen lined up in the street. There were voices crying out too – the other old soldiers who had ridden out with Ezra tonight, hollering to find their companions.

Somewhere out there, gluts of Young Bloods moved. Somewhere, just beyond them, Albie Crowe was shackled to a roof beam, waiting to be rescued – or waiting to be killed.

Abraham climbed to his feet, made for the motorcycle, whose engine still hummed. He was not back in the saddle before the men crowded him. He drove hard at the pedal, swung the steed around.

'I'll go round you, Ezra,' he said, 'or I'll go through you. It's all the same to me.'

'Get him off the bike . . .' Ezra ordered.

Some of his sergeants rushed to the command, but Abraham lifted his good arm to fend them off. One of them reached around, snatched at his torn shoulder – and, for a moment, he could not breathe. A final tremor shook the skies, and the last of the planes ripped through the clouds.

Ezra came slowly forward, his palms open as if to show he concealed no knife.

'Abraham,' he said. 'What's going on? Where did he go?'

It was finished. Abraham allowed his greatcoat to fall open, saw the almost imperceptible flicker of Ezra's eyes when the old man recognised the revolver.

'You can't take him, Ezra.'

'If you've been plotting something, why have you kept me in the dark? Elsa was my granddaughter . . .' He uttered the last words like an oath. 'Did you let him get away?'

Abraham seized his chance. 'Better that than have to take you in as a murderer, Ezra.'

'Take me in?' The old man was incredulous. He turned to his companions, the last of them only just rounding the street. 'Take me in, he says, as if it's me with his daughter's blood on my hands ... You're the watchman, Abraham. You decide what's wrong and what's right.' He stepped forward. 'You'll give me the boy?'

'You don't understand ... This isn't just Albie Crowe any more ...' He stopped. There was no time, he could not explain, the beats of this night were numbered – and he had sworn he would reach the end of Meanwood Road. 'He belongs with the Night Watch ...' It occurred to Abraham that the words were his own mantra. He snarled them in the same way Albie Crowe offered up his self-penned prayers. 'He's mine, Ezra ...'

'The Great Captain Abraham Matthews!' the figure at Ezra's side announced. 'Honour and Duty inscribed upon his shield! Who was it told you to be so chivalrous? Well, you don't sit at a Round Table, Abraham – and we're not here to joust ...'

'I'm taking Abraham back,' said Ezra. 'Letting him see what this damn crusade of his is costing me. The rest of you, take these streets any way you can – the little craven can't have got far ...' The men crowded Abraham's shoulder, shepherding him to the motorcycle still spluttering dark fumes. 'This is the way to hunt the boy, Abraham. With a battalion behind you – not some lonesome ranger ...'

'I still have friends in this city,' Abraham said. 'Stalwarts of mine from the old days. They're still at my side, even if they don't ride with me tonight.'

'There's one who doesn't ride with you, though, isn't there, son? One who'll never sit at your side again, now she has the measure of you ...'

Ezra might have been right in that. There was only one thing Abraham wanted more than Ada to take his hand again or throw him a smile – but even the best conjurors in the land did not know how to bring back the dead.

'Put him in the sidecar, boys.'

The house had not changed since that day Abraham first walked the kerb to confess his love. They came through the door to the familiar smells of onion and sage. The paper that hung in the hallway was the same, the carpet at his feet worn by thirty years of tramping boots. At the foot of the stairs, there loomed a picture of him and Ada, taken on the eve of their marriage. He gazed at her for a second too long, and then followed Ezra.

At the foot of the stairs, Abraham peered into darkness above.

'Does Sarah sleep upstairs?' he asked.

Ezra stopped. His wife's had been a long, slow illness that claimed her by degrees. When the rest of the terrace had gone to the hills, she had not even descended the stair.

'Sarah's dead,' Ezra breathed, turning in the doorway. 'We buried her this morning.'

The darkness at the top of the stair was absolute.

'You bastard. You didn't say a thing. Just because Ada's gone, it never meant . . .'

'Don't get honourable on me, Abraham. We tried to tell you. There were a dozen messages sent to the stations. But you don't walk those paths any more, do you? The drudgery of police work isn't enough for Abraham Matthews and Albie Crowe . . .'

Ezra directed him to an old wicker chair, and obediently Abraham sat down. In truth, he was glad of the respite; the pain was dull in his eye, but resurgent in his arm. He tightened the tourniquet, thankful for the momentary release.

'I remember the first time you came to this house, Abraham. You were older then than you are now. That's how it seemed. How old were you? Twenty-eight? Twenty-nine? Fresh from the killing fields and looking for something else to do with your life. Police work was one thing – but the rest, well, you found that in my daughter. Sarah always said you wanted to save Ada from every ill thing in the world, that you hadn't saved her that night you met and you wanted to save her, piece by piece, every day after that – but the truth is, Abraham, that you wanted *her* to save *you*.'

His own story bored him, so often had it been told. It had not been as cynical as the old man made it seem, but he had always known that Ada was the one saving him. Without her, there would have been nothing, just an endless procession of grey days; a past, but no future. He had torn a caul on that day he walked into the Violets tearoom to make her acquaintance – but that had been twenty years ago. Tonight, he was the hero of the story; he did not need to be saved.

'What would you do with Albie Crowe tonight, Ezra?'

'That's my business. You've had your chance with him. Unless I'm mistaken, this wouldn't be the first time you've turned a blind eye to Albie Crowe.'

Abraham did not need reminding; it was a year ago, but he knew what he had done.

'You let him make up the rules, son. But you're a watchman. You're bound to keep this city safe. There isn't any shame in forcing the rules down the boy's throat.' Ezra paused, studied Abraham's face as if he might see the impressions of his words upon it. 'That's something my father taught me. What did your father teach you, Abraham?'

There was not a thing Abraham had learnt from his mother and father that had not been torn to shreds in the fields outside Mons, the years of dirt and deserters and groping in the mud.

He had learnt new lessons, then – and if he had himself torn those to shreds in the years of his roaming, it had not been his father's teachings to which he had returned before coming back to Leeds.

'I want you to trust me, Ezra. I'm not the fool you take me for . . .'

The old man scoffed at the words. 'I've trusted you before. I trusted you with my daughter, and I trusted you with my grandchildren too. Now, one's in the ground and the other's running with Albie Crowe. And Ada – you've destroyed her . . .'

Abraham took the blow, like he had taken a thousand blows before, the better to keep what fragile peace remained.

'You didn't trust me with your daughter,' he returned. 'She trusted me with herself.'

'And where is she now?'

Abraham did not reply. He pictured Ada on the shores of the lake. She was sitting with Kate, and the fisherman Wilbur had described was beside her, telling her the tales of his own life, growing warm with each of her smiles. Perhaps she was thinking the same things about him that she had thought about Abraham, in those first days, when he turned up at the Violets tearoom, unknown and unannounced.

'She's upstairs,' Ezra whispered. 'She came back for her mother.'

When Abraham stole through the door, Ada was curled between her blankets, pretending to sleep. He had known her too long not to read the signs. Gently, he let the latch fall, looked up to see the framed embroidery of the Lord still gazing down. It was not worth his ire tonight.

'Most of us are sad,' he whispered, venturing close to the bed.

Ada turned. In the guttering light of a candle, he saw that she had been crying. The tears were dry, but they stained her cheeks in wild, webbed patterns.

'You should be in the shelters,' he began.

'I heard it said you were there earlier tonight.'

As she moved, Abraham saw that she had not disrobed to go to bed. She was dressed in black, the same robes she must have worn as they scattered dirt upon her mother.

'You should have told me. I'd have been there, with you. I'd have lowered her into the ground.'

Momentarily, Ada's face creased. 'I did tell you, Abraham. I walked from Burley Park to Woodhouse Moor. I left messages at every station. I left messages at home.'

'I haven't been there in nights.'

'I know it. I'd wanted Edmund there too – but he doesn't call that place home any more than you do, does he, Abraham? He even sleeps in the dens of Albie Crowe, doesn't he? Even after Elsa . . .'

Abraham listened to the footfalls retreating along the hallway. He had no doubt that her father would turn at the head of the stairs and creep back silently to listen at the door, but that mattered little. He took the small frame chair from beside the dresser and jammed it beneath the door handle. There were blackouts in the window, but they were easily peeled back.

'Is it true?' she went on. 'You've got Albie Crowe hidden in one of your bolt holes out there?'

'It's true,' he admitted. 'I'm taking him to the station at the end of Meanwood Road.'

Some ghost moved across Ada, contorting her face.

'It's time these streets were safe again. It's time the Crowe got what was coming to him.'

'The Crowe?' she questioned.

73

'Albie,' he replied.

'It seems to me you'd have just called him that, seven months ago. It seems to me you wouldn't have called them Young Bloods or Whisperers or . . .' At last, Ada stood. 'I went back to the old house, Abraham . . . I read your ledgers.'

On the threshold, Abraham stalled. In those tomes he had written their histories, had inscribed the way he might bring each Young Blood to his knees. The phantoms did not only walk the streets at night; they staggered and reeled across every page.

'What's a Stalwart, Abraham? You kept writing about Stalwarts . . .'

'Ada,' he began, daring to turn at last. 'You don't understand. I've seen my head brought in on a platter. I've seen it a hundred times, but it never made a difference – every time I took one on the chin, every time I turned a blind eye, took a sucker punch just to keep the peace, the world kept on turning, just as before.' He stopped, willed her to let him go. 'But I can't spend all my life down at heel, Ada, not like that, not any more . . . I had to do something – and he, he has his Young Bloods. I needed help . . .'

She lifted a sheaf of papers from the dresser at her side: torn and crumpled things, but each bearing the impressions of his words. At the head of each leaf, a name was written, over and again. Elsa. My daughter. My dear girl.

'They weren't addressed to you.' Abraham tore them from her grasp. It was the first time he had sniped so at his wife, but she did not flinch. Scraps of the letters remained between her forefinger and thumb.

'There were others. Letters meant for me.'

There had been more than that. Scrawlings he had been making since the days he first returned to Leeds. Words for Edmund, written upon the day of his birth. Passages scribbled on the backs of envelopes, things that came to him in the dead of night and refused to leave until he forced them out.

I don't want to wake you, but I want to tell you that I love you.

The boy flies ravens at night.

My dear girl, you are less than nothing, now; you are dust.

Abraham had been writing down his thoughts for as long as he could remember.

'You were never meant to read them.' Abraham shook as he spoke.

'Why won't you talk to me?'

'I tell you everything there is.'

Ada let the fragments of letter slip between her fingers. 'You don't tell me a damn thing, Abraham. You've been telling yourself you do for twenty years. But you come in from the beats and you put your arm around me and you tell me all the things that you did – but you've never once told me the things that you think. And – and you're writing letters to a dead girl. Telling her things you've never told me . . .'

He grappled for the page still in her hand, but quickly she withdrew. It had been torn from the leaves he had written to Elsa. Night after night, holed up in that stagnant back bedroom, surrounded by the books and stuffed animals of her childhood, the words had poured out of him in a frenzy of paper and ink. On one side: the ledgers in which he narrated the Young Bloods' history and announced their end; on the other, everything he wanted to say to her, every day he ever lived that had brought him to this night, that had put her six feet under the sod.

Before dawn, I knew what must be done: I knew I did not return to the same England I had left, for my brothers were gone now and there was nobody there to remember the boy I used to be; and if I could not go back and be him, I would not go back and be the man I was now – the man who knew how to dodge the strafing pattern of mounted guns, to lure his enemies forward into the spewing fire of his fellows' flamethrower, to draw his blade across a boy's neck and think nothing of being drenched in his warm arterial spray.

Instead, I roamed.

For months, I rebuilt the obliterated roads of the Ardennes. There were months I kept guard for a young family who trailed the decimated townships, trying in vain to bring their lost brothers and fathers back into the fold. After that: springtime in a home for convalescing soldiers, a summer tilling land ravaged by gas; a winter spent searching for some sorry girl's lost love, a boy who bathed in the blood on the Somme and then disappeared, a wraith, into the snow. There wasn't a beggar on his knees or German boy trapped and running for his life that I didn't bend down and prop up and travel with until they chose to make their own way back home.

And, one by one, I slit the throats of all the people I had been. Some had already been smothered for me – the older brother, the younger brother, the son and grandson both – but the rest, I took a knife to myself: the soldier and servant; the killer and saviour; the hero and villain.

Ada had spent the nights since her return lost in those letters, delving deeper and deeper into those ledgers and chests. That Abraham had spent his years of war driving bayonets into boys' breasts she had always known, but to see each death drawn so vividly, scored into the page as if with a blade, was not something for which she had been prepared. And here were written the stories of every boy Abraham ever killed, how it was done and with what ease he lifted his gun or unsheathed his dagger. There were dozens of tales, but not one of them bled into the others like the blood of those boys had done; each one Abraham had inscribed in intimate detail: the parrying of a blade; the sinking of teeth into some sorry lad's groping arm. Where he could, he had listed names – and if not names, then regiments and insignia, sketching in words the best descriptions his wearied mind had been able to muster.

'You think it's only Albie who has fantasies? Well, you have a fantasy of your own, don't you, Abraham?' She flung the paper at him; when he did not reach out, it only drifted to the ground. 'Being a good man on a dark night.'

Abraham said nothing, drifting instead to where the blackouts hung.

'You're bleeding . . .' she finally said. It might have been that she had noticed it some time before, for she stalled his reply with fingers dancing at the wound. 'I could stitch it for you.'

She reached into the dresser at her side, and fumbled there to produce balls of thread and a needle used for stitching shirts.

'All I wanted was for you to come to the hills with me. You and Edmund, up and out of the city.' She paused. 'Tell me what you have planned for Albie Crowe,' she said. 'Tell me what's happening at the end of Meanwood Road. He thinks you're just arresting him – but it isn't that, is it, Abraham?'

It had touched her already, but there was nothing he could say to staunch it now. There were Young Bloods in her streets. Whisperers. And now, some other monster to whom he himself was giving birth. She would bring him back to earth, if only he would let her, reacquaint him with bricks and mortar and slate; that was what her eyes were pleading, even if her words were not.

He reached out to finger the blackout blinds. There were still planes pirouetting over the city. The morning had not yet come, and Abraham was not yet ready to face the real world.

The carnival had to go on – at least for another few hours, another two miles. He had to finish what he had started.

'Are you going to come back to Leeds?' he asked, not daring to turn around.

'I only left because of the bombing,' she said. 'You made the rest up. You're making it up still. I didn't leave because I hated you.'

'But Elsa . . .' Abraham began, the final word wavering as if he meant to go on.

'I couldn't bear it when you brought her back that day – but I never hated you for that, you old fool. Just like I never hated you for that night we first met. You hang yourself high. I don't know why you get such a thrill out of it, but you put your head in a noose every morning – and, Abraham, I'm not sure I can look at it any more . . .'

Abraham froze. The wind was pawing at the glass, beckoning him on.

'That's the real reason you left,' he said.

From the other side of the wall: a stifled splutter. Abraham thought he heard fingers scratching at the door handle, but when he looked over his shoulder, the handle did not move. He shifted, bent low to kiss Ada's brow.

'He's worried about you.'

'If you kiss me on the forehead one more time, I'm going to . . .' Ada fell still. 'I don't need him looking over me. I don't need you. I want you. That's all. And . . . and what do *you* want, Abraham?'

Abraham would have sacrificed anything to have walked with Elsa tonight, to have huddled with her and Ada and Edmund in one of the Anderson shelters in the yards across town – but the living did not feast at the banquets of the dead.

'You want to be a hero in your own life,' he said, 'but it doesn't work out that way, because you're only some man . . .'

At the window, he peeled back the blackout blinds. He was a mile or more from the attic where Albie Crowe hung from the rafters, straining against his bonds. He lifted one leg through the window, turned back when he heard Ezra's first cries.

'I'll stall him,' whispered Ada, holding his gaze for the first time.

'You were better off at the lake,' Abraham replied, breaking from her eyes. 'Whoever you were with, you were better off out of this.'

Abraham hurtled along an alleyway, reining himself to a halt as he reached its jaws. At first, he thought he could see Ezra's men rampaging along the road beyond – but it was only another string of blitz scouts headed through the ruin. Once they were gone, he loped over the thoroughfare and followed another alley, emerging at last onto the thoroughfare of Meanwood Road.

He could feel a furnace already, and squinted back along the road. There was no sign of the devastation, but surely the streets were ruptured further along the terrace, for black smoke surged upwards, and orange light swelled. He took a step in that direction, but a wall of heat drove him back. He had walked that road with Albie Crowe only hours ago – but there would be no returning by the same path tonight. The thought buoyed him: even the falling bombs were telling him not to turn back.

Watchful, he hurried along the terrace. When he came, at last, to the house where Albie Crowe was gagged, he slowed. Looking back, lest he had been followed, he pushed through the broken door and scrambled up the stairs. The bedroom where the mattresses were piled seemed untouched and, with his one good arm, he reached up to dislodge the trap door above.

When he rose through the portal, the silence was oppressive. In the corner, from shattered crates, the dog rose – but did not dare approach. Shameful, its head hung low.

Abraham heaved himself up. Above him, the rafters were bare. Only the shirt dangling from the wood told Abraham that Albie Crowe had ever been shackled here.

He turned with a long, aching breath. At his feet, the handcuffs lay open, as if left there in taunt. He stooped to pick them up and, as he did so, the dog slunk out of its hiding to grovel at his feet.

'Girl,' he began, 'what happened?'

Abraham scrambled to the rent in the roof. There came a shower of fire from somewhere over the terraces, and orange light rushed in. He pushed forward, the dog whimpering softly at his side.

'Was it Shepherd? The boy from the alley?' he began. 'Or . . .' He paused. 'The old men?' he asked, imploring the hound. 'It can't have been the old men . . .'

Abraham clawed at the tiles and forced his way out onto the roof. Up and down the street he looked – but the boy was nowhere to be seen. Hot wind flurried, streamers of ash moving like tumbleweed along Meanwood Road.

A fire truck appeared from one of the neighbouring avenues and came to a stop, its drivers debating the best way through the devastation, before taking off again, circling in the street to head back the way it had come. After that, there were only black birds, frightened out of their gutter roosts, skittering up and down the pavements, and a feral cat to stalk them.

The emptiness around him was vast.

Abraham sank to his haunches, steadying himself on the hound. A single roof tile loosened beneath his boot, and he kicked it away. For a second it hung in the air above the guttering; then it disappeared, shattering somewhere below.

He started to cry. He did not know it at first, but soon hot tears tracked down his cheeks – and great spasms racked his chest, so that he had to cling onto the dog or risk slipping down the tiles. He drew the hound close, breathed in its earthy scent, murmured incomprehensible apologies over and again. Then, when at last he was still, he sat there shivering, watching the city come back into focus.

Beneath him, Meanwood Road banked toward the devastation at the heart of the city. The station was waiting there, beckoning him on – but the shackle hung freely from his wrist, with no boy bleating at his side. He could reach the end of the road, if that was what he wanted – but there was no point in walking that road alone. There was no point in walking any road alone – he believed that with all of his heart now, in a way he had only tried to convince himself before.

He pictured himself turning around, following the path along which he had walked and going back to his wife. She would come to the door and take his hand and lead him within, and they would lie together in the sheets and talk about their daughter, the first words she had spoken, the tears she used to shed, the face that would be pressed against the glass every time Abraham returned from his beats. And then, come the morning, they would find their son and say their farewells to the city.

There would be another chance to catch the boy. He could not disappear completely, no matter what he thought. He was flesh and blood, just like every other crook Abraham had condemned. Perhaps it was only the way his wife's eyes had implored him, the way he had walked again in her scent – but it seemed clear to him, now, that a man lived from day to day, without having to shoulder his past. He could go to her now and not damn himself in the morning. Elsa was dead and gone; there could be life after that, but only if he let it.

Wearily, he turned. As if in understanding, the dog rose gratefully and beat its tail.

Before he could stoop back through the rent in the roof, something drew Abraham's eyes to the churning sky. For a moment, there was silence – and then a plane banked sharply out of cloud, so low that Abraham fancied he could see the clusters of leaves daubed in white paint on the fuselage. The plane roared as it rose, disappearing again into thick smoke.

Abraham stared until long after the plane was gone. He pawed the tears from his eyes, and squinted further down the valley. Yellow beams rose from the horizon, searchlights beyond the city limits tracking planes as they hurtled on. One set swung toward the terraces before another station picked up the call. When Abraham turned, he saw other beams tracking planes over the northern streets. The barbarians were at the gates.

The night, it seemed, was not finished yet.

Ada's words rang starkly in his head. *You have a fantasy of your own, don't you, Abraham? Being a good man on a dark night.* It was a foolish fantasy for which she justly chastised him – but, no matter how great the temptation, he could not denounce it yet. The boy out there, running free of his chains, was crafting his own legend too – and if it took that fantasy to make him ride out, recapture Albie Crowe, and get him to the end of the road, well, he could indulge the nonsense a little longer.

He took the dog's snout in his hand and fixed it with a gaze. It had been a wearisome night and its eyes glimmered hopefully.

'Not yet,' he said, as if to convince himself as well. 'I can't give up yet.' He thought of Elsa and he thought of Edmund, and he thought of every other Young Blood, rushing to Albie

Crowe's banner, being dragged into his world. 'Not when there's only one mile left to go . . .'

* * *

The mirror was cracked from side to side.

If he stood in the right position, above a knot in the boards, Albie Crowe could see his reflection twice over, two identical visions considering themselves in the looking-glass. If he twisted his body slightly, the image fractured again, his body contorting as if in some cheap fairground hall of mirrors. It was this effect that the boy remembered so vividly from his earliest days: one minute a monster, one minute a saint.

His trousers were buckled at the waist, but other than that, he wore nothing. The old army greatcoat was draped over a chair in the empty hearth, of all the things Albie owned the only one over which he took any care; on the boards underneath the unmade bed, his battered hobnailed boots and a pile of ragged shirts. He lifted the knife from its rest on the mantel and, spinning it between forefinger and thumb, turned back to the mirrors. He murmured the same three words over and over – 'Don't fall asleep, don't fall asleep' – and then he dropped to his knees.

It is said that, left to its own devices, a child will find its own rituals and superstitions in the world. Albie Crowe looked into each of his reflections, brought the knife to his breast, and carved a small notch there to sit alongside the rack of pointed scars he already wore. One day, his body would be daubed with all of the things he had done, the triumphs and disasters both. A thin trickle of blood cut its course down his trunk. He staunched it with a finger and admired the texture of his crimes in the glass.

When he went out that night, the wounds were not yet dry. This, he had learned, was the way it had to be: an open sore for an open crime. He had walked with others on the last of his forays – a boy named Shepherd, who matched him at dominoes in the Packhorse taproom – but, tonight, Albie prowled alone. This was the way he had prowled on the night he smashed his first glass; there was a purity in it he still liked to savour.

He had picked his mark a dozen nights before. There were opportunist thieves working these streets – but they were the ones who would rot in cells. Albie Crowe worked at his craft, offered up his prayers to the demons that looked after him. He dropped to his knees in front of the gate, made the sacred gestures from head to foot, and fixed on the glass that he would smash. The window was a portal to him tonight, and he longed to step into that other world, become the creature on the other side of the glass. One day the people of these towns would see what manner of man walked among them.

Through the glass he went, into the family home beyond. The houses of these streets had all been built to the same design, and he palmed confidently along familiar scullery walls. That was the first lesson a boy embarking upon this endeavour ought to learn: the world craved its order – and all it took to make your mark was to dare to be different. There were silver spoons in the scullery, and he found places to secrete them in the folds of his clothes. He had a knapsack over his shoulder, and he tossed other trinkets into it as he went.

Albie was not so unlearned that he did not know this was the house of a watchman. Books and blackboards were not the only places a boy could learn his lessons, and Albie was not so stupid as the watchmen of this city dared to think. They were called Abraham and Ada, and tonight they celebrated an anniversary that was not the date of their wedding, but the date they confessed their honeyed love for one another instead. It was not difficult to learn such sentimental stories, if that was what you wanted to hear.

He took his first steps upon the stairs. He took them three at a time, prowled into each of the rooms on the landing above. Here, the marital bed where the watchman's wife slept in the protection of her captor; here, the small dresser with its drawers of necklaces and pearls. He took everything he could find, crowned his spoils with the ornate frame of a photograph whose portrait he scattered in fragments upon the bed.

'Sleep well tonight,' he whispered to the empty room as he retreated.

There was only one room left to scour. Albie Crowe lingered a little on the landing, breathing in the smells of this family, imagining that in doing so he might discern something of their habits, their hatreds, the people they purported to be. Then, satisfied at last that he had the measure of this brood, he followed the passage to the final room.

He came through the door. Upon the window-ledge, a girl with brown hair had her face buried in a book. She was wearing her night-shirt, and held the book in the pool of light from a candle whose lavender scent filled the room. She did not see him, at first. Hushed, he shuffled into the shadows around the door. He looked at the words illuminated on the cover of her book, those inscrutable symbols that would never mean a thing to a boy like Albie Crowe. He hated her, then, for the secrets those symbols kept from him.

Slowly, she turned around.

The girl did not shriek. She did not claw at the glass and holler for her father. She merely lifted the candle, dribbling molten wax at her feet, brandished it aloft so that the light might fall upon the intruder.

'Who are you?' she asked; the words were soft, but still it was a demand.

Albie froze. He had had a vision, upon his first foray, of the way he would one day be: a thief so talented that he might live for seasons at an end in the very rooms from which he was thieving; so silent and skilled that he might be seated at the head of the table while the family dined around him, lifting the food unseen from their plates.

'My name is Elsa,' she said.

'Albie Crowe,' he answered, bowing his head low.

He sat with Shepherd in the Packhorse taproom in the week that followed, playing at dice. It was one of the few haunts across Leeds that he still frequented. There were inns here where every man knew the name of every other, but that was not Albie Crowe's way. Better a back room where no man cared to introduce himself than a room full of beaming faces and hands to shake.

He called her the Girl in the Night, for something stopped him from using her real name, and when he described her to Shepherd, the boy's lips turned.

'I haven't heard you talk like this before. Don't tell me you're in love?' Shepherd ventured, uncertain how the taunt would go down.

'I didn't use the word,' said Albie. 'But there are things I want to do, things I haven't done yet, and it might be she's the girl for it.'

'There's a place in Chapeltown you can get that without having to make an effort.'

'I'm a thief, Shepherd. It isn't my style to pay for the things I ought to get free.'

It was not Albie's style to make any man his confidant either, but he supposed there were some things over which a boy might seek counsel. He and Shepherd had already run on a dozen or more nocturnal forays together, and though he would never deign to call the boy a friend, perhaps he would stoop so low as to use the word 'ally' instead.

A gust of cold wind flurried through the doors, and a stranger crossed the room to reach the bar. He was a lean man, a year or two older than Albie, and he walked with a strange gait, as if walking was an action he had been late in coming to. His brown hair was long and unkempt as a tramp's.

'Shepherd,' the boy murmured, nodding his head as he passed.

'Who's that?' asked Albie, following the stranger with his eyes.

'They call him Doonan. A lad from Salford, who pitched up here last winter. He doesn't have many friends. They don't breed them for making friends that side of the hills.'

'I jumped a train there once,' Albie returned, not caring to explain the nature of his voyage. 'A monotonous lot, the boys over there. No imagination. But the girls . . .'

Shepherd downed the dregs of his drink. 'That's the second time you've mentioned girls tonight. I'm beginning to think you're trying to make a point.'

They stayed there through the afternoon. It was the middle month of winter, and darkness came early. Workers drifted back from their haunts in the city, traipsing the roads to the outlying towns, and a steady stream of them passed through the taproom for whiskies to warm them on their way.

There was much to discuss. Albie had marks in mind, and there were fences in the city whose enterprise demanded to be fed. Shepherd would run with him in the next weeks. There would be a division of labour: Albie to spirit treasures from the houses he had marked, Shepherd to ferry the goods to the fences and collect their dues – and, in the end, a division of the spoils.

'We should bring Doonan in. Drew too. He's simple, but he's loyal, Albie. He wouldn't let you down.'

Albie's eyes widened, but Shepherd did not yet know him well enough to understand the warning.

'I'll tell you when it's time for a gang,' Albie breathed. 'There's too many already. You see that man in the third hearth?' Shepherd's eyes flickered in that direction. 'He's another one wants in. Reckons he used to run a racket when there wasn't even a city, riding from town to town like some highwayman of old. He thinks he can curry favour in the constabulary, pull strings for us – but I heard tall tales about him from one of his turncloak friends. He calls himself a Whisperer, but he'd turn us in for a nugget of gold, and we can't protect ourselves against the likes of him. So listen to me when I say it, Shepherd – I'll tell you when it's time for a gang.'

A shadow fell across the table. Shepherd was the first to look up, for Albie insisted on draining his drink before looking around. The Girl in the Night stood beside them. She had not even had the decency to be sheepish in her approach. Shepherd knew, before being told, that this was the girl of which Albie had spoken. She had an indistinct prettiness, that much was true, but she was not a girl much to Shepherd's tastes. He nodded to her vaguely, and kicked back his chair.

'Crowe?' he began.

'Don't call me Crowe.'

Shepherd did not respond to that.

'Get out of here, Shepherd. I'll let you know when I'm ready.'

'Take your time, Albie. I've got a life outside of you.'

Shepherd disappeared into one of the back rooms, and from there out into the night. Thin trails of snow were falling, and they spread in calculated patterns on the glass. Albie imagined he could predict how each pattern would spread and grow; the world was built on patterns waiting to be exploited.

He turned to the Girl in the Night. She was different than he remembered, but that was no surprise; it had been the Albie on the other side of the mirror who had met her last – but, tonight, he was on a different side of the glass.

'People tell me I should be frightened of you,' said Elsa.

Albie Crowe must have liked the sound of that, for it was the first time he looked her in the eye. His own were suddenly aglow, and he turned his tankard to her, as if to offer her a taste.

'Who knows you came here?' he asked.

'My brother Edmund,' she said. She allowed herself to smile, as if she had caught the arch-manipulator Albie Crowe off guard. 'He doesn't know I know it, but he's watching us from a yard across the street.'

Albie's eyes darted viciously around.

'He thinks he's your father, does he?'

'He dreams of being a watchman.'

'You should tell him there are better roles a little whisperer might play.'

Albie offered to get her a drink. She admitted, without any embarrassment, that she had never before ordered a drink in a taproom, and that perhaps she would like the experience for herself. Albie sat back then, and spread his arms wide to show her the bar. 'You'll buy me a drink, of course,' he said. 'It's only polite.'

When she returned, she put two glasses on the table before them. Albie thought about thanking her openly, but only nodded quietly instead.

'I've been thinking about you,' she said, taking her seat.

Albie raised his shoulders.

'You're supposed to say you've been thinking of me too.'

'That's the way this goes, is it?'

'That's what happens when a boy meets a girl in a book.'

Albie tensed, taking the first draught of his drink. 'I haven't a head for books,' he began. 'But I'll take your word on it.'

Elsa took the first sip of her drink too. She had tasted wine before, but only on Christmas days, and the taste was not entirely pleasant.

'So – have you been thinking of me?'

'I've been thinking what made me give you my name. I've been thinking what you might have told that father of yours that he hasn't already put me in a cell. I've been thinking why you didn't scream, when I walked into that chamber.' He paused. 'I suppose *that might mean I've been thinking on you more than your father would think proper.'*

There was flattery in that, Elsa decided. That would do – for a start.

'I've been thinking of you too,' she admitted.

'And what have you been thinking?'

She was not shy, or at least she feigned confidence more strongly than any girl Albie had known. Albie liked the uncertainty in that. He said little to her that night, playfully rebuffing each leading question with an observation of his own. Albie bought a second round of drinks, and by the time they were finished with those, the barkeeps were shovelling the men they did not like back onto the street, and shepherding those they did into one of the back rooms. Albie had watched the ritual before, but not once had he been invited through those doors. The night drinkers here were too set in their ways to understand what a boy like Albie would one day do for these towns.

They walked. The snow was too wet to settle for long, and the drifts that gathered along the banks of the road would be gone by morning. Though Elsa drew a shawl around her, Albie Crowe walked in torn shirt-sleeves and did not make complaint. They came to the Otley Road and walked in the shadow of the Moor.

'You came here tonight to decide whether you'd rat me out or not,' Albie deduced. He had been weighing the thought in his mind since she appeared, but he was not yet certain which way her decision had fallen. There was something inscrutable about Elsa Matthews. A girl who did not scream when a lone stranger stalked her bedroom at night deserved special attention.

'That might have been part of it,' she conceded. 'But there were other reasons too. I've heard your name whispered in the terraces. Do I really have to spell it out?'

Albie curled his hands into the loops of his belt. His chest was searing now, where last he had carved it.

'I suppose there are things you don't see in life when you grow up a watchman's daughter,' he mused. A trap passed them, an elderly couple huddled beneath blankets in its back. 'Will you tell him who took his things?'

'I haven't asked for them back.'

'They're long gone by now. There's a man ferries coaches to Manchester. They'll buy any old thing over there, if you tell them what it's worth.' He paused. 'What would he do, if you told him it was me?'

Snow iced the braids in her hair. Albie was surprised to find himself noticing.

'My dad's a straightforward man.' Elsa was not certain, but there had seemed a certain thrill in Albie's voice when he asked the question. 'He'd come looking, once he'd taken it to his station. There wouldn't be any malice in it. I'm not sure there's a malicious bone in him. He'd come for you, but out of duty, not revenge . . .'

Albie walked with a different bounce in his step then, as if he had stumbled upon some private magic whose meaning had long evaded him. Duty, not revenge. Perhaps he could understand the watchman, now.

'No fire in his gut, that's what you mean.'

Elsa tensed. She controlled it well, but still Albie noticed. The snow curled more thickly and seemed to draw a veil between them.

'No fire?'

'A man with fire in his gut doesn't become a watchman.'

Elsa folded her arms. She might have thought Albie would take umbrage at that, but if he did his pale blue eyes did not change.

'A watchman's what he wants to be. He grew up dreaming of doing something good – being a knight in armour, or a brave Antarctic explorer, or a man saving drowning wretches at sea . . .'

'Those dreams will get him nowhere. They're just fantasies his parents gave him when he was a kid. And I didn't have parents to hold me back like that, not ones who'd fill my head with those notions.'

'You must have had dreams,' insisted Elsa. 'What did you dream of being?'

Albie smiled for the first time that night. 'A pirate,' he said. Once he realised the way she was looking at him, he stalled. 'You're laughing at me.'

Elsa furrowed her brow; she had not raised even the flicker of a smile.

'I'm not laughing,' she said.

'See that you don't. I dreamt of manning the guillotine as well.'

They reached the corner of the Moor, that parting of the ways where the lights of the Violets tearoom still shone. Though Elsa strayed on, Albie drew to a halt. He stood there, shivering for the first time, until Elsa turned to face him.

'Are you going to kiss me?' she asked.

'Not tonight,' admitted Albie Crowe.

If she was perturbed at that, she kept it hidden well.

'Or even walk me home?'

She realised that Albie was not looking into her eyes as she had thought. He was looking beyond her, instead, into the shadows of the great oaks beyond. There was another shadow there, hunched against one of the trunks as if he was hidden.

'I think there's another to shadow you home,' Albie said. He danced his fingers up and down her arm in deliberate patterns, zig-zags he had been plotting all night. 'But I'll see you again, no doubt. I have a place in the terrace. Might be I'll show it to you. Might be there's a room for you there.' He paused. She had shuffled a little closer to him, but he drew his hand away. 'And tell your brother there's a place at my table too,' he breathed, turning

*away to drop down the ledges, 'if that's what the little spy
wants . . .'*

*She came back to him only three nights later, and together they
walked the highest stretches of the Moor. Edmund lurked in the
lower pastures, too frightened yet to cross the scrub his parents
had forbidden him to walk, too courageous to turn and leave his
sister to this strange boy without a home.*

*It was Elsa who did the talking. Albie was content to
listen, drink in her words and, in doing so, come to know
her better. He asked her which parts of the city she had seen, and
it did not surprise him to learn that she had lived her whole life
in the stretch of terraces that reached from Burley Park to
Woodhouse Moor. There was, he decided, time to rescue her from
all that.*

*It took some coaxing, but he told her of the little empire he
dreamed of building, down in that run of the Sheepscar terrace
where he had been holing up, and she agreed that she would
follow him there. She asked if that was where he had been raised,
but his eyes told her that he did not want to say. He led her
through the briars at the Moor's scrub end, and from there they
dropped down lanes she had never followed before. She followed
at two paces behind and tried to take his hand. Their fingers
touched, but not once did they intertwine. Albie Crowe was
saving that for a later hour.*

*Before darkness was completely descended, they came to a
crooked row where the windows were boarded and the gardens
left to go wild. There were gaslights along the row, but only one in
five glowed with any light.*

*'They never came back to these houses, after the fighting,' Albie
explained, running his fingers idly along the bars of every fallen
gate they passed. 'Whole families just gone, and no one to fill the
void. Until me and my kind came along.'*

He had chosen as his lair a house at the end of the terrace. The bottom windows were boarded up, but fractured glass remained in the windows above, and the rooftop slates had not perished yet. Within, the bottom rooms had been gutted – tables and chairs hacked to pieces for want of firewood – while, upstairs, life of a sort went on. It was unlike any home Elsa had walked in before, but there was something appealing about the patchwork life Albie Crowe led.

Albie threw himself onto the old mattress. Elsa looked over him curiously.

'You call this a home?' she ventured.

Not once in his many months of bedding down here had Albie Crowe called the place home. And yet, as he saw Elsa peering into every corner, running her finger along the mantelpiece dust, inscribing a line through the dirt that stained the window, he saw that that was what it was. There had been a dozen different places his mother called home when he was a boy, but he had bedded down here longer than in any of those.

He stoked the remnants of last night's fire. There was no seat in the room, but they sat on the end of the bed together and watched the fire daemons dance.

For the first time, she asked about his family. She looked at the bare walls, unadorned by photographs or portraits, and found herself wondering aloud where the rest of his brood were. There must have been a mother; there must have been a father; no doubt there were brothers and sisters, older and younger, who had once run and squabbled with Albie Crowe.

'They're gone,' Albie returned.

He saw her eyes widen. There was a wildness in this girl – some throwback, surely, to a generation that was not her father's. And if she wanted to know where the rest of his brood were, well, he would not have been able to tell her, even if she had begged. He had exorcised those ghosts already, left them far behind.

'Dead?' she asked.

In the year since he last looked into his mother's eyes, he had been searching for the way he could make the severance complete. It was not enough to never see them again – not when he still spoke with her voice, not when his words still echoed those of his stepfathers, not when he laughed with the same derisive sound as the brothers that once surrounded him. It had been twelve months, but he had not yet lost faith: soon, he would discover the rite that would change him beyond recognition.

'After a fashion,' was all he could muster.

Elsa recalled the story of her father's return to the city. 'You don't have to live alone,' she began. It was not pity that she felt for the boy, but something in her did reach out for him; it was not only her hand that inched across the crumpled bedsheets. 'There are people out there who think they do, but that's a ploy they play.' It was something her mother believed. They had spoken of it often, while her father was out pounding the beat. 'But there's a perfect world to be made, if you go out and get it – one where no one falls asleep alone. My dad has friends. Good men, but they go to bed alone every night and wake up the same way the next morn. And they'll tell you they're happy in that, but you see them in the taprooms, and I watch them walking the beats with my father . . . and it's in their eyes, Albie.'

He paused. He had not expected her to understand. Yes, he had a mother, somewhere out there. Yes, there was a father flitting from one side of the hills to the next, siring his bastards as if he alone was charged with populating the earth. And, of course, there were brothers and sisters scattered from one end of the city to the other. But not one of them was with him. He alone had set out on this great adventure, begun again without any of the trappings of his past.

'Stay the night,' he said.

She looked at him. 'They'll wonder where I am . . .'

'Let them wonder,' he went on.

His words must have thrilled something in her, for she smiled and said that there was nothing she wanted more than to wake in a room with boarded-up windows, in sheets that had not been changed for months, with a breakfast of stale toast and milk lifted from some poor soul's doorstep.

'Another time,' she began. 'For now, you can be content in walking me home.'

'They're coming down the road, Crowe.'

Shepherd stood idly at the foot of the close. November was already nearing its end, and flurries of snow whirled over the terraces. Shepherd and his slow-witted hound Drew had run strings of yellow lights through the hedgebacks of the abandoned houses, and spent hours hurling tin stars up to crown the tops of broken gaslights – and, through the strange shadows of those decorations, two boys lumbered forth. It was rare for boys to venture into this part of the terrace, but there was always some poor wayfarer who strayed onto the wrong path. Tonight, for the first time, the strangers were expected.

Albie pitched his cigarette out of the upstairs window and drew back into the room. In the bed behind him, Elsa was reading some tome of fairy tales that had been in her family for generations. There were more and more books in the lair these days: histories and Shakespeares and books of Greek myth. She was fond of reading aloud, though often it took a bitter and bloody scene to make Albie listen. She had read to him the night before of the old commander Fairfax, who long ago gathered his troops upon Woodhouse Moor before storming the city. Albie had listened attentively to the tale, but bristled each time she turned the page.

'You'll stay here,' he murmured, sitting briefly at the foot of the bed and running his hand along her leg.

Shepherd had already admitted the two stragglers to the barren halls below. There were candles lit along an old mantelpiece and, with the windows still boarded, no other light to see by. When Albie took his seat, he saw that the boys were younger than he expected – barely out of short trousers, and already holding cudgels in their hands.

'Who are they, Shepherd?' he asked, looking over their shoulders to see his cohort prowling the boarded-up bay.

'The ugly one's Browning. The other? His lackwit, perhaps.'

'He's my brother,' the first began. He had a weasel's snout, and his hair was a dirty kind of red.

'And what would bring you here?' Albie asked. 'What could there possibly be for boys like you in these roads of town?'

The Browning boys were not men of many words. Albie liked that in a man.

'We have a little problem,' one of them began. 'We'd heard you were the sort of a boy who might help. It's with a . . .' He spent a moment floundering for the words. '. . . an associate of ours,' he decided. 'A man named Allgood. A slaughterman.'

The Slaughterman worked in a butcher's shop at the end of the Meanwood lanes, with a small killing parlour out back where he bled pigs and goats and sheep. It had long been the racket of the Browning clan to rob from the herds of the outlying farms, and bring their stolen flock to the Slaughterman for his blade. The arrangement had extended between Browning the elder and the Slaughterman's father before them but, with the coming of war, the butcher, though more and more eager to accept their wares, was less and less eager to spend his hard-earned shillings on them.

'You brought this on yourselves,' Albie began. Shepherd cast him a quizzical look; he was not aware that the Browning boys had come to hear Albie pronounce his first decree. 'If there was another slaughterhouse competing for your wares, you wouldn't have this on you.'

'We shouldn't have boys coming here, spilling all their secrets,' Shepherd interrupted. His eyes, wide with warning, lifted, quickly, to the ceiling boards. 'She might be listening. All it would take was one wrong word – to that brother of hers, if not her father – and these boys could be hauled over the coals.'

'Bedding the watchman's daughter . . .' the larger Browning snickered. 'You play a dangerous game, Albie Crowe.'

'Who whispered that in your ear?'

Albie was not angry, only curious. The Browning boy shrugged, but his brother was more eager to turn his cloak. It was all over the terraces, he said. The words came from the girl's brother, Edmund, who rode his bike from one end of the terrace to the next. It was certain that the girl's father knew which boy she had taken up with, for Edmund was an obedient boy, and too straight to keep a secret.

'I'll help you with the Slaughterman,' he conceded. 'But I'll want something in return – and it seems to me you came to my terrace with empty hands.' For the first time, he stood. 'It seems to me that, if I came to a man asking for his help, I might offer something up to him. Some sort of payment. Some sort of thanks.'

'Some sort of tribute,' murmured Shepherd, though his words went unheard.

The Browning boys shifted uneasily. They were not stupid, they had ripped off the Slaughterman for long enough to know that nothing came without its cost, and yet there was a glimmer in Albie Crowe's eyes that told them his would be a steep price.

'We'll cut you in. Give you a third of what we get the next time we make a run.'

'I don't want your cut,' said Albie. 'There'll come a time for that – but that time isn't now.' He paused. 'All I want,' he said, 'is your promise. You boys know stretches of the terrace that I don't. You'll know watchmen who pound different beats. I want you to come to me with everything you know.'

'You want me as your spy?' the Browning boy asked.

'Let's call you my Whisperers,' he said, recalling the old fool in the Packhorse taproom. In the corner of the room, Shepherd's eyes lifted at the word. 'Somebody to spill the secrets they hear out there on the terrace, somebody to keep me one step ahead of the constabulary.' He paused. 'I trust we have an understanding in that,' he breathed.

The Slaughterman did not trouble the Browning boys again. The next time they came for him, he spoke only when he was spoken to, gritting his teeth behind lips swollen and red. He was ready to accept almost any kind of load from them after Albie Crowe's intervention – whether prime mutton rustled from one of the strongest flocks, pheasants lifted from some farmer's doorstep or pack mule meant for the feed of pigs. The Browning boys were grateful for the service Albie performed, and eager to show their thanks. At dawn, on each Sunday that followed, a freshly blooded grouse hung from the gatepost of Albie's lair.

After that, there were more and more gangs that came for the service of Albie Crowe. A trio of brothers from deep in the Kirkstall terrace asked for help in the sacking of a forgotten school. Some midwife with a trade in stolen coals came from as far as Otley to make her allegiance. The word spread, through taproom and cobbled market, that here there was a boy of talent, a ragged man extending his hand to every other ragged soul who cared to come his way. One by one, they drifted to his lair on the Sheepscar terrace – and, one by one, they discovered the new law of Leeds: for everything Albie Crowe gave, he exacted a price in return.

'Your boy Drew has a way with birds, doesn't he?' Albie asked Shepherd one crisp midnight, with Christmas nearly upon them. A flight of starlings perched upon the gutters above, lit from below by the flaring Christmas lights.

'Simple things love a simple mind,' Shepherd replied.

'It might be we can find a use for him, after all. It might be he's just what we're looking for.'

After it was agreed, they took Drew to the Packhorse taproom, and introduced him to the delights of whisky and gin. The Brownings were there too, and in the back rooms some of the other boys who had come to Albie Crowe. When Elsa wended her way through the revellers to find them crowding one of the flaming hearths, there was a seat waiting for her at Albie's right hand.

'We won't be seen like this together again,' said Albie, a dozen heads crowding to hear his words. 'Not all in the same place, not all at the same time. There'll be ravens to ferry our messages and loose tongues out there, whispering to us whenever a watchman comes our way.' Elsa's fingers found his beneath the table. He squeezed them as she no doubt wanted, then let them go. 'From this night in, we have never been friends.' He spat the word, for it was not one he had often used. Then, he looked to Elsa.

He had not told her yet, but these were to be the last nights they spent in the abandoned terrace. There were too many out there, now, who knew which roads to walk, too many loose tongues who could whisper of which doors hid Albie Crowe; there were grander halls for them to walk when the New Year came.

Some of the boys had brought gifts. Christmas was only days away, even the Packhorse taproom was bedecked with streamers and lights, and they lay across the tables amidst boxes and balls of crumpled paper. Albie, too, had provided presents of a sort: there were trinkets he had been saving from his most intrepid expeditions, and cold cider waiting for all of his boys behind the bar. Elsa's gift for Albie lay unwrapped among the remnants of the rest, but she was not discouraged by that: later, in the night, she and Albie would unwrap that old tome together, and she would read to it from him – and he, no doubt, would bestow his present upon her.

'You're the one calls himself Crowe?'

Albie looked up. He had not seen the man before, and for that he swore an oath – he knew the faces of almost every man who drifted through the taproom, and took pride in the knowledge. The figure who loomed before them, angular as a man made out of sticks and meant for a bonfire, looked old enough to have seen the better part of his days in the century before. He wore a greatcoat that was frayed around the edges and belted with rope, the insignia of his battalion still clinging to the breast decades after the man last saw battle. Albie had taken note of his kind before: they clung to their relics, lived inside their heads.

'What can I do for you, sir?'

'You can go back to whatever brothel you was birthed in.'

Albie looked from his right shoulder to his left. Beside him, Elsa shook her head slowly – but the Crowe was not a boy to be admonished.

'Speak of my mother how you will,' he said. 'She isn't in me any more.'

'Why aren't you boys fighting?' the stranger snarled. 'Why aren't you signed up? There's decent boys dying in droves for you, but they leave the shit behind, just like it was the last time around – and here they sit, drinking and dancing and whoring around. I've seen you in the alleys, son . . .'

'Say hello the next time, won't you?'

'You've never been blooded, that's all it is! You haven't seen a thing of the world, so you think you can raze it all and start again . . . But kick out, and everything that came before, it'll kick right back . . . You young bloods won't last for ever . . .'

'Young Blood,' smiled Albie. 'It has a certain ring to it, I'll admit.' He turned. 'Barkeep!' he called, gesturing vaguely to the man who tended bar. 'Is this man one of yours?'

The man behind the bar was older than Albie – but by months, not years. His father had kept the Packhorse taproom before him, but now he wasted his nights in the rooms upstairs, leaving his son the rule below.

'Bothering you, is he, Albie?'

Albie Crowe softly shrugged. 'He's troubling me some,' he murmured.

The barkeep vaulted the bar to appear at the old man's shoulder.

'Then he's out of here, Albie.' His hands fell upon the old man. 'You heard the boy,' he said. 'I won't have you attacking my patrons.' They turned. Somebody had already opened the doors, and outside streamers of snow turned through the dark. The old man might have said something, then, but instead he only craned back to look at Albie and his acolytes.

'Time to find another taproom, I think,' Albie Crowe muttered as the winter whipped in.

Back in the lair on the Sheepscar terrace, Shepherd and Drew played at sticks while Elsa brewed tea. Weeks ago, she had taken the boards down in the windows, and hung threadbare curtains in their stead, salvaged from the other abandoned homes – but, soon, all of that would be gone.

Abandoning the game, Shepherd crumpled a week-old newspaper and threw it into the embers that glowed in the hearth. For a moment, the coals flared brightly; the paper curled, and then it was gone.

'They say there'll be bombs over London soon,' he said. 'Manchester too. It won't be long before they're here, Albie.'

'The watchmen might have something more to think about than some young bloods out on their streets,' he began. 'There'll be good days.' He stopped. 'Better days,' he observed, parting the ragged curtains to see the starry vaults above. The night was clear, but in the months to come, surely the sky would be streaked with smoke. The fire would fall upon the factories and mills and the people of Leeds would flee into the hills. They would leave their treasures behind, of that Albie Crowe was certain. The city would be his. 'Elsa,' he said, taking her hand. 'Let's leave these little boys to their games.'

In the bedroom, he told her that he loved her. They were not words she had been expecting. In the sheets they fell together, quick as dogs; then they sprawled there together, the cold night air blowing in.

'Have you been with anyone before?' she asked him softly.

He had come close. It had been in the days before he left home, when there was still a woman he called mother, with brothers and sisters wheeling around. She had been some cousin of a half-cousin banished to lodge at whichever hovel his family was holed up in, and he must have clung to the ends of her coat for three months before he understood it was only a game. He had thought he could ensnare her, had practised on his sainthood so that she might come to his side – but it had earned him nothing.

Now that he practised only on himself, Elsa was his. He wondered what it was that she loved in him: was it the things he inherited from his mother and his father, or was it the man he was becoming, now that he was carving all of that away? He shivered at the thought that she might have been falling for some part of his family that still remained.

'I've never had anyone,' he admitted.

She curled into him. As he looked down, he tried to remember how he had felt only last night, wondering when it would happen. It was a foolish notion, but he had thought he would feel differently after the fact. He had hoped he might have found the right incantation to erase, at last, the dregs of his old life.

Lying with her had been well enough, he supposed, but the quest was not over yet. It was going to take something bigger.

'It's coming, Elsa. You know that, right?' She cocked him a look, and it moved in him. 'And it isn't the bombs and it isn't the boys. It isn't even you. I'm not the boy I was five years ago. I'm not the man I was five months past.'

Elsa checked herself in the tall mirror against the wall. It was cracked from side to side, and identical reflections faced each other across the divide. Albie's arms were around her, and in the glass their eyes met: the real Elsa Matthews and the mirrored Albie Crowe; the real Albie Crowe and the mirrored Elsa Matthews.

Elsa turned and kissed him. He did not kiss her back, but was happy to drink in the moment.

'You look so serious every time you kiss me,' she whispered.

'I know,' he said, closing his eyes to sleep.

When Albie finally emerged to face the day, Shepherd was waiting. He had been pacing that stretch of the terrace since their appointed hour, and when Albie admitted him, he did not mumble his thanks.

'I've been waiting for hours,' he mouthed. 'You were the last person I thought might lose it over a girl. You count her as one of us, don't you?'

'She's helping me change,' Albie grinned. 'I know what I'm doing, Shepherd.'

They had a mark in mind that night, the first of a crusade they were planning against the lower reaches of the Sheepscar terrace. It would be the first night Albie had carved himself since he broke the seal of Abraham Matthews' house, and he found himself wondering if there would be a girl waiting for him in every home he broke into now, if it was more than trinkets and treasures he would steal from every family he loathed.

'You can have anything you want, if you only say the right thing, Shepherd. I want you to remember that. Last night I told

Elsa I didn't know I was so lonely until the first moment she left my side. She looked at me like I was the only thing in her world. There's not a soul ever looked at me quite like that – and I knew it, then, like I'd only suspected before: you can take anything you want, if only you have the right words. And . . . I want you to teach me how to read, Shepherd. I'll be stronger if I can read. The page won't mock me any longer.'

'The page doesn't mock Drew, Albie, and he can hardly read his own name.' Shepherd knew he was chancing his arm, but he skulked by the taped-up window and warmed his hands around a chipped mug of tea. 'Drew lives in a house full of books – and it doesn't touch him like it touches you. You want to know why? It's because you want it. You want to be mocked. It thrills you to think the whole of humanity is ranged up against you.' He dared to look into Albie's eyes. 'But I'll teach you to read, Albie, if it pains you so much. I have a book of fables I think you'll like. Cutpurses and vagrants and vagabonds on the march. That would be up your street, wouldn't it?'

* * *

The Final Mile

Reaching the middle of the thoroughfare, Abraham delved into the pockets of his overcoat and produced Albie Crowe's shirt. When he presented the rag, the dog recoiled. Grinning that even a dog might find the boy's scent odious, he whispered a command and, tentatively, the hound returned to draw in the scent.

Snout to the ground, the dog scuttled forward. Ten yards along Meanwood Road, it looked back to give Abraham a shrill yap.

That they had marched toward the jaws of the station itself was something he could not yet believe. There had to be an alley they had taken, some other bolthole in which they had gone to ground.

The dog yapped again, and started to run.

This deep into the sprawl, Meanwood Road was still. There were no blackouts pasted in the windows they passed, but there were few families clinging on this deep among the factories and mills, and the houses had already been ransacked or blown apart.

And here was the heart of the devastation: the street carved apart, vast sprawls on either side where towers had been felled and only the skeletons of iron girders remained. Along the edge of the road, pylons still stood – defiant even to the end – but the cables they once trailed had severed and whipped across the road, clawing up clods of rock as they came.

When they reached the shelter of a shattered bus stop, they paused. The planes were soaring south, drawn to the old battlefield over the centre of the city. Abraham presented Albie Crowe's shirt once again, and the dog pushed its snout to the ground and followed one of the avenues that led from Meanwood Road. Half-way along, it stopped, rising on its hind paws to scrabble at a low brick wall skirting one of the yards.

Abraham commanded it to heel – and, with great reluctance, the dog obeyed. Around the blackout blind in the house's uppermost window, he could see a faint halo of light.

Abraham pushed through the gate and crossed the narrow stone yard, where refuse was heaped around a gutter pipe fallen from the roof. Gesturing for the dog to remain behind, and returning its reproachful gaze by running his fingers through its fur, he tried the back door and found it locked. Eyes to the sky, he counted down the seconds until another plane thundered over – and took his good elbow to the glass.

Fumbling within, he lifted the latch and pushed through. It did not take long to become accustomed to the darkness – he closed his eyes and counted to five, as he had been taught as a soldier – and realised, upon opening them again, that he was standing in a narrow scullery, kept in pristine condition by some proud housewife. Against one wall, crockery was presented on a series of racks, as if never to be used – while, on the other, a larder was brimming with cans of dried egg and whalemeat steak, enough to make Abraham believe a mountain of ration books had been collected and put to good use.

Abraham followed a hallway until he reached the foot of the stairs. There came no sounds from any of the chambers he passed, but he thought he caught the smell of something half-forgotten wafting in the air. It had been so long since he last savoured a decent cup of coffee that he did not recognise it at first. He took his first step on the stairs, determined to follow the scent.

At the top of the stairs, he turned and pawed his way along a banister rail. The first room was just as empty as the rooms below – but he peered in all the same, saw the marital bed made up neatly with only one pillow, the dressing table with its gilt-edged mirror and array of powders and perfume. He saw, too, the fur hanging on a stand against the fireplace, the polished shoes sitting underneath as if to create the impression of a woman glaring back.

At the end of the hallway, a thin sliver of light shone between the door and the floorboards beneath. Abraham approached slowly, pressed his back against the wall and listened for the voices that must have communed within.

For a long time, there was only silence. Every time he thought that he could hear movement, another plane set the roof slates to clatter, or some shuddering moved deep in the earth and worked its way through the building. He crouched, old knees creaking, and fancied he could see shadows crossing the sliver of light. He watched them pass once, twice – and only at the third crossing did he understand that it was only the wavering of a lantern on the other side, trembling every time a tremor worked through the street.

He put the flat of his palm against the handle and pushed. Under his weight, the door flew inward. The lantern light flurried, lapping up the walls behind – but the room before him was empty.

It was a child's bedroom. Token efforts had been made at stripping it away, but lead soldiers still lined a shelf above the bed and, half-obscured by a rack of shirts, a rocking horse stood proudly. Against a closed chimney breast there lay a dresser, upon which three mugs sat. The dregs of the coffee Abraham had smelt were still inside, with an empty half-pint of whisky at their side. When Abraham lifted the first mug, it was warm to the touch. Two of the mugs had been laced, but the third was dry.

Abraham opened the first drawer of the dresser. Inside, a stack of ration books were tied up with string. He opened the first. The name scored into the inside cover was familiar, a young widow from the lower end of the Sheepscar terrace who, he vaguely recollected, had fled to the hills. In the second, he read the name of a secretary who worked out of the station at Harehills Heights. Each one of the books thereafter had come from some other corner of the city.

Dropping the bundle into the pocket of his overcoat, he shaded the lantern and peeled back the blackout blind. The street below was barren, but the dog still sat obediently at its post. If anyone dared to approach, Abraham would quickly know.

A row of photographs hung on the wall beside the door, family portraits of mother, father and two sons. Abraham lifted the first from the wall, catching it on its hook. Turning to the lantern light, he studied the faces of the two boys. The younger he had not seen before – but the elder, fourteen or fifteen years old, stared out of the picture frame as if knowing that Abraham was staring back.

Abraham looked up, as if he could judge the hour of night by the patterns in the ceiling tiles. A scant few hours had passed since he had cornered the Crowe in that air-raid shelter, the other boys stumbling in after. And yet – here was the same face: the gangly youth whose eyes had lit up to see his hero appear was staring out of the frame with his lips curled as if, even when the photograph was taken, he had anticipated the joke.

Abraham turned back to the coffee mugs – one, two and three. The Moor was two miles away, the bombs had pounded the streets between here and there into the ground. Albie Crowe had come here looking for shelter, but he had not found it. The boy was gone – but somebody knew where.

Photograph still in hand, he hurried back along the landing. In a room at the end, a window of frosted glass over an old bathtub looked north, away from the fires flourishing at the city centre. Peeling back the blackout blind, he might almost have been tricked into believing the city was not aflame only a mile away.

Out there, the yards were silent. Over a fence built high, he could see a snarl where the alleyways between the houses fed into Meanwood Road itself. He tried to judge which way the boys might have run after they had dallied here.

Momentarily, the cityscape was illuminated, as if lit by sheet lightning. The clouds above flashed white and crimson red, some explosion colouring them from the battle played out above – and the light, refracted through the cloud, spilled in spectral hues over the rooftops. In an instant it was gone – but it had been long enough.

In a backyard, where a family had once strung their washing in the factory smoke, there crouched an Anderson shelter. The residents had heaped it high with stones and earth, like one of the lonely cairns over Woodhouse Moor, but there was no disguising it. Through a rent in the corrugated steel door, lantern light streamed out.

Abraham fixed the blackout blind back into place and thundered down the stairs.

The yard was small, the shelter set into a trench carved into its furthest side, and he crossed the bare earth quickly to rain his fists at the door.

'Night watch!' he bellowed. 'Open up!'

There was shifting inside the shelter, but still nobody came to the door. He thundered again, kicking out this time, and heard a woman's voice screaming that there was no room at the inn.

'I don't want your damn shelter!' Abraham bellowed. 'I want your help . . .'

'Sir,' the muted voice on the other side trembled, 'I've got three children in here. I can't help . . .'

'That shelter's built for six,' Abraham answered. 'You'll open this door, or I'm coming back for you in the morning.'

Slowly, the door drew open. Abraham took a step back so that he could look fully through the entrance – and saw, then, that there were only two figures in the shelter. The woman, red-haired and not unpretty, might have been forty or forty-five years old, and her face was smeared with make-up as if she had been crying.

On a bench piled with blankets at the back of the shelter, a younger man was scrabbling back into his trousers, pulling braces over his shoulders before he had even donned a shirt. Taking advantage of Abraham's momentary alarm, he scrambled past, and disappeared into the alley.

'My husband's ARP,' the woman trembled, fixing her blouse. 'He's out on patrol every night. I get frightened in the shelter on my own.' She paused. 'You wouldn't tell him. He wouldn't understand . . .'

Abraham was not interested in who kept her warm at night. He strode down the shelter steps and wrenched the door shut behind him.

'This shelter isn't meant for just you. There are houses down this row where they must be cowering in cupboards . . .'

'Look around you,' the woman returned. 'Those houses are abandoned. They all went to the hills. There's hardly a family left this far along Meanwood Road.'

'What do the words Young Blood mean to you?'

Abraham saw the knowledge flicker in her eyes. He had not spent the long years of his life pounding the beat just to let a little clue like that go unnoticed.

'You have children . . .'

Her face twisted. Advancing across the shelter, Abraham produced the framed photograph from a fold in his overcoat. He held it out so that she could see, drawing back when her fingers fluttered to take hold.

'You've been into my house . . .'

'I wasn't the only one. The boy on the left – who is he?'

She seemed loath to respond. 'It's my boy,' she finally said.

'And where is your boy tonight?'

The woman did not reply. Too late, she found the words. By then, Abraham already knew that she was lying.

'He stays with his grandparents. They have a house outside the city. I sent him there myself, sent his sister too, as soon as the bombs started falling . . .'

'He's holed up in a shelter on the scrub end of the Moor,' Abraham interjected. 'I saw him there myself. Came blundering in when I had my charge just waiting to be shackled up. You know about them, of course. I've seen the way your larder is stacked. Albie Crowe and the rest?'

'I don't know what you're . . .'

She drew the ragged blankets up around her chin, but Abraham lashed out to snatch them away. Still clothed underneath, nevertheless she scrabbled back. Abraham was aware, for the first time, that he was blocking her way out of the shelter. Her eyes seemed to dart at either side of him, like some rabbit in the shadow of a hawk, picking her best route of escape.

'I don't care that your son's one of them,' he began. He had to force himself not to step aside, revealing the portal to her. She would have to suffer him a little longer. 'I don't care that he brings home ration books he's plundered from houses, or big crates of steak and eggs they've lifted off the back of some passing truck. But I know they came here looking for sanctuary tonight . . .'

The woman blanched, shuffled as if she might charge him to get out of the shelter – but then relented.

There had been two of them, she began. Two boys, hardly even men, who had rained their fists at the shelter, just like Abraham had done, demanding to be let in. When she opened the door, one of them was holding the other one up. The second looked weak, as if he had only just risen from his sick-bed, and though he was wearing a heavy overcoat, he was not wearing a shirt. There were scars all over his breast.

There had been three in the shelter when the boys arrived: the woman, whose name was Redmond and who had lived in these streets for all of her life; the man who had scrambled away when Abraham first appeared, who lived alone in one of the ruins down the road, and worked in a munitions factory on the city's edge; and her youngest son, Tomas. Perhaps Albie Crowe and the boy who rescued him had come looking for the elder brother – but this younger one suited them just as well. Tomas himself had been thrilled to see them appear.

'I told them they could shelter with us, but the boy just balked . . .'

Abraham understood that well enough. Albie Crowe had already been cornered in one air-raid shelter tonight; to be trapped like that a second time would have been criminally careless.

'Your son took them away. They went into the house. Running across the city, through the smoke, had worked up a thirst . . .' He paused. 'Then they took off. The question is: where?'

'You don't think I . . .'

Abraham let the photograph drop from his hands. When it landed at his feet the glass splintered, a fractured web spreading to obscure the family on the other side.

'There's a place they go, both of my boys,' she began. Her eyes flitted from one corner of the dug-out to another, but Abraham did not follow. 'Their father used to patrol the place. He helped keep the barrage balloons down there. Too old to go out and fight – but he wanted to play his part. The balloons still fly, but they don't have anyone to tend them any more. The factories that way are still dead – they fight battles over different parts of the city . . .'

There were places like it all across the northern burghs. The mills and factories there had not come back to life like they had in the south. The balloons flew sentry over them still, but they were guarding nothing.

Abraham urged her on.

'They used to go down there with their father. They idolised him, back when it began. He fought over the water the last time around, had stories to tell of the things he'd seen. They thought he was a hero – and then that boy came into the city, and suddenly they didn't care about being a hero any more. Suddenly it wasn't wars and battles and triumphs they wanted to hear about . . .'

Abraham had heard it a hundred times before. The same story was scrawled across the pages of his ledgers. Heroism had had its day; boys grew up wanting to be villains, now.

'When I was his age, I dreamed of fighting a war . . .'

The woman dared to smile. 'Look how that ended up,' she said. 'I had brothers die in that war. They dreamt about being heroes too. How can you blame our boys for not having the same dreams we used to have after that?'

Abraham did not have an answer. He pushed back the door and stepped out of the shelter, careful to put himself between the lantern light and the open air. He breathed in deeply, filling his lungs with the dry smell of mortar and smoke.

'You'd better get yourself one of those lovely furs,' he said, looking up at the house. 'You're coming with me.'

They cut a comical sight, a man smeared in blood and dirt, a woman dressed in fine furs, as they crossed Meanwood Road and took one of the snaking lanes toward the city's heart. Perhaps, an onlooker might have mused, it was one of those marriages made in hell, each soul ill-suited to the other but bound together by an unbreakable contract. Abraham led the way, but he kept the woman close at heel, listening to her directions.

The lane broadened where the houses fell away. On one side, where workers' houses once stood, there was only rubble – but, on the other, the land had never been built upon, and an expanse of scrub gone to seed stretched out. In places, a fence separated the road from the scrubland but, more often, the stone simply petered into earth and tussocks of thick grass.

On the other side of the grass, the factories rose, great shells where men had once toiled but which had, long ago, been abandoned. Abraham remembered men traipsing this way from the days of his own youth. When he had come back from his roaming, the mills had been silent. Perhaps it was only that, once peace returned, they were no longer needed – but it had seemed to Abraham that they sat empty because nobody had returned to work them, because the boys who should have been turning their wheels were drowned in dirt somewhere over the water.

Between the factories, the barrage balloons sailed lower than he had seen. They were grouped in close clusters here, like they were grouped over the munitions factories on the southern side of the city – as if even these stagnant shells were deemed worthy. Their cables creaked at the side of the road, winch wheels shifting each time a gust drove at the balloons suspended above.

'Which one?' asked Abraham, squinting into a flurry of ash that twirled up the road.

The woman looked from one factory to the next. 'Dear,' she began, 'I wouldn't know where to start.'

There were three great hulks pitting the scrubland. One stood apart from the rest, on the downhill slope with the city furnace flaming on its shoulder. Beyond that, a tumbledown warehouse of redbrick and timber stood windward of what had once been a sprawling gunpowder mill. Smoke lounged over each, but it was only smoke that had drifted in from different parts of the city; the bombs had not fallen here, tonight.

Abraham pushed Mrs Redmond forward, a hand in the small of her back. Crouched low together, they darted through thistle and tall grass to reach the northern wall of the first factory. They were shielded from the view of the other buildings here, and crept together along the wall – until Abraham found an open door. Inside, coarse weeds had broken through the factory floor, so that the tiles now rose in hummocks and dark shoots grew in between. Street dogs had fouled the earth freely, and a platoon of small, black rats scattered at Abraham's approach. The smell in the air was stale, but at least it was different from the acrid air without.

They crossed the factory floor, where a great press for tin cans slouched in the earth, its cavities a den for the rats that still skittered each time Abraham took a step, and looked into each of the storerooms in turn. In each, there was nothing but the remnants of fires that vagabonds and runaways had once stirred.

'You're certain the boy would come here?'

Abraham craned out of one of the dank rooms and turned to see Mrs Redmond, huddled in her fur.

'His father found him here a hundred times before – him and his brother.' She looked back. Through the doorway, across the slouched steel press, she could see the cable of one of the barrage balloons creaking back and forth. 'He thinks it's safe when the bombs fall.'

Around the rim of the great hall there ran a gallery, with rickety stairs climbing to it on either side. Abraham ushered Mrs Redmond that way and began to climb. The stair was bolted to the struts that held up the factory walls, but still it teetered as they rose. When they reached the gallery, they paused to catch their breath. Already, the rats were beginning to return.

Abraham pushed into the rooms that opened onto the gallery, offices where foremen had once worked and nightwatchmen once dozed. Though Albie Crowe was nowhere to be seen, he saw fresh litter gathered beneath a window patterned in cracks, the core of an apple the rats had not yet discovered, and wax paper that had once wrapped biscuits or bread.

Something thundered overhead. Instinctively, Abraham dived, wrapped his arms around Mrs Redmond as if to swaddle her from the falling bombs. His arms still entangled with hers, he craned a look through the shattered glass of the window just in time to see one of the Stukas scrambling high between the barrage balloons. The great hulks turned in the slipstream, straining at their tethers.

He had held her for too long and, as the silence returned, Mrs Redmond flailed to get away.

'If those bastards are going to flatten me,' she said, 'I'd as soon not have my insides mingling with yours . . .'

Abraham did not look at her. His eyes, instead, were drawn to the fractured glass. Across the upturned earth, he could see the warehouse sitting in the shadow of the gunpowder mill, like a cub huddled close to its mother. The land between them was narrow. There had once been a road to join the two, but the stone had come apart and across it the thistles grew wild.

A boy emerged from the mill, looked furtively one way and then the next, and scuttled across the broken causeway with a satchel over his shoulder.

Abraham dragged Mrs Redmond to the window. She did not squall, this time, when he clutched her.

'Your boy?' he demanded, as the figure disappeared into the warehouse doors.

'I couldn't tell at this distance,' she insisted, at last working her arm free, 'but I . . .' Already, Abraham had crossed the room, clattering down the factory stairs. 'Captain!' she called after. Her voice echoed, metallic, from the roofs. 'Just what are you trying to prove?'

Abraham ignored her and vaulted the last few stairs, the pain in his joints suddenly forgotten. He reached the doorway and, there, he stopped.

It did not matter what he was trying to prove. The night had started, the night was not yet finished – and that was all that mattered. It was not only about reaching the end of the road, but reaching the end of everything else. He supposed, suddenly, that it was a lesson he had learned from Albie Crowe himself: you could change the way you felt, the way you were. You decided your destination, mapped out your route, and then – if you had the courage to see it through – you would stand, victorious, at the end of the road, a different man from the person who set out. And if he ensnared Albie Crowe and got him to the station – well, only then could he go back to Ada and not be the coward who set out at dusk, the man who let his own daughter die for want of speaking out or saying a word.

Mrs Redmond was at his side.

'He's a little boy,' she began. 'He only wants to be like his brother.'

Abraham took a step, but just as quickly recoiled.

'You'd hang him high for that, would you? Because he's a little boy and he wants his adventure?'

'Your boys ever tell you that you talk too much, Mrs Redmond?' Abraham raised his palm, forcing her back through the factory doors. 'Don't breathe another word.'

'What is it?'

Abraham glared over his shoulder. 'We're not alone,' he breathed.

After a moment, he dared to push out again, craning first to his left and then to his right, to spy upon the broken road along which they had walked. Beyond the ruins of the outhouse and the fence, a figure on horseback trotted, wreathed in the smoke that drifted languorously by. From this distance it was only a silhouette, appearing and then disappearing through the grey reefs – but, where the fences petered away and the road widened into the factory yards, the rider drew his mount down and pitched the beast onto the scrubland. Soon, the silhouette emerged from the veil. A sudden fountain of fire broke over the rooftops behind, and oranges and reds flurried in its wake.

It was Ezra's rider – but somehow the steed seemed stronger than it had only hours ago, as if the beaten old nag had walked through the fire and come out, on the other side, a fierce destrier. Abraham tried to shake the image, but then the fire fell again over the rooftops and, lit like that, the beast and its rider seemed demonic. In his mind it bucked and brayed at the devastation – but, in truth, the rider merely cantered the length between the factory and mill, surveying the land.

This, too, was part of Albie Crowe's disease. Albie Crowe would have taken one look at that rider and decided it was some bounty hunter come from the underworld to collect him. Abraham felt that image thrill in him. It was only an old man, he told himself, just some old butcher sitting astride his nag.

The rider followed the line of scrub behind the warehouse and reappeared at the apex of the thin strip of land between that building and the gunpowder mill. For a second he seemed to be staring Abraham directly in the eye – but then he passed on, disappearing again as he rounded the gunpowder mill. For a long time he was gone, only to reappear, having followed the walls of the factory and come back to the broken road.

He was circling them. There could be only one reason for that. No doubt he, too, had seen the boy crossing from warehouse to mill.

'Who is it?'

The rider drifted with the smoke along the edge of the road. Endlessly, he moved back and forth, gazing up at the dark towers of the mill.

'There's only one,' Abraham whispered. 'We've got time yet. He can't send for the others, not without riding away . . .'

'What others?'

'They're hunting for Albie Crowe as well.' Abraham hesitated to tell her more. He saw the horseman turn again, like a general parading his first rank of soldiers before they dropped their spears and charged. 'I need to get to the mill,' he said. A hundred yards of tall grass and crumbled brick stretched between him and the warehouse into which the boy had sloped. 'You'll need to draw him away.'

Over his shoulder, Mrs Redmond gave him such a withering look that he might have asked her to take a bullet in her side.

'Do you want them to catch up with your boy?' he demanded. 'Is that it?'

Mrs Redmond hesitated, her furs falling apart to reveal the nightdress underneath. 'What does it matter,' she ventured, 'whether it's them or it's you? There's neither of you means any good for my boy . . .'

Abraham took her by the shoulders and forced her around. A pain, sharp as the bullet that gored his arm, shot into his shoulder when he clenched his fist around her wrist. He ignored it and angled her to face the horseman.

'He's not a watchman,' he hissed, 'and the men who'll come after him, they're not watchmen either. They're soldiers. They've come to make their kill. They don't mean for Albie Crowe to live through the night. Whether he's buried under the bombs or whether they drag him into the ruin themselves, they don't care. And I can't vouch they wouldn't cut the Crowe's companions down with just as much relish.' He stopped. 'So which is it to be?'

Mrs Redmond felt suddenly limp in his hands. When he understood that all the tension was gone from her body, he slowly released his grip. Shuffling back, she tightened her fur. Over her shoulder, the horseman disappeared to make another circuit of the scrub.

'What would I tell him?' she asked.

'You'll work it out,' Abraham answered, pushing her forward. As she took her first step, a plane scrambled overhead, and the barrage balloons that surrounded them surged, suddenly, from left to right. 'Get back to the road,' he said. 'I'll be watching . . .'

Abraham did not watch as she darted back across the scrub, body bent double. Instead, he tightened the tourniquet at his arm, buttoned his greatcoat, broke back the barrel of the old service revolver and checked each shot. Only when he could hear the horse's canter again did he return to the doorway.

The rider had made his circuit of the mill and warehouse. When he reached the factory yards, he spurred his steed onwards, heels kicking viciously for want of any spurs. Abraham ducked out of the factory, flat to the wall, and saw

Mrs Redmond standing in the middle of the thoroughfare, fur coat flying. A reef of grey smoke curled around her, and into it the horseman plunged. Though Abraham could see the rider drawing his mount down, hemming in Mrs Redmond in tightening circles, both seemed ethereal to him now – grey ghosts who had no business being in the same world as him.

When he was certain that the rider was facing the other way, he scuttled out of the factory doors, taking huge strides until the towers of the gunpowder mill loomed above. Without looking back, he came to the thin tract of land between the warehouse and the mill. On either side of the jaws of that overgrown alley, two great winches were set into the ground, with thick steel ropes ascending from each. As Abraham came between them, they felt like ancient stone sentries guarding the entrance to some mountain pass.

Plunging between the mill and warehouse, it was suddenly graveyard cold.

The doors to the mill had been chained shut, but over the years the chains had slackened and there was enough room for a boy to contort his way through. Opposite that, the way into the warehouse stood open, a brick arch with doors that had rotted away. Abraham crept to its edge and, listening out for footfalls on the other side, hurried through.

The way was dark. He came into a wide, barren hall, with partitioned alcoves at either side, where crates and wooden pallets were still to be found. The air smelt of smoke and dry rot. He pushed further, back against the wall, and scurried past the first of the alcoves. Light streamed in from huge tears in the roof, and he skirted the pools as best as he could. Squinting up, he could see the tail end of one of the barrage balloons, turning in a wind flurried up by some plane banking sharply above. As it swung out over the warehouse, he was momentarily in pitch blackness again. He hurried on.

Half-way along, the warehouse broadened on either side, with further alcoves set against the back wall. In one of them, there sat what had once been a motor car, with a pallet jack chained to a wagon at its rear. Abraham slipped into the alcove, and saw that a thick, khaki sleeping roll was crumpled inside. He delved inside, but the bedding was not warm; the nest had not been slept in tonight.

He came back out and stole left. He supposed it must have been goods from the gunpowder mill that were once stored here, for many of the stalls that he passed were encrusted in thick grey grit. He came to another stretch where orange light streamed in from the rafters and saw, for the first time, the trail of footprints he was unwittingly following.

At the end of the row, shadows moved in one of the stalls. He pushed as close as he could, his own shadow cast long, and at last he heard voices: one boy, and a second – but neither of them Albie Crowe. He scuffed his boots in the dust and listened.

'No,' the first one said, 'you're not going anywhere.'

It was the boy from the other side of the wall. The boy named Shepherd, who had followed Albie Crowe from the first days of the Young Bloods.

'She'll wonder where I am,' a younger voice protested.

'I'm sure she has other things to be thinking on,' Shepherd said. 'That man in her shelter – who was he?' A silence lingered between them. 'He wasn't your father.'

There came the sound of another plane arcing far above the warehouse. Its noise was distant, but still strong enough to muffle, momentarily, the voices from inside the stall. Abraham took the chance to scuttle back, ferreting in one of the other alcoves for a stone. The first crumbled when he lifted it – but, against the wall, he found a half-brick. Holding it in his fist, he scampered back to his station.

'If you left now, you wouldn't make it back anyway. Sit down, Redmond. It'll be over by dawn.'

Abraham judged the weight of the brick in his hand. Then, bringing his good arm back, he let it fly. He watched as it sailed high, over the stall in which Shepherd and the other boy bickered, until, caught fleetingly in the light from above, it disappeared. Seconds later, it shattered as it struck the ground.

In the stall, the boys ceased their chatter.

'What was that?'

'It wasn't a goddamn rat . . .'

Abraham slunk into shadow, finding a shelter in the neighbouring stall. Drawing the revolver from his belt, he watched as a silhouette emerged to follow the sound. He was not certain, at first, whether it was Shepherd or the other boy who had set out. He did not know if he cared. When he was sure the boy had disappeared into the darkness, he rounded the corner and stormed the stall.

Boys had camped here before. Against one wall, there sat a bench, Albie Crowe basking upon it, draped in blankets; against another, the remnants of a dead fire and a knapsack, spilling out the same cans of whalemeat steak that Abraham had seen in the Redmonds' house. When he rounded the corner, a young boy was staring at him with eyes opened wide. Neither said a word.

Abraham stared down the barrel of his gun – but, instinctively, he lowered the weapon. His eyes darted at Albie Crowe, but the boy just lay there, eyes closed, oblivious to the world.

'Redmond?' he began. 'Tomas Redmond?'

The young boy opened his lips as if to cry out, but Abraham hissed him into silence. Drawing the handcuffs from his belt, he tossed them up. The boy fumbled to catch them.

'Lock him to the bench,' Abraham ordered, gesturing at Albie Crowe. He wheeled around, listened out for the sound of Shepherd in the warehouse beyond. 'You two are here alone, are you? Just babysitting your overlord over there?'

'How did you find us?' the boy ventured.

'I had some help.'

Over his shoulder, Abraham saw the boy kneeling at Albie's side.

'Exhausted, is he, after tonight's little trip?'

'You had him locked up in an attic!' the boy trembled. 'With a shirt stuffed down his throat!'

'That's right,' Abraham replied. When he was certain that Shepherd was not about to pounce, he wheeled around. Albie Crowe seemed to be stirring, but he froze for a second, and again the boy stilled. 'Now get out of here . . .'

Rising back to his feet, the boy paused.

'I'm a Young Blood too!' he protested. 'Didn't you come for me as well?'

For a second, Abraham was still. He supposed he should not have been surprised that boys wanted to be counted with it, even if it meant prison or death – but the boy standing before him looked so young as to make the idea absurd.

'I said get out of here,' he said. He reached forward, clawed out to grapple with the boy's collar. Taking him up, he forced him to the opening of the stall and threw him down. When the boy landed, he skidded forward on hands and knees. He lay there, motionless, for a second, crying over a grazed knee.

When he was certain that the boy was gone, Abraham turned back. He thought he heard something tearing over the warehouse roof and, instinctively, he cowered – but no explosion sounded. He was starting to flinch at shadows. On the bench, Albie Crowe turned. Only a boy as oblivious to the real world as Albie Crowe could sleep through a night like this.

Abraham reached down, drew the blanket down from the boy's chin. He looked vaguely at peace, eyeballs flickering behind their lids, lips parted. Abraham brushed the hair out of his eyes like some loving father. Then, he brought his hand back and, with an open palm, brought it down against the boy's face.

The Crowe started, rearing suddenly and pitching back when the handcuff snapped at his wrist. Bucking on the bench, he twisted until he saw Abraham staring back down.

Abraham crouched suddenly, stifled the boy before he could cry out.

'Captain . . .' the Crowe began, his breath warm on Abraham's fingers.

'You've been testing my patience tonight, son. But I suppose I can forgive you that. If I were in your position, I could think of places I'd rather be.'

Abraham slowly released his grasp on the boy.

'How did you find me?'

It was the wrong question. 'I wasn't the only one, Albie. The old men – they're here too. Circling the factories until Ada's father can find his way here . . .'

'And?'

'And I mean to get you out of here before . . .'

Abraham saw the boy's eyes brighten – but, by then, it was already too late. For an instant, he felt like a lamb with a vulture on its shoulder. Then, he reeled sideways, pain blossoming in his temple. Instinctively, he curled against the unseen blow, crashed down into the wooden walls of the stall. He lay crumpled for only a second, turned to see Shepherd striding toward him with a length of piping in his hand.

It had been like this, once. Like all of the other boys he had soldiered with, he had thought it would be guns and shells and gas – but, when the day came, it was all about knives and fists and thumbs pushed into some other boy's eyes. It came back to him, now. When Shepherd swung the pipe, he caught its end, strained to stop the boy dead. From his bench, Albie Crowe was barking out indecipherable commands.

'Son,' Abraham breathed, drawn back to Shepherd's eyes. 'You're not like the rest of them. You're cleverer than that. You never went brawling on the Moor. You've never really believed Young Bloods are real.'

Perhaps it stilled Shepherd. Perhaps it brought back memories of his first days with Albie Crowe, before the fatherless boys of this city had put him on his pedestal. Perhaps – but only for a second. With a sudden effort, he heaved the piping back and thrust it forward, jabbing like it was a blade.

Abraham scrabbled backwards, but the wall was already at his shoulder. He looked up, saw Shepherd bearing down and launched forward with his feet. When the flat of his boot piled into Shepherd's shin, the boy tumbled. Abraham tried to roll out of his path, but the piping clattered down and he threw his arms up to fend it away.

Already, Shepherd was sprawled upon him, grappling with Abraham's arm. The wound there screamed out as viciously as the scars on the Young Blood's chest. Abraham brought his other arm back, tried to connect with the boy's head – but all that he could do was wrap himself so tightly around the boy that neither could deal another blow. For what seemed an age, they held that strange embrace.

At last, Abraham rolled. It was only when he brought back his fist to finish it that he understood the boy was already unconscious. Slowly, Abraham stood, kicking him softly in the side to make certain he was not playing dead. He had seen boys playing that trick before. He himself had been one of them, the first time his trench was overrun by boys from the other side of the wire.

Abraham lurched to the other side of the stall. Albie Crowe was watching him keenly from where he was shackled, but he did not breathe a word. The brickwork in the outer wall was crumbling here, and he peered out of worn holes to see the scrubland beyond. Though they were hidden at the furthest end of the warehouse, he could just make out, through thick thistle, where the factory yards broadened.

The horseman appeared from the road, drawing his mount around to make another circuit of the yards. On his tail, Mrs Redmond hurried, crying out words he could not hear.

Abraham fell, limp, against the brick, braced himself to stop sinking to the ground. For a second, he could not focus. The room swirled in blurring, amorphous colours. At last, he saw a canteen poking out of the knapsack on the ground and fumbled to lift it to his lips. He had expected whisky or rye; it was only water – but water would do.

'Captain?' Albie Crowe ventured.

'Don't worry yourself on my account, Albie. I'll be OK. I've been hurt worse.' He gestured at Shepherd, still lying prostrate on the floor. 'He came for you, did he, up in the attic?'

'He was watching when the old men moved in.'

Abraham reared, determined to swallow the sickness. 'He wasn't watching well enough. They followed you.'

'And they're out there, now?'

'Not Ezra,' Abraham conceded. 'Not yet. It's the horseman, the butcher – but there'll be others, if we don't get out of here soon . . .'

Albie lifted the shackle, teasing Abraham with a finger.

'I need a moment, Crowe. I'm not as young as you.'

'That's the point, isn't it? That you had your chance at being young, and you ruined it, and now you want to ruin mine . . .'

Abraham was bored of Albie Crowe's philosophies. He took another draught of water from the canteen and, the pain in his arm spreading, breathed deeply until he started to feel some life again. All the while, Albie Crowe kept his eyes on him. Abraham might have been wrong, but it seemed, then, that the boy was almost grateful for the reunion.

'What did you find at her grandfather's house, Captain?'

'I found my wife,' Abraham began.

This, at least, was mildly curious to Albie Crowe. 'Come back from the hills?'

Abraham did not turn around. 'For a funeral,' he replied.

'They say death brings families closer together.'

Abraham turned back to the wall. The horseman had reappeared, but he was not alone. Another man hurried after. Behind him, there trailed the young boy. Mrs Redmond rushed to him, snatched him up in an embrace; then, she dropped him to the ground and slapped him hard across the cheek.

'I should have been there with her,' he began. 'Even you were at Elsa's funeral. Even you know how that feels.'

'Captain, I've told you before – whoever it was lurking at the churchyard, it wasn't me. You've started seeing ghosts.'

'You were there, Albie. I wouldn't dare to wonder why. Gloating or rejoicing or just pressing on a wound. Maybe you just wanted to see how normal people grieve, to see what a family looks like.' Over his shoulder, Abraham eyeballed him. 'Did you even grieve for her, son?'

'Some of the lads in the Young Bloods were sorry. They were dressed up and wanting to go and spy as you put her in the ground. You'd have laughed, Captain. A sorrier lot you've never seen, dolled up in Salvation Army rags like a king was being crowned. Shepherd himself barely said a word when I told them the news. The lad Monmouth was blubbering like he'd been told it was his own sister.'

Perhaps Albie Crowe went on – but Abraham did not hear. Out there, the horseman tore himself from conversation with the Redmond boy. When he cantered forward, the other old man hurried in his wake, but could not keep up. Moments later, the horseman disappeared from view.

Abraham drew back from the wall.

'What is it, Captain?' Albie asked.

Abraham cursed his own weakness. Rushing to Albie's side, swallowing his nausea, he held the boy back with his good arm and strained to unfasten the shackle with his bad. When the boy was securely fastened at his wrist again, he heaved him aloft. Shepherd was still lying prostrate on the ground, and he made certain that Albie trampled the boy's body as he dragged him to the door.

'It's the horseman,' he said. 'He's coming for the warehouse.'

'We could cross to the mill,' Albie began. 'He couldn't force the horse in there . . .'

Abraham heard the questioning tone in Albie's words – and, though he knew it pathetic, found himself cheered. The boy, it seemed, was asking for his help.

'And be trapped in there, without a way back out? You've got more nous than that, Albie Crowe.'

Abraham advanced along the body of the warehouse, the open stalls gaping on either side.

'Then what?' Albie asked.

Together, they stood in the middle of the warehouse. Suddenly, the room seemed vast. Abraham's words drifted in the rafters somewhere far above their heads. He reached, slowly, to his wrist and stroked the shackle hanging there.

'Then I'm giving you to him,' he said.

Abraham flashed an arm down and, with a twist of the fingers, slid his own wrist from the shackle. As he did so, he brought his bad arm back and, bracing himself for the pain that was sure to come, felled Albie Crowe. When the boy crumpled, Abraham took off, finding shelter in the darkness of one of the great stalls. There were still packing crates piled here, and he found a hiding place between them where no light streamed in.

He was crouching there, only seconds later, when he heard the hammering of the horse's hooves as the rider made his way between warehouse and mill. He held to his arm, kneading at the wound, eyes fixed on Albie Crowe. The boy was rising awkwardly when the silhouette horseman appeared in the warehouse doors. He froze.

The rider did not speak. He pushed the horse through the warehouse door, head scraping the beams, and trotted slowly forward. Albie stood, cupped a hand to his eyes to squint at the intruder.

'I'll want to know who you are!' the boy demanded. Though his voice trilled, quickly he reined it in. Abraham recognised the trait well: here was a boy who was well rehearsed at hiding his every weakness. 'You're with the old man? Is that it?'

The horseman did not reply. From his hiding place, Abraham saw him advance, the horse nosing, for the first time, into his line of sight. The steed was blinkered and wore a harness that he had not seen earlier in the night.

Albie turned, scrabbling backwards as if he might find some secret passage at the back of the warehouse. When he slipped out of view, Abraham moved through the crates, craning that he might see the alcove into which the boy was disappearing. The horseman drifted slowly forward, hooves sounding dully on the open earth. At stages he stopped, and Abraham could hear the skittering of Albie Crowe's feet as he careened around the far walls of the warehouse. The rider seemed to be shepherding him into some corner Abraham could not see, guiding him as deftly as a dog with its herd.

The horse passed out of his sight – and Abraham knew he had but seconds before Albie was lost. Lifting the service revolver, he kicked through the crates and strode out of the alcove.

'Get off the horse!' Abraham roared.

The rider reined the beast in. On the other side of him, Albie Crowe had his back against the wall, lurching from one flank to another.

The rider contorted to look over his shoulder, but Abraham was lost in shadow.

'Captain Matthews?' a low voice began.

'I said get off the horse,' Abraham repeated. 'It's been a long night. If I have to tell you a third time . . .'

'You don't get to make the . . .'

Abraham lifted the service revolver and squeezed the trigger. The pistol bucked in his hand, and the shot exploded into one of the warehouse walls, barely a yard away from where Albie Crowe was standing.

Between them, the horse suddenly spooked.

It was only a pack-horse, Abraham had told himself. It was not some fierce destrier bred for battle – but a butcher's nag instead. If ever it had heard the shooting of guns before, it was only in the yards of some downtown abattoir.

The horse rose on its hind legs, kicking wildly at the air, head whipping from left to right so that blinkered eyes might see what demon stalked it. On its back, the rider held firm, threw himself close to the horse's body and tightened his hands around the reins. For a moment, it was enough – but then the horse twisted, trying desperately to turn for the murky light at the warehouse doors. Its front hooves smashed back down to earth and it kicked out with its rump. The rider trailed uselessly behind, one foot caught momentarily in its stirrup, before plummeting to the ground. There he lay, unmoving.

As the horse took off into one of the warehouse alcoves, its braying ebbing away, Abraham hurried forward. Over the recumbent rider, Albie Crowe was frozen, caught in one of the beams of light that tore in from the rafters. The boy was tensed, shoulders hunched high, but Abraham stared at him until he relented.

'You didn't really think I was giving up on you, did you, son?'

'Is he dead, Captain?'

It struck Abraham as odd that it was Albie who had asked the question. Together, they looked at the rider, spread-eagled in the dirt. The service revolver still trained on the boy, Abraham knelt and turned the body over. The man groaned, blinking back dirt and sweat. Abraham stroked the hair out of his eyes and dropped him to the ground.

'Come on, Crowe,' he said, climbing back to his feet. 'There are still others out there. They'd start moving as soon as they heard that shot . . .'

Albie stuttered forward, out of the pool of light. 'Two of them, Captain – and two of us . . .'

'Don't dignify me by putting us on the same side, son. It doesn't work that way.'

Abraham snapped the dangling handcuff over Albie's naked wrist. Then, with the gun in the small of his back, he kicked him toward the alcove into which the horse had taken flight.

Still spooked, the horse shifted up and down the outer brickwork – but Abraham came forward coolly and ran his open palm along its snout. When the beast had calmed, he turned and gestured for the Crowe to join him.

Albie shuffled to the horse's flank, and Abraham forced him up into the cloth saddle hanging there. The boy had clearly never ridden an animal before, and he sat there awkwardly, hands grasping uselessly at the beast's thin mane.

Throwing himself up behind the boy, his feet found the stirrups and he kicked the horse around. He wrapped an arm around Albie Crowe, holding him tight, and trotted the nag back through the warehouse.

The rider was still lying on the earth, but it would not be long until he came to. Abraham guided the horse past its fallen master and toward the open doors.

'Captain,' Albie Crowe began, his throat still raw, 'you made it this far – but it's still raining hell out there. I've listened to them flying. It's going to get worse. The night isn't finished yet. But . . .' He paused, cringed from his first sight of the roiling sky. 'We can find shelter until it's finished, Captain. They'll soar out west, the ones that are left, go harry some other towns as they make their way home. And there'd still be time, before the dawn, to get me to the end of the road . . .'

Abraham looked at him from the corner of his eye. The Crowe was right – the night was not finished yet, but there was only one mile left to go.

'You're not giving up now, are you, Albie?' he murmured.

Arms around the boy, he pushed the horse into the night. Ahead, the chained doors of the gunpowder mill creaked sadly.

'Captain!'

Abraham turned, the horse restless underneath him. At the end of the lane, where a dead winch sat with its cable heaped high, Mrs Redmond stood. Wind was funnelled along the land between the warehouse and mill, and it blasted at her, whipping her fur coat wide.

Instinctively, Abraham looked over his shoulder. At the other end of the lane, no figure blocked his path. The two great cables still rose into the smoke above the warehouse roof.

'Captain!' Mrs Redmond called again. He looked back to see that she was slowly advancing through the long grass. Emerging from the cross-wind, she reached up to brush hair out of her eyes.

Abraham was about to turn the horse and head for the open scrub when he saw the other man appearing behind Mrs Redmond. There was no doubt, now: he was one of the company who had harried him earlier in the night, loyal courtiers to Ada's father. The face was familiar enough, but he could not dredge up a name.

'Abraham . . .' She stopped, as if trying to trick herself into believing the words. 'They said it was only Albie Crowe they cared about. That it isn't about plundering and looting, Abraham. It's about your daughter . . .'

Abraham tightened his arms around the Crowe, drew the reins up. Something in him wanted to lift the horse high, send its forelegs flying at the woman, trample her underfoot and make quick his escape. She had no right to breathe a word about Elsa. He knew what the night was about more than any man alive in the city.

'This isn't just about my daughter,' he said. In the corner of his eye, he saw Ezra's man pushing past Mrs Redmond. 'This is about the city. This is about every boy who clamours to be a petty thief, instead of signing up to fight.' He stopped, dug in his heels to spur the beast forward. 'This is about me,' he breathed.

The horse took flight, the man behind hollering as it ran. Past the doors of the mill it thundered, past the tussocks of thick grass and outbursts of thistle. In seconds, the end of the lane was looming. It seemed to bear down upon him: the barren scrub, the squatting factory shell, the endless terrace beyond.

One of the barrage-balloon cables whipped past, and Abraham wrenched on the reins. Braying manically, the horse reared up, hooves clattering against the side of the mill. Straining to hold on, Abraham wrapped an arm around Albie Crowe's throat, fought to keep hold of the reins with the other. The leather slipped from his fingers as the horse crashed down – but, somehow, he still sat astride its back.

Abraham looked up, uncertain as to what he had seen. Where the cables had once been wound into their winches, now they trailed freely, great iron ropes with clubs on the end, like spiked maces, clawing up the ground wherever they hit. Somewhere above, the balloons still floated – but every time they were caught in a gust of wind, every time they were dragged into the slipstream of the turning planes, the balloon shifted, its heavy leash tautening and snapping at the earth.

'Captain!' Ezra's man called out. 'It doesn't have to end this way . . .'

'Don't you understand?' Abraham returned. The cables lashed around him like a lion tamer's whip. 'Ezra wants him dead. I only want to get him to the end of the road.'

'He's only one boy, Abraham.' There was something conciliatory in the old man's tone. 'Ezra just wants what's best for his granddaughter. He wants the same thing as you . . .'

Abraham strained to speak. Not a thing that any of them did tonight was best for Elsa. She was dust, now. She was less than nothing.

Albie Crowe let out a sudden cry.

Too late, Abraham turned. Over the factory roof, the clouds frothed and came apart, spewing out a ball of flame. The plane, trailing dark black smoke, climbed steeply, its tail flickering vermilion – and, in its wake, another fighter screamed, sputtering out bursts of rapid fire. Abraham squinted up, his eyes streaming. The planes rose between the two barrage balloons, one after another. In the roiling air they left behind, the barrage balloons bobbed and turned, cables snapping wildly beneath. The two cables came close and then parted again, like a doorway inviting him on.

Albie kicked out, tried to turn, a shoulder at Abraham's throat.

'Crowe,' Abraham said, holding him fast, 'you get off this horse and they'll kill you . . .'

'I've seen boys maimed by them,' Albie gasped, eyes glimmering at the great cables cutting back and forth. 'I've seen them tear through houses more viciously than any bomb.'

'And I've seen boys drawn and quartered for being cowards,' Abraham whispered. 'You'll just have to pray to those daemons of yours . . .'

Abraham kicked down and the horse bolted forward. As they emerged from the lane, through the great winches, there came a groaning from somewhere above, the balloons finally grinding against each other. One cable caught momentarily on an outcrop of rubble and reeds, tautened – and then sprang back to dance, viciously, with the other. For a second they entwined, and then – the balloons parting above – they scythed apart again, a fountain of sparks bursting forth where the cables caught. Roaring in the boy's ear, he dug the point of his boot deep between the horse's ribs, and came pounding through the two thrashing cables.

They cantered beyond the reach of the cables, slowing only when they came past the factory and ruined outhouse. Abraham did not mean to – but, as he joined the broken road, he looked back a final time. The first of the balloons was drifting over the warehouse, now. Its cable ploughed into the wood, and the figures in its shadow scattered out of sight.

'Albie,' he said, shaking the boy with his bad arm. 'Crowe – you're still with me?'

The boy gurgled a reply. Abraham imagined it a razor-sharp riposte, and it cheered him to know the boy was not gone yet.

'This night has done you some good already, son. You can't imagine your way out of everything.'

By the time they came back to the terraces, the horse was starting to flag. Abraham slowed it to a trot and lost himself in a labyrinth of alleys. He was not certain, at first, to which part of the terrace they had returned; the roads had been recast, and more than once he found himself following some causeway that the bombs had opened up, or turning away from some intersection now closed by a landslide of red brick and timber. In front of him, Albie Crowe sagged, rising only to murmur intermittent oaths and be silenced by an arm at his throat.

He reached, at last, a stretch of the terrace that he recognised, bringing the horse windward of an omnibus half-buried in the road. Further down Meanwood Road, there lay the house in which he had gagged and bound Albie Crowe – and, beyond that, the hulks of fire engines still battling the blaze that blocked the paths back to Woodhouse Moor. Abraham wheeled the horse around and followed the road until he came, again, to the buildings opened like doll's houses.

At the end of that row, Abraham whistled out – and, from a snicket, the dog careened. When it reached them, panting so wildly that it looked to be beaming with joy, it rose on its hind paws, scrabbling to reach Abraham on the back of the horse. For the first time in what must have been hours, he felt serene. Ezra's men surely still hunted him, but somehow he knew he was beyond them. He hushed the dog, and commanded it to walk at the horse's side. As they went, it looked up merrily at Albie. Perhaps it had grown fond of him through the endless night – or, perhaps, it was only salivating at the thought of reaching the end of the road.

In one of the yards they passed, a single Christmas tree stood. Planted there some seasons before, somehow it had flourished in the barren earth and factory air. The needles were still a vibrant green, the trunk broad and strong.

'Scarcely half a mile left,' Abraham remarked, nosing the horse onward.

'Let's be done with this, Captain,' Albie began. 'After tonight, I'll be thankful for a cell and a decent meal. I'll rest easy, I shouldn't wonder. Tomorrow can be another day.'

The road swung again, rising steeply to leave the endless terrace behind.

'Here we go, Albie . . .' whispered Abraham, as if in regret.

Albie looked up.

In the barren stretch below them, the station at the end of Meanwood Road was a ruin, just like the rest of this blasted land. Where its outhouses once stood, now only rubble remained, twisted monoliths of brick standing monument to some fallen civilisation – while, beyond that, the fortress smouldered.

'Captain,' Albie ventured, feeling new fire. 'Captain, you lost . . .'

Abraham ushered the horse gently onward, toward a low stone wall banked with debris. For a moment, and even with the dog close to his heel, Albie smiled. Then, he considered the land.

'Are you really so sure?'

Back down the hill he looked, back over the terraces that grew against the Moor. The planes had pirouetted this way, that much was true. They had dropped their bombs and wiped out lives, carved new craters in the streets and sent tall columns of fire high into the skies above Leeds. But fires did not flicker in the gutted rooms of Meanwood Road, orange light did not rise from the station's heart, nor did smoke curl from the crumbled walls. The land had been razed, but the destruction had not been tonight.

Abraham guided the horse to a gap in the low stone wall and, steeling himself with the revolver in his hand, he dropped from the beast. The horse shifted, unsteadily, on loose shale – and Abraham reached up to draw Albie Crowe down. Dazed, the boy stumbled from the stirrups, finding scant purchase on the rubble-strewn road.

Instinctively, Albie tried to turn. Perhaps he might even have run had he not seen, in the corner of his eye, Abraham lift the revolver high.

'Son,' Abraham began, 'I told you already, back in the air-raid shelter – there's no place left to go.'

The dog snarled.

'How long?' Albie asked, turning back to see the shell that had once been the constabulary's proudest station.

'Four nights ago, the Stukas soared over, the fire fell,' Abraham replied. 'We lost a lot of good men. I thought, at first, that the news might have reached you – but the thing to learn about turncoats and Whisperers, Albie, is they've always got a price.'

'And now?'

'Now?' breathed Abraham, striding forward to face Albie down. 'Well, now, Mr Crowe, there's only the two of us.' He stopped, before he too turned to face the blackened walls. 'This is it, Albie Crowe. We've reached the end of the road.'

* * *

Elsa Matthews was gone to the Young Bloods for ever before the new year was old. When she kissed her father and scurried along the terrace to meet the boy lurking at its end, Abraham did not understand that she was leaving him for ever. It was just another in a long line of daily goodbyes, and to his later regret not once did he believe he would not see her again.

There was a school in Kirkstall where Ada would wait at the gates with the other mothers, and cluck around her son when he emerged. That day, a false dawn for the spring, it was Abraham who stood there, smoking a rolled cigarette while Ada's friends eyed him curiously. Bells rang, and children tumbled from windows and doors. Most of the mothers rushed to meet their sons and daughters, with only the wise ones holding back and waiting to be found. Edmund did not seem to think it odd when he saw his father at the gates instead of his mother. They took to the small roads together, and talked gently about their days. Like his sister before him, Edmund was a boy in love with his schooling, and Abraham was happy to hear it; he remembered little from his own days in front of a board.

'Have you seen your sister, son?'

It was a moment before Abraham realised he was walking on alone. He turned to look back at his son, saw him swinging his satchel with what might have been ire.

'It's all right if you've seen her, Edmund. I'm not cross.'

'Don't you think I'd have told you if I'd seen her?'

Abraham knew, then. His son had never bitten back like that before.

'Not if she asked you not to,' Abraham replied. He waited for Edmund to catch him up and then, together, they went on. They were walking detours from their natural route home, but that in itself was not unusual: Abraham often took his son on long meandering strolls, as if to show him the parts of the city that any other boy might miss. They came to the wide thoroughfare of Kirkstall Lane, where the viaduct loomed above, and there they stalled. 'She's gone to Albie Crowe – that much I know. She's been honest enough, but your mother's sick with it. She just wants to know how she is.'

'I can't . . .' Edmund breathed the words softly, torn between two oaths. 'Albie told her not to. Because . . . because you're a watchman, Dad.'

At last, Abraham could smile. There was some comfort in the reasoning.

'I know why it is, son. I know she'd bring him to us, if she could. We'd sit down and your mum would make tea and there'd be cream and jam and . . . But I know it can't go that way. I might even understand. You can't help who you throw your hand in with. Elsa didn't choose Albie any more than your mother chose me.'

'Albie says that too . . .'

Abraham did not warm to that thought, but he tried not to let it show; Edmund was not old enough yet, and there was too much to ask of him today already, without starting to quibble over every little thing.

'I want you . . . I want you to go to him.'

'Dad?'

'He said there was a place at his table for you too, if that was what you wanted.' Edmund tightened his hand on his satchel. 'Don't look so surprised, son. I hear all sorts of secrets. I've been a copper for longer than you've been a . . . thing.' He grinned, was gladdened to see his son grinning back. 'I know where he is, but I can't go there. I'd be crossing a line, and then Albie would have to build walls – and then he'd have turrets, and guard posts, and garrisons of men – and, soon enough, we might have lost her for ever. So, Edmund, I need you to look out for her now . . .'

Edmund thought he understood. 'Become a Young Blood?' he asked. There was the same thrill in his voice when he said the words that there had been when Abraham first heard other boys on the terrace whispering of the gang. 'Really?'

'Don't call them that,' Abraham answered. 'They're not Young Bloods. They're unemployed and down and out, they've known too many years of this . . .' He floundered for the word. '. . . greyness,' he decided, 'to know how to do anything else. They're thieves – don't forget it. Not cutpurses or highwaymen or brigands. They're just boys with nothing better to do.'

They started to move, stepping together into the darkness beneath the viaduct's towers, stepping together into the light on the opposite side. The sun was growing low over Kirkstall, just as it was growing low over the terraces Elsa now called home. 'I'll do it, Dad,' he said. 'I'll bring back word from her.'

Edmund went to the Young Bloods that same night. His mother tried to pack him sandwiches, as if he was embarking on a cycling trip with friends, but Abraham would not allow it. 'A young thief does not set out to learn his trade with biscuits from his mum,' he whispered, and watched his boy set out along the terrace.

They were suspicious of him, at first – but he dined with them, that first night, on a casserole of meat the Browning boys had lifted, cooked and prepared by Elsa herself. She was glad to have him with her and, after they had eaten, she showed him around the land she now called home.

After Albie yoked the other gangs of Leeds to the Young Bloods, they had abandoned the old terrace in Sheepscar and crossed the Moor to their new home at the low end of Burley. Albie kept the old lair, still, but only as a trove in which to store their plunder. They lived, now, in what had once been a schoolhouse. Like the terraces in Sheepscar, the windows had been boarded in 1919 , the few children left shipped out to schools scattered across the other townships of Leeds. Now, for the first time in decades, it lived again.

Elsa led Edmund from room to room. There was industry here, but not of the kind that seemed so inevitable when he watched workers tramping the Otley Road each night, coming home from whichever factory or mill in which they wasted their days. Many of the Young Bloods were old enough for just that sort of a trade, but instead of taking up their fathers' tools, they had come here, to the halls of Albie Crowe. There were boys coming back and forth, and in a small yard set back from the narrow road, a bank of motorcycles sat under the indifferent gaze of the Brownings' nag.

There was a patch of land, between the schoolhouse and its caretaker's lodge, that had once been a paddock, claimed in the long years of stagnation by briars and thorn. Elsa had cleared the undergrowth already, and marked her plots with stakes and string. There was not much she could do until winter truly died, but she led Edmund up and down the rows and explained to him the vegetables she hoped to plant here. It was her hope, she said, that Edmund would work the poor strip of land alongside her, that they might even take a barrow of their runner beans and beets back to their parents – as an apology, of sorts.

'I don't think they need you to say anything,' Edmund began. 'They just wonder why you don't come home. If it's him that makes you stay . . .'

Elsa smiled. In the frosted windows that overlooked the garden, some of the boys were smoking cigarettes. Albie himself had never entertained the habit, though he liked the taste of it on Elsa's lips.

'You can tell them it isn't so. I like it here, Edmund. That's the only truth there is.'

They sat, together, on an old bench propped up by stones, and watched as some of the Young Bloods tramped back into the halls, carrying a cargo wrapped in rags.

'They were out all night,' Elsa began, noting their drawn expressions. 'The skinny one's called Monmouth. He comes out of Meanwood. Not a typical one of Albie's boys – can hardly run in a straight line, his knees are so crooked – but Albie sees something in him all the same. Neither of them have families of their own. Lost boys like Monmouth, they're always welcome here.'

'Out . . . stealing?' asked Edmund, as if thrilled by the idea.

Elsa pondered the question. 'Not stealing,' she answered, and watched as Edmund's face crumpled in what might have been disappointment. 'There's been sightings. Some of the boys think a man's been following them, some night-stalker wandering the terraces long after dark, all dressed up in grey like some villain out of a story-book. It got Monmouth more spooked than most – but he's got what Albie calls a temperament. What he means is he's nervous as hell. But nervousness spreads, and some of the other boys have caught it now.'

In the doorway at the foot of the garden, Albie Crowe appeared. It was Edmund who saw him first and, furtively, he nudged his sister in her side. She nodded to him, and then went to join him in the open door.

Though Edmund could not hear a word, he followed the pantomime as best he could. Elsa had a hand curled to her stomach, and when Albie wrenched it away, instinctively she drew her hand back. One of the other boys, the one named Shepherd, appeared in the doorway behind them, lingered there for only a moment and then disappeared into the halls. A motorcycle revved its engine, a horse whinnied and Albie Crowe retreated to deal with whichever boys had arrived in the yards.

'He seems angry,' said Edmund, when Elsa returned.

'That's just Albie. What you see isn't what you get.'

Edmund recalled, suddenly, a favourite saying of his father's. Everyone's a moron for a mystery, he had often remarked.

'I know what they think, Edmund.' For the first time, his sister's voice was stern. 'But he isn't the way they picture him, not really. On the night I came to stay, he told me something. He said you could just sit back and take your lot in life – or you could strike out and take somebody else's.'

She had seen, in those words, a different sort of boy to the one who had pushed open her bedroom door, his knapsack brimming with her family's stolen treasures. Albie often spoke of mirrors. He made Elsa gaze into her reflection, and read back to him the things she saw there, and how they differed from her real, waking self. He had set out on a great voyage when he turned his back on his family, erasing every memory of them, every inherited inflection in his voice, every mannerism or tic whose lineage he could trace. He was becoming a different Albie Crowe, the one he saw when he peered into a looking-glass – and he would blaze that trail for anyone who cared to follow.

'He isn't there yet,' Elsa admitted. 'He can still feel them in him – his mother and his stepfathers and the rest. He's searching for some rite to perform – that he can get rid of them altogether. Something to push him through the mirror and trap him on the other side. He'll be free, then.'

'Is that why you won't go to Mum and Dad?' For the first time, Edmund sniped at his sister. 'You've got a mirror of your own to tumble through?'

'This is Albie's quest. Not mine. But . . .' Elsa floundered for the words. 'He's all alone in the world. Just because he put himself there, that doesn't mean it's any less harsh. He's got nothing – nothing except what he makes up. And I want to be there for him, when he comes out the other side.'

And so, she spent her nights and days in his company, watching him warp the world. She and Shepherd were teaching him the things he had missed out on in those days of the childhood he had erased for ever. Often it riled him to fits of spite, but she read with him every night from any book he cared to choose – and, slowly, he was beginning to learn the sounds and shapes and meanings of words. He knew by heart, now, the story of Peter Pan, spiriting children away from all the houses in Kensington Park. Albie Crowe was fond of those chapters, though he forbade Elsa from confessing his secret to Shepherd and the rest.

Albie reappeared at the end of the garden and gestured for Elsa to join him. She bent low and kissed her brother on the cheek, asked him to wish their parents well – and then, lifting her skirts, she followed Albie Crowe.

'You told him, didn't you?' Edmund heard Albie ask, when she ducked into the house.

'Not yet,' Elsa replied, laying her hand on her stomach. 'Not until we've decided what we're going to do.'

The end of February brought with it new gusts of snow. For days, the roads that led out of the townships and into the neighbouring hills grew high with impassable drifts. The Browning boys, spying bounties in the valleys, set out into the white, taking with them a flurry of the younger recruits who had flocked to Albie Crowe's call since the New Year came in.

On the night the Brownings set out, the fires burned brightly in the tumbledown halls. The drifts lay too deeply across the terraces to risk leaving a trail for watchmen to follow, the man in the grey cowl had been seen only two nights before – and so, instead of venturing on their nocturnal forays, the boys gathered together to share a banquet Elsa had prepared. There was steak and roasted chicken, rashers of bacon with fat sausages of blood, potatoes baked in an oven, plates piled high with parsnips and carrots and beets, all offered up to the Young Bloods by grocers they had brought into their trade. Some fool had brought along his guitar, but by the time the first dish was served, Albie had already severed its strings. It was a certain kind of fool, he explained, who liked to hear the sound of his own voice warbling out some clichéd song of love.

On the cusp of the second course, the door slammed and footsteps pounded in the hall.

'I saw him again,' said one of the Young Bloods, shaking the crystals of ice from his overcoat as he tore into the room. 'Out at Drew's rookery. Just watching from one of the ledges higher up the terrace. Standing there like some gargoyle. And for what, Albie? What does he need to know about ravens and rooks for?'

'It can't have been him,' said one of the other boys. 'We sighted him on the Meanwood trail when we come back in. Prowling the

147

thickets down that end of town. He couldn't have covered that much ground in that little time.'

'I don't care what you say,' the boy retorted, gesturing for Elsa to help him yank off his boots. They were made of brown hide, and lifted from a cobbler's down some Headingley backstreet. 'It was him, I'll testify to it. There's something gets him from one end of town to the next. He's the sort who'd ride a goddamn horse. I saw into his hood tonight. I saw his eyes just shining out.'

'That's enough,' barked Shepherd. The room fell silent, and boys from one hearth to the next laid down their forks. 'He isn't a ghost. He's just some man, and we don't even know he's hunting us. A loner out late every night, peering into people's houses. Does that remind anyone of anything? In all likelihood, he's just another thief.'

'If he's another thief, he ought to be one of the Young Bloods,' the elder Browning boy piped up. 'It isn't right that he'd be out there, stalking the streets on his own. These are our streets, aren't they? Isn't that so, Albie?'

'They're certainly not his,' Albie murmured.

The man in the grey cowl had been on their tongues for weeks. Some of the boys considered it an honour that they had crossed the path of that highwayman, others that it was a special omen of ill luck that the streets had dredged up for the Young Bloods alone. Drew's grandmother had reported a visit from the stranger in the dead of night; Shepherd's mother herself had demanded to know what her son might have been doing that a man draped in grey had been ferreting through their rubbish like some common tramp. And so it went that the Grey Cowled Stranger moved through the ranks of the Young Bloods, appearing on thresholds in lands as far apart as the Otley downs and the heights of Harehills, traipsing after boys on their midnight routes.

'We should be rid of him, Albie. You should take a knife to him.'

It was a pale-faced boy who had spoken. When he breathed his last word, a host of faces craned toward Albie Crowe – but Albie, as was his wont, merely shrugged, as if ridding himself of a persistent itch.

'You can't go round killing . . .' said Monmouth. 'We're thieves, not killers.'

The silence compelled Edmund to lay down his fork. Across the table, he caught Elsa's eyes glimmering at him secretly, and for a moment that settled the whimpering in his gut. Somebody lifted their knife to carve out a piece of steak, but a dozen gazes fell upon him, and quickly he withdrew the blade.

At the head of the table, Albie stood.

'This phantom does not exist,' Shepherd scolded.

'Oh, he exists,' Albie said. 'But he's just a man, only blood and bone – and there's nothing to be frightened of in some frail old man wandering the terraces wrapped up in an old woollen frock. Don't you see?' he asked – and there must have been something funny in that, for the grin widened his face. The boys sitting before him, he was certain, had not invented the man – but the spectre, well, that was undoubtedly theirs. 'Edmund,' he went on, turning to face the boy. 'What do you think?'

A strange silence. Edmund screwed up his brow. 'I haven't seen him,' he shrugged.

'You're a slippery sort, Edmund. That wasn't the question.'

'Leave him alone, Albie.'

Even Edmund cringed at that. Shooting Elsa a look, he shuffled the chair back so that he might stand – but Albie Crowe's hand was on his shoulder, pressing him back down.

'The meal isn't finished. Didn't your parents teach you a thing about manners?'

Elsa lifted a hand, stroked Albie's forearm as she tried to entwine her fingers with his.

'He has to go, Albie. You know he doesn't bed down here.'

'The snows fall deep,' Albie began. 'It wouldn't do the boy any good to catch a chill.'

'It's all right, Albie,' Edmund ventured, squirming into the arms of his overcoat. 'It isn't so deep that it could stop me. There'll be drifts on the Moor, but if I keep to the low trails . . .'

'No, little brother,' Albie went on. 'It's cold out. The foul are abroad. These streets are full of vagrants and cutpurses and Grey Cowled Strangers getting ready to spring their traps. It wouldn't be right of me to send you against all that.' He paused, and when next he spoke he was glaring at the girl, instead of the boy. 'I think it's time things changed for you,' he said.

'He says I can't carry on, fluttering back and forth every time that I want. He says it's time to make a decision.'

Abraham put down his coffee and folded his paper. There was toast in the rack, but he had let it go cold, his appetite waning with each week Elsa was gone.

'He's predictable as a one-dog derby,' he murmured. There had never been any doubt that this would be Albie Crowe's ploy. Abraham was only a rudimentary player of chess, but even he was thinking that far ahead. 'What prompted it?'

'He rowed with Elsa last night.'

Abraham tried to disguise the twisting of his mouth. 'Does he hit her?' he asked.

Edmund shook his head.

'It doesn't matter. Boys like him have other ways of beating a girl.'

He folded his newspaper, and trudged from the scullery into the halls upstairs. Edmund followed closely, not breathing a word. 'You'll need to pack a bag – and do it before your mother comes back. She'll only persuade you there's a warmer bed for you here. You know what she's like with that silver tongue.'

They moved into the bedroom Abraham and Ada shared.

Edmund had spent many warm weekend mornings in here when he was still a small boy, he and Elsa crawling under the covers with their mother and father. Family portraits lined the walls, faces of men who had come before Edmund, but in whose features he saw a dozen different versions of his father.

On a hook against the far wall, there hung a hooded cowl, woven in grey and stitched along the seams with thick black thread. As Abraham came into the room, he lifted it from its peg and stashed it inside the chest beneath the bay. Hovering on the threshold, Edmund watched him closely.

'Would you think me a coward if I said I was frightened?' he asked.

'I'd think you were a simpleton if you said that you weren't.' Abraham smiled at his son. He had not often told Edmund about the days he was a soldier, but he imagined the two of them, then, crouching low in some foxhole with the sky shattering above. 'I won't think less of you if you don't want a part in this any more.'

Edmund shifted, uneasily, from one foot to the next. 'It doesn't matter. I'd think less of myself.'

Abraham knew that feeling well. He lifted a small knapsack, began to fill its pouches with whatever useful oddments he could find.

'There are places you can go to, if you need to escape. If it happens, don't come here. That's what they'll be expecting. They'll rally themselves to cut you off. But I have friends.' Abraham was whispering himself, now. 'Old stalwarts of mine, men who ran in my battalion when there was war the last time, men I've pounded the beat with since before you were born. We can trust them, at least . . .' He paused, lifted from his greatcoat a small, yellowing roll. 'I've written them down,' he said. 'All their names and addresses. Read it, over and again,' he went on. 'Then burn it.'

Edmund's eyes flickered over the words.

'We'll have to keep our distance now, son. But there'll be times we have to meet, things I'll need to know . . .' He stopped, moved slowly to the window-ledge. 'If you need to see me, well, I'm easily found. I'll pound the beat by the Kirkstall viaduct at dusk every day. And if ever I need to find you . . .' He opened a small chest beneath the window. From its cavities he lifted a bundle of beeswax candles. Pushing one into a five-pointed candelabrum on the ledge, he flicked a match against the wall and held it to the wick. 'Should I light a candle in the window, you'll meet me on the Moor,' he went on, coaxing the candle to a tall, bright flame. 'There are people listening in the streets. The trees and the scrub – it's the only safe place left . . .' He described the place, where the brambles grew wild at the conflux of trails, a depression in the land beyond the plots where men were building allotments in preparation for the sea blockades to come. 'You must be careful, Edmund. You know what they'll do if they think you're whispering on my account. And if it ever comes to a time you need to denounce me – well, don't think twice about it. Just look after your sister, son.'

It was colder in the house, now that Edmund, like his sister, was gone to the Young Bloods. Abraham sensed the change in Ada from the first week. When he returned from the beat, she had set the table for four. He did not ask her why, nor put the knives and forks back into their drawer. They ate in silence.

Edmund descended, in the third week, to the Viaduct, and convened with his father, there in its shadows.

'You have to move against him,' he said, stepping out of the undergrowth that banked the road.

Abraham put an arm around him – because, in spite of everything else, he was still a father.

'What happened, son?'

'I wanted to run, go find sanctuary with one of your stalwarts . . .'

The word sounded strange when it tripped from Edmund's

tongue, as awkward and out of shape as the words 'Young' and 'Blood' had once seemed.

'I've got a secret I don't want any more. I'd tell you everything, but I'm too yellow, I'm too loyal . . .'

Abraham's eyes lifted. 'Loyal?'

'To Elsa, Dad . . .'

'She asked you not to tell me?' Abraham did not want to rail against his son, and he paused to gather his thoughts. 'I thought we had an understanding, son. She wasn't to know we still meet.'

The sky was overcast, threatening rain. There had not been snow in a week and sludge ran in rivulets along the banks of every road. Edmund's trouser legs were sodden when he came fully out of the brush.

'They're moving against you, Dad. Albie's going to hit the homes of every watchman, make them answer for being who they are. Seven nights' time. You can't let it happen.'

A great rumbling told Abraham that a freight train lumbered along the tracks overhead, and he ducked back to face Edmund.

'If he did that,' said Abraham, 'he couldn't go back. I couldn't keep all the constabulary at bay if he went for them. And I'm trying, Edmund, I'm straining to keep the peace – all for Elsa's sake.' He hesitated. 'He'd be starting a war.'

Abraham saw Edmund's face twist, as if exasperated.

'Don't you get it?' his son cried. 'He's already started a war! He took your daughter! Like he was some barbarian, he came into your house at night and he took her away . . . She might not see it like that – but, I swear it, Dad, he does. He's gloating about it. He's mocking you, Dad . . .'

Abraham cared little for the mockery of boys like Albie Crowe.

'It's not his taunts I'm worried about.'

'Why do you let him do it?'

Abraham was silent. He was not being a coward; he was being a decent man.

'I'll see to the Young Bloods,' he finally began. 'You see to your sister. That's the understanding, Edmund. That's what we agreed on. And don't you let her down.'

There were seven nights to prepare the defence. On the first, Abraham sent out messengers; on the second, convened meetings in the homes of the watchmen whose homes would be hit. The third day was for shipping each family's treasures into the cellars of his own house; the fourth, for finding bolt holes to hide away each watchman's wife and children. On the fifth and sixth days he worked hard to empty the cells of the station at the end of Meanwood Road, let the turnkeys who dwelt in darkness there spend an idle afternoon out in the sun, in preparation for the long night to come. Then, on the seventh day, he pounded the beat from one end of the city to another, following every old patrol, feeling the cobbles and stones and earth underneath his feet, dreaming that he might see his daughter again soon.

Abraham's was not among the houses that would be hit that night. It had taken him a little while to understand that the young king had already stolen through his home. He caught himself wondering what Elsa might have seen that night that had drawn her to the boy.

Wilbur was wishing farewell to Kate when he arrived. The sun was already down, and the last of the day's light spilled golden from the rooftop slates. Kate nodded coldly at him as he came down the garden path.

'Don't worry about her,' said Wilbur as they sloped inside. 'She doesn't think what we're doing's right. She thinks we're trying to instigate something.'

'By defending our homes?' asked Abraham, a half-dead cigarette lolling between his lips.

'It's more than that, Abraham. You don't have to pretend.'

Three mugs of coffee later, Wilbur ran a patrol along the terraces of Woodhouse Lane, and came back to report that the boys were on the move.

'One of them dropped to his knees in front of a window. A man might have thought he was praying.'

'Was it a watchman's house?'

Wilbur nodded. 'And there are ravens flying,' he said.

Where Albie Crowe and his cohorts had conjured up the idea to ferry messages by raven, Abraham had not yet discovered. There was a boy named Drew who tended to the birds – that much he understood – and he supposed there was a certain posture in sending out flocks of black birds to do a boy's bidding. A boy like Albie Crowe would have found some splendour in that.

'Edmund didn't let us down,' Abraham said.

Long past midnight, Wilbur set out on another patrol. He had not been gone long when there came the noise of shattering glass. In houses across the city, the act was already unfolding – and, at last, it had reached their door. In a small terrace house at the height of Harehills, a boy named Browning took a bandaged fist to a window-pane, only to see, in the shards' reflection, a watchman looming on each shoulder. In Chapeltown's heart, Shepherd crept into a starlit chamber to find an old service revolver levelled at his head. A stream of Young Bloods shuffled, now, along Meanwood Road and into the station there.

Abraham ground his cigarette against the bare brickwork, and fell into a chair by the dying fire. There was little warmth in the room tonight, but he did not feel the cold.

The handle turned, the door opened only a fraction – and then the boy curled through the narrowest of gaps, barely touching the walls. For a second, he froze, his back to them, his head low. Abraham could not be certain, but he thought he heard words being whispered. 'Don't fall asleep . . .' the boy seemed to be murmuring. 'Don't let them catch you . . .'

'Albie Crowe,' said Abraham. 'I want to talk to you.'

At last, he was alone with the Crowe. Looking at him now, he considered that he was not a very remarkable boy. He was not good looking, but nor would he turn heads in the street for his ugliness. If there was anything extraordinary in the way he looked, it was only in the curious glimmer of his eyes.

'Congratulations, Captain,' Albie began. Abraham had been opening his own lips to break the silence, and cursed himself, now, that the boy had got there first. 'You must have been working hard.'

'Even now, there are men sitting in each of the houses you put a mark on. They're taking your friends to the cells at the end of Meanwood Road. Have you heard of the cells they keep there?' Abraham paused, but Albie Crowe did not respond. 'How is Elsa?' he asked.

'She's the same as ever she was.'

Abraham did not believe that. If she was the same, she would not be with Albie Crowe, bedding down in his hideout every night without her family at her side.

'I'll want to see her.'

Albie knew the words were framed as a command, but he was pleased to hear the plea in the watchman's tone. His shoulders dropped a little, and he crossed his ankles as he leant against a shelf of books.

'You can get almost anything you want, if you say the right things,' he said, hearing some memory of himself whisper into Elsa's ear, watching her slowly disrobe. 'The question is: do you have the right words?'

'What would you have me say?' he asked. 'She's my daughter.'

'What are you going to do with my boys tonight, Captain?'

Set them free? Even Albie Crowe would not suggest such a thing. But, as Abraham listened closely, he saw, at last, what Albie had understood from the very beginning: Abraham Matthews would not put chains around Albie Crowe tonight; not when his daughter was at stake, not when there was a chance she might still come back to him of her own accord, without retributions and justice getting in the way. If he put a stake through Albie Crowe, there was no way back to the peace of before; if he played his hand with caution, there was still a chance he could salvage all he had lost.

'They'll pay for the crimes you had them commit. For most, there'll be a choice. There are men needed for fighting a war, and boys like Shepherd shouldn't be rotting in a cell while other, decent folk are dying on their account.'

'I wouldn't want Shepherd in my battalion. He'd stab his commander in the back and desert soon as the guns started to sound.' The boy seemed proud of that, as if he had instructed all of the Young Bloods in those bold, valiant ways.

'That, Crowe, is why your little enterprise won't last for ever.' For the first time, Abraham felt the pull of pity toward Albie Crowe. 'You wouldn't trust anybody with your life, would you, son?'

Son, he said, and that made Albie smile. The old fool did not know in whose company he cast himself.

'Sometimes, she asks about you. She wanted Edmund to start telling her stories of the old times, when it was just the four of you, when you'd spend every night holed up there together, fires roaring, telling tales.' Even the memory of it riled Albie Crowe. Abraham pictured his son and daughter, beaming at the memory of those happy days, while Albie Crowe prowled the peripheries of the room. 'But, all of that, well, Captain Matthews, all of that's in the past. And I've drawn a line under the past. For Elsa and Edmund, just like the rest of the Young Bloods.'

'You talk around every question anybody asks, Albie. So I'll make this thing simple: what is it going to take?'

'If you mean to see her, you'll end this Grey Cowled Stranger madness, of course. It has the boys all spooked. They're simple enough to believe in portents and wraiths. Shepherd tries to drum it into their heads that there's no such thing, but too many of them have seen you tramping their streets to be quelled like that.'

That they had given him a name at all was a surprise to Abraham. He had not donned the cloak as any disguise; it was they who had decided that.

'I suppose,' said Abraham, 'that if they can believe there's romance in thiefdom, in something so foolish as a common racketeer dubbing himself a Young Blood, it isn't such a flight of fancy to start seeing Grey Cowled Strangers on every street.'

They had to call this shadow who stalked them something, he supposed. But there was a power in nicknames that stretched far beyond the borders of the schoolground. Call a boy 'Runt' and it was not only his feelings that took a beating; soon the name would stick, and soon it would spread, until some day his friends would look upon him and not know him by the name his mother had called him at all. And, from that day on, the name would turn against its owner, like some parasite starting to devour its host. Slowly, by degrees, he would become the thing that they named him. Call a boy 'Hero', and suddenly he would be leaping in front of bullets, rampaging through buildings consumed in fire; call a boy 'Coward' and soon he would be shrivelled up and sobbing under any petty slight.

Call a boy a 'Young Blood', and he would become the daring thief of the legends Albie penned.

'I'll hang the cloak up,' he began. 'But I'll want one night with her. After that, well, Elsa has her own mind to make up.'

Albie Crowe nodded. 'Have you thought,' he began, 'what your constables might think of you if they thought you were bartering with a thief?'

'I suppose,' Abraham conceded, 'that they'd think me as bad as you.'

Albie Crowe smiled. 'Well, in that case, Captain,' he said, 'I believe we have a deal.'

Abraham curled, that night, around Ada – and knew, for the first time in many long months, that she was sleeping alongside someone who deserved her. She rose before him and, perturbed at the dark impressions growing around his eyes, insisted that he stay in the sheets until his beats began at midday. She brought him tea and toast and yesterday's news, and he promised her she would see Elsa soon.

'I didn't mean to let her go to him,' he said as she left his side. 'I didn't know it would go this far.'

She turned at the door and came back to the bed.

'If you keep looking for things to hate about yourself, well, you're going to find them,' she said. 'You did well last night.' She kissed him softly, then, and left him to his thoughts.

A messenger came for him before noon. He had been bathing away the night's grime when the knock came at the door, and Ada admitted a weasel of a boy, the bastard son of one of Abraham's commanders who lived with his mother in Armley and performed duties, when it suited, for watchmen in need. It was a summons, but beyond that there was no explanation. Ada welcomed the weasel to the house and led him to the chamber upstairs, where Abraham lay in a tin tub.

'To the station?' Abraham wearily asked.

'Not there,' said the boy in his usual flinty tones. 'To the Packhorse taproom. Wilbur's going to be waiting.'

Abraham hurried over the Moor, with the weasel following in his wake. At the banks of Otley Road, Wilbur was waiting. When they met, they did not need to greet each other. They set off at a march, following the broad thoroughfare toward the labyrinth at the city's centre.

The Packhorse taproom sat sullenly along that road. Though it was early in the afternoon, the drinking hole was alive. In the corner, a lean young man was already drunk, bawling over his game of cards. In the first of the hearths, a huddle of boys raised their glasses high. Abraham had always been under the impression that this was a tavern for an older generation, where night-walkers warmed themselves before their long shifts began. He saw, now, that only a handful of the old-timers remained, shuffled into closed rooms, or bundled into the shadows at the back of the halls.

The gang of boys sang out their toast and drained glasses. When the closest of them set down his tankard, Abraham tensed.

Shepherd's eyes met his. He felt Wilbur's hand on his shoulder, shook himself free, only for the hand to fall and check him again. And here were the rest: the Browning boys, the raven keeper Drew, the countless little ones to whom Abraham could not ascribe a title nor name. As one, the gang looked upon him – but it was Shepherd upon whom his own gaze was fixed. Last night, as he had watched them bundled into cells, the boy's eyes had seemed the least odious of the lot – but even they were glimmering with mockery, now.

'How did this happen?' he breathed.

They made haste to the station at the end of Meanwood Road, hitching a ride with a tinker as he made his rounds. It was the proudest of all the stations of the city's Watch, and stood above the terraces of Little London and Woodhouse both, the clock tower at its heart a sentry that might be seen from every alley and close for miles around. There were traps and motorcycles lined up in the yards, where a glut of younger constables gathered to smoke, and high above men scrambled along ladders and gutters, taping up windows and checking them for signs of weakness. When the bombs fell, they could not afford the station to fall.

Abraham came through the doors, but the watchman keeping the desk only shrugged vaguely, as if to shake off the meagre burden that had been laid on him the night before. Ada had once told Abraham to beware of swallowing his anger, for one day he would choke upon it, and today he decided to follow her advice. Vaulting the desk, he bundled the sergeant out of his path, snatched a dozen rings of keys from their hooks on the wall, and turned to an archway of brick that disappeared into the black vaults below.

Abraham turned a key in the lock and raised the portcullis. From here, the steps plummeted into the bowels of the earth. The stones underfoot had long since eroded away, but Abraham had walked that path too many times to let himself fall. He came to the first level, lifted a brand from its bracket on the wall, and turned into a passageway whose roof, thick with dirt, brushed the top of his head.

This deep underneath, the air was thick with damp. Thick pipes in the roof warmed the rooms above, but in the tunnels below it was dank; condensation trickled down the walls, so that it seemed the stones were bleeding, and even the ground at their feet ran slippery where the effluent gathered. At the end of the tunnel, he stooped to pass through a final gate, and dropped at last into the deepest layer of the warren.

Here the cells sat, nine narrow chambers hewn from clay and rock, constructed so that none faced another. The prisons were of varying size, some fit to hold only a single man, chained to a stake, others broad enough to imprison a murder of Albie Crowes. In Abraham's long knowledge of the cells, not a man had fought his way back to the light of day.

A turnkey sat slumped in his chair, passing his cudgel idly from hand to hand, as if to stave off the boredom of his shift. When Abraham loomed in the shadows, the sound of Wilbur's footfalls still rising at his shoulder, the man scrambled back, climbing rashly to his feet.

'Abraham!' he called. 'Captain . . .' he said, catching himself.

'Don't stand on ceremony on my account,' Abraham sniped. 'I'm not your commander.' He strode to the end of the tunnel and back, shoulders hunched low, peering into each of the vacant cells in turn. 'There isn't a man here,' he said. 'They bawled at each other last night. They cursed every watchman they could number. What happened?'

There was a fraternity of turnkeys kept these cells. Rarely did they mingle with the watchmen who roamed the streets above, lurking in their own taprooms and feasting in their own halls. Abraham cursed himself, now, that he had not lingered long enough among them.

When he turned, he saw Wilbur emerge from one of the cells. He was wringing his hands slowly, breathing only shallow breaths.

'It's as if they knew what was coming,' he muttered. 'They made a mess of the rushes in there, smeared their own dirt up and down the walls. They were mocking us, Abraham. They knew they wouldn't be trapped for long.'

Abraham considered it quietly. 'This wasn't a turnkey's call to make,' he said, lifting a palm in silent apology to the old wraith who sat there. 'There must have been a man to authorise this. There had to be a command.'

'Somebody in the constabulary, Abraham?' Wilbur began. 'A Young Blood in the station?'

Abraham looked up. 'Get me a list,' he said, 'of every man who pounded every beat last night.' He paused. 'And Wilbur – don't let a man among them know what we're hunting . . .'

He spent the day in deliberation. In the Violets tearoom he sat, tearing uselessly at the newspaper in his hands, trying to keep his courage up by applying coffee and tea and whatever secret spirit he could find to liven it up. He was still there, long after closing, when one of the waitresses had to send him on his way. When she *ushered him out of the door, she did not call him by his name. She was young, and it occurred to Abraham that he had not seen her before, that he could not put a name to the face, that she knew nothing of him and Ada and the moments they had shared in this place. Tramping the road home, he saw the faces of the young peering at him from every doorway and yard. They were throwing their stones on the Moor, flicking their knives in every alley and lane, dreaming in attics and bedrooms of the things they would do when they threw off the shackles of their home towns.*

It was late when he reached the old house. He let himself in, still uncertain how he could face his wife, and, in the scullery, tore the boots from his feet. Through the walls, Ada called out his name.

He found her in front of the fire. There was a tray at her feet, but the plates on it were still full, and the tea in her mug had not been touched.

'It's late,' was all that she said.

Ada looked at him – and, damn, but she was beautiful. He wanted to go to her, but he took a step and could go no further. His eyes darted, feverish, into the many corners of the room – but none of it was familiar, none of it was his, he should not have tramped the earth from his boots across her carpets, should not have carried armfuls of books to her house and asked her mother to let him through the door.

At last, he found his voice.

'They let them go,' he breathed. 'Shepherd and Drew, the Browning boys, every little bastard among them. Somebody threw them out.' He lifted an empty mug, checked himself from hurling it against the wall. 'They're back in the taproom now, laughing at me.' He stopped. 'And you know what this means, Ada? It means there are men in the constabulary, men sucked into this illusion of Young Bloods ruling the streets. It means I can't trust them any more.' His voice cracked. 'And he still has our daughter. Whatever happens now, it's on me.'

'Edmund must have known,' Ada whispered. Her fingers scrabbled at the arms of her chair as she strained not to shout. 'How could he not know a thing like that? Is he one of them, now?'

Abraham went to her. He bent low and kissed her on the forehead, as if a simple gesture like that might undo the last year of their lives. Then, slowly, he retreated.

In the bedroom upstairs, where once his son had read his books and lined up his toy soldiers, he pressed a beeswax candle into the holder and watched it flare.

High on the Moor, Abraham waited.

The hour had been and gone. The candle on the ledge would surely have whimpered and died by now. It might have been that the message never reached Edmund. Abraham prayed it was so. He looked above, saw the silhouettes of ravens lining the Moor's ancient trees. Even the birds were whispering their secrets to Albie Crowe. Another man knuckled through the darkness, stalking one of the lower trails. A year ago, Abraham would have followed, waited for him to show his hand. Tonight, he stood restlessly against an old oak and thought of all the things he had not done.

At last, there was shifting in the undergrowth, the murmuring of bramble briars and rustling of leaves. By the time Edmund emerged from the scrub, Abraham was ready.

'I thought you weren't coming . . .' he began. Until he spoke, he did not know how broken he had been. 'Damn this city, Edmund, where have you been?'

'The Young Bloods are on the move,' said Edmund. He urged his father to follow him, deeper along one of the old drovers' roads, into lands where the trees and scrub might better protect them. 'One of the lads who raises recruits down the Meanwood lanes, he says he's getting out. Monmouth, they call him. He says it's got too big, gone too far – that when the bombs start falling, we'll be finished for sure. But Albie has other ideas. He took

164

Shepherd out of his home, put him down in the old lair on the Sheepscar terrace. And the Brownings, and every other Young Blood there is, he's giving them all hideouts now, calling it the sacking of the city . . . Elsa keeps ledgers, Dad. He had her meet with fences on his account.'

'You're saying she's one of them? Do they carve her chest too?'

'She's still Elsa, Dad!' It was the first time Edmund had snarled so at his father. 'You're panicking. You're panicking like you told me never to panic – and she's still your daughter, and she's still my sister, and she's still the same girl she ever was, no matter who's around her, no matter what she's . . .'

Edmund's hesitation was too long. Abraham rounded on him.

'What she's what, Edmund?'

'You frightened them, Dad. That's all you did last night. But they know, now – they know they're above the Watch. You had them manacled in your stations, and you let them go. What went wrong!? And why didn't you take him? Why didn't you arrest Albie Crowe?'

'He promised me he'd send Elsa back.' Abraham tore wildly at the low branches of an elm, flaying his hands as they flew.

'But if you don't have the Watch on your side . . .'

'If I don't have the Watch with me, I have to find another way!' He tried not to yell, but there was a thunder in his words that would not be controlled. 'It isn't finished yet. There have to be some people I can call on. Some grey cowled strangers I can hunt them with . . .'

'Who, Dad?' Edmund demanded. 'You don't have any friends . . .'

Abraham shifted. 'I used to have friends,' he said. 'I used to be a soldier. I'll spirit my own army up if I have to.' He looked at Edmund – but the heath was dark, and Edmund's face was cowled. Perhaps there was yet a caste of men he could call on. 'Son, I want you to tell me where she is. I have to go to her now. I'll drag her out if I have to.'

'I'd tell you if I knew,' Edmund breathed, 'you know I would, but she's gone, she went before dawn, as soon as the rest were released, deep and deeper into the Rubble. And Dad, I think he knows, he has to know what I'm there for . . .'

Abraham prowled. Of course Albie Crowe knew. He had spies of his own all over this city, of that Abraham was certain. And yet Elsa was gone now, the boy was in her head, she was staying of her own accord – and he had let the boy go.

'Did he tell her to forsake us? Is it him? Is that why she's gone?'

'No, Dad . . .' Edmund whispered. He did not want to go on. 'It's . . . it's because she's pregnant.'

* * *

The End of the Road

Inside the building, Abraham untethered the hound and called it to heel. There was a bundle in the corner of what had once been the entrance hall, where a locked grille led to the prison cells below, and he lifted from it a bone. The dog received it gratefully. There were three bones in that bundle, but Abraham supposed it was little recompense for the way the bitch's brethren had died.

They came down a narrow passageway. If it was difficult to see where the walls once stood, that was not Albie Crowe's concern. Much of the interior was still standing, but the brickwork was charred, the doors hanging loosely in their frames. A peeling poster on a wall declared that 'The People of Leeds Will Go Forward Together'.

They came from the entrance hall along a dark corridor. At the end, where stairs climbed into the stories above, the way was blocked by a landslide of timber and brick; it was here that the bombs had pounded the station into the earth. Opposite the foot of the stairs, a side room still stood, an oasis in the ravaged shell. Old army boots had trailed footprints through the dust in the past days, heaving cabinets and tables against the bare brick walls. In the middle of the room, glowered upon by the proud portraits of watch commanders whose time had been and gone, sat a lone wooden stool.

Above that, a noose dangled from a rafter exposed by shells.

'You saved me from her grandfather,' Albie whispered. 'Let your dogs die on my account. Rode me away from those old soldiers. It doesn't make sense.'

'It makes sense.' Abraham kicked at the stool. 'Have a seat, Albie.'

Leaving Albie shackled to a pillar of stone with the dog standing sentry, Abraham ventured back through the doors. Unwilling to meet the dog's watchful gaze, Albie listened to the Captain's footsteps fade. For an interminable time, he was alone.

He bellowed. Thundered out words. Cries for help. The names of the Young Bloods who might have been tracking him down: Shepherd, Drew, the Brownings, Redmond and the rest, all the little ones who ran his errands and hit his marks. In reply, there was only the echo of his own words, reverberating about the abandoned station.

Through the tumbled brick, there came the tolling of bells. He fell silent, listened to them peal. When the ringing was done, and only the air-raid sirens remained, he opened his mouth to bellow again – but no words would come.

The dog howled out a greeting when Abraham reappeared. Shackled to his pillar, Albie's eyes were wide.

'What do the bells toll for?' he asked.

'They toll for the end,' Abraham answered. 'Come on, Crowe, there's something I want to show you . . .'

He locked Albie back to his arm and pitched him back into the fallen tunnel. In a room back along the passage, a bedraggled man was sitting, still wearing the rags of his watchman's clothes, hands shackled to the iron pipe on which he rested. He did not look up when Abraham dragged Albie through the door. It seemed, to Albie, that he had been chained there for days. His face was ruddy where he had cried himself to sleep, and the smell of retching was thick in the air. Bluebottles danced around a pail that sat just out of the captive's reach.

Abraham barked out a name, and the old fool stirred. He tried to speak, but his throat was raw from the sickness.

'He isn't one of mine,' Albie began.

'I have a full and frank confession.'

'Tricked out of some sorry bastard, strapped to a rack down there in your dungeon?'

Abraham tugged at Albie's chains. 'Shepherd filled you in on our cells, did he? I don't suppose he was there long enough to soak up the atmosphere that night, not with this Whisperer waiting to set them all free.'

'I'd have been there myself if you'd only arrested me, if you hadn't been such a noble coward.' Albie stopped. 'I'd have sent Elsa back to you, you know. Did you never think she just didn't want to come?'

'You sent her back, in the end,' breathed Abraham. 'You sent her back dead.'

The Whisperer ventured to speak once more.

'Shut up!' Albie flailed. 'Keep your mouth closed!'

'You got to listen to me, Albie – you don't know what he's got planned, what he's been plotting since his wife ran off . . . It's the cells, Albie, the black cells . . .'

Abraham lifted the pail from its rest and launched it at the bars. Drenched in his own piss, the Whisperer fell silent. It took him a moment before he would even dare gasp for breath, and for that Abraham allowed himself a smile. There was to be little pleasure in what he did tonight; it was only proper that he should savour every petty delight.

'Back through here, Crowe . . .'

He forced Albie back along the passage, toward the landslide and into the chamber where the noose gently swung.

'I took him three weeks ago. Three weeks, Albie, and word didn't reach you. I'd known from that night, of course, that you had a man in this station. But you got too involved thinking about the grand romance of the story you were building out here, and forgot to pay attention to the little things.' It had been a dull, drawn-out process of spinning lies and watching as they made circuits around the city, but eventually Abraham had identified the man who had released the Young Bloods from the cells that night on Meanwood Road. 'Just what do you think I've been doing since my daughter died, son? Pounding the beat and shining my shoes?'

'I didn't kill your daughter.' The sound of it was beautiful: real fear trembling in the throat of Albie Crowe. There was no posture to his terror, no pose to which the other Young Bloods might aspire. 'You think I did, but it didn't go that way . . .'

'Oh, you did it. Not with your fists, I'll grant you that. Not with a knife or a needle or a rope around her neck. But you killed her all the same, Albie. Words were always your weapon. You learnt that at a very early age, didn't you, son? Words,' he scoffed. 'The most powerful thing you had – and, until she came along, you couldn't even read.'

For the first time, no words whipped out of Albie's lips.

'What did she say before you took her to that woman?' he asked. He spat the last word like a vile oath. That woman had been the last face Elsa ever saw.

'It isn't a question you ought to be asking.'

'I'm asking it, all the same,' Abraham returned. 'What did she say to you, when you led her out of the carriage and showed her into that room?'

'She asked me if she had to do it,' he said. 'She said it didn't have to be that way, there was another path, there didn't have to be Young Bloods and Whisperers and boys all over the city held to my account. There could be a family – just me, her, and the baby . . .'

Abraham pressed forward, so close to Albie Crowe that their breaths mingled like that of two lovers.

'And what did you say to that?'

'Well,' grimaced Albie, 'I still led her into that room, didn't I?'

Who they waited for, Albie Crowe did not know.

The darkest watch always came before the dawn. Abraham remembered an old captain murmuring those words, somewhere outside the little town of Le Bizet, the evening he and his fellows had poured out of their holes in the ground. Intermittently he stood, peered through the blackouts into the ravaged yards outside. Out there, the city still cowered, families still hunkered in their Anderson shelters. And though he knew the night was not yet finished, Abraham felt a strange stillness, as if he had already put right all the things he had done so wrong.

At last, he saw the shadows.

'Albie,' he said. 'I wish you could see this.'

A host gathered. They were coming from the north and the south, the east and the west. He saw them appear where water tanks once stood, watched with one eye on Albie Crowe as the men there exchanged stories and lined up to face the shell. Five, ten, fifteen and more . . .

'Who are they, Abraham? Watchmen? Home Guard?'

The shadowy host closed in on the station. Even at this distance, Abraham could hear the tramping of boots upon shattered stone. He remembered marching, in the days of his own youth. He remembered its rhythms and joys, and wondered how it was for the ghosts who rallied to the fallen station tonight.

He dropped back the blind, and rounded on the boy.

'I make it twenty,' he ventured, dangling his key just out of Albie's reach.

'Twenty men to take one boy?' Albie asked. 'What are you doing, Abraham?'

Abraham came forward to unlock his shackles, but Albie kicked wildly out. The boy, Abraham supposed, had been kicking out at something his whole life. It was only misfortune, in the end, that he had kicked out at the wrong man.

He caught Albie's whirling boot, pulled back so that the boy crashed down, with his hands still shackled around the pillar of stone. As he lay there, Abraham unlocked the cuffs and snapped them back shut, this time binding the boy by his shins. Listening to the advancing men, he commanded Albie Crowe to rise.

'You want to know what I thought about your daughter?'

Outside, the first door slammed, the murmur of voices growing as the host moved along the crumbled hall.

'You want to know her last words?'

Abraham did not care. 'I'm ready for this, Albie. Are you?'

Albie threw him a pained look.

'I'm just a boy,' he said, the dangling rope brushing the top of his head. 'And I didn't kill her. She didn't have to come to the Packhorse and find me. She didn't have to go for walks on the Moor. She didn't have to get in that carriage and go to the woman in Armley . . .'

Abraham lifted the revolver high, closed his fist around the trigger, refused to wince as the wall behind Albie exploded in an eruption of plasterboard and brick.

'Put your head through that noose,' Abraham said.

He stumbled towards the stool.

'It was you who changed the rules. Remember that, Albie? You started making things up. And if you can do it, son, well, so can I.' The footsteps were heavy in the hallway. Abraham watched as the boy craned his head into the rope.

'Whoever comes through that door,' Abraham whispered, 'you are Albie Crowe, caught on the wrong side of the looking-glass. Remember that, Albie, and we won't go wrong.'

The door drew back – and in walked Edmund.

It had been long months since Abraham last crossed his son's path, and though their eyes instinctively met, neither troubled to hold the gaze. He was standing with Young Bloods on each shoulder, like the projections of some twisted conscience, and as he came forward, Albie Crowe suddenly stood tall.

'Abraham,' Albie began, lifting his head from the coil. 'Looks like your watchmen lost the race . . .'

Abraham lowered the revolver, turned to face the ranks of Young Bloods who poured into the room. His son seemed to be wavering; his shoulders shrank, as if he was about to be scolded, his eyes opened fractionally wider, as if in apology or fear.

'Edmund, please,' Abraham began. 'You understood me, Edmund. You understood it, once.' And now his son towered above him, taller and broader than he had ever seemed, sitting with him and Ada for breakfast, riding out with them for weekend walks. 'You promised, son, you swore it to me – and you never forgot a promise in your life. Edmund,' he breathed, 'please?'

Edmund turned his back on his father. In the rooms behind, the Young Bloods moved.

'Shepherd!' he cried. 'Drew!' he yelled. 'He's here . . . Albie's here . . .'

Young Bloods piled into the room. First came a gaggle of little ones, boys twelve and thirteen years old, whose families were no doubt huddled in their Anderson shelters or else long buried in the ruin. One of them was wearing the cap of a blitz scout – for not even they were immune to the lure of Albie's world. Over their shoulder, the older boys started to loom. Abraham had names for them all, inscribed in the long pages of his ledger – Shepherd and Drew, the Browning brothers,

Doonan and Hyde. He saw each face in turn, and something hardened in his gut. Every Young Blood who mattered had flocked to his summons tonight.

'Cut him free,' said Shepherd, pushing the Brownings aside as he came to the head of the crowd. 'And put the manacles on Captain Matthews before he pulls another rabbit out of his hat.'

'And won't somebody kill that miserable hound?' Albie spat. 'It's got its slobber on me now.'

Willingly, Abraham lowered the gun. On either side of him, little ones advanced.

'Shall we take down the noose, Albie?' asked the younger Browning boy.

'Leave it up,' Albie returned, descending from his stool. 'We might have use for that, yet.'

'You can't kill a watchman . . .'

Albie's eyes did not flicker at that.

'How did you know which roads to take?' he asked, turning to Shepherd and kneading at his neck as if the rope really had tightened there.

'He hasn't made a secret of it,' Shepherd replied. The flow of Young Bloods into the room had stopped. 'He tolled the bells, didn't he?'

Albie's eyes snapped back at Abraham. The old bastard might have had the decency to look frightened, but instead he just stood there.

He gestured sharply and, from the pack, Edmund emerged. Their eyes locked, and Abraham opened his palms, as if pointedly refusing to curl a fist. They had met only once since the day they bore Elsa's body home, cold and with the blood still staining the insides of her legs. On the day they had put her in the ground, with Ada ghosting through the well-wishers at the churchyard, he had exchanged only three words with his son. 'Don't give up,' he had mouthed, and then drifted on.

'Somebody hold him down,' Albie murmured, half-obscured by Edmund's shoulder.

Two of the Young Bloods, boys too insignificant even to be named in the long pages of Abraham's ledgers, emerged from the throng. They did not need to grapple at his arms, for Abraham did not mean to fight back.

He craned so that he could see the Crowe.

'The bugler plays, and you will join the dancing, Albie – that's the way it goes, you won't change that with what you conjured up in these streets. You and all these boys whose heads you've filled with your shit – you're still a part of the world . . .'

The first punch was soft, a glancing blow without any real finesse. After that, things changed.

Abraham had been beaten before, but never had he felt his own son's fists. Edmund was not the strongest boy he had known, but he threw a good punch; somebody had evidently been teaching him the value of a good follow-through. He used his weight well, and cut a smooth arc. Under the second blow, Abraham crumpled. When he hit the cold stone ground, the room whirled, the colours blurred, all sound momentarily stopped. An instant later, when he found his focus, he scrabbled backwards, smashed against the open brick at his back. Reaching out, he grappled at Edmund's shirt. Where the collar tore away, he saw the mark carved into his son's breast: three little notches, each deeper than the last, the scar tissue still fresh and black with blood.

'Edmund,' he whispered. 'What is it? What did you do?'

'Where did you disappear to, Dad?' Edmund hissed back. 'I've been searching. I've been prowling the streets.'

'For me?'

'You just disappeared, you bastard . . . What have you been planning?'

'I couldn't tell you, not with Whisperers on the streets – and your mother, your mother came back to the city . . .'

Edmund hesitated – but, after only a second, he reined himself back. Lifting his knuckles, bloody and raw, he pummelled forth one final time.

Abraham crashed into the stones.

'Enough?' Edmund cried. Through the parting boys, he faced Albie Crowe. 'You want to bloody your own fists, now?'

Shepherd momentarily closed his eyes. Even in the mist through which he peered, Abraham noticed it: the boy had almost cringed.

'Albie doesn't bloody his hands, not since . . .'

Abraham did not know, at first, from which direction the words came. It was a small voice, and when his swollen eyes finally found the speaker, he saw that he could have been no more than eleven or twelve years of age.

Edmund rounded on the boy.

'It seems to me,' sniped Edmund, 'that it's only been a week since Albie bloodied his hands for ever. Or are we all just forgetting what happened to Monmouth?'

A new fist flew. For the first time, Abraham did not see it coming. Albie Crowe was slight, but there was something feral in the way he streaked across the room and clawed for the Captain. Instinctively, Abraham tried to raise his arms – but there was never any need; before Albie reached the Captain, he stayed himself, so close that Abraham could feel the dewy warmth of his breath.

'Shall I tell you a story, boys?' Albie breathed, looming above Abraham as if he pressed a sword to the old man's throat.

Though not a boy replied, the Crowe was not deterred.

'The Captain came after me tonight. He came after me alone. He came after me alone because he has nobody left. Not a watchman. Not a daughter. Not a son. Not the wife who rode by his side since the days he stopped his own killing. What is it you once said to me, Shepherd?' Albie leered, wild and alone. 'You need the whole of humanity ranged up against you. Isn't that so, Abraham?'

Something in Abraham relented. He had been alone, once, that much was true. He had roamed France and Flanders and come back to England a blank slate of a man, without a past or a present or even the idea of a future. But Albie would learn, tonight, just as Abraham had learned, that a man could not march away from the person he was. Abraham would teach him that lesson himself, throw his arms open and feel the old days rushing back: the trenches and the shells and the simple joy of taking another man's life instead of giving up your own.

'There's something in him thinks he can undo this year of his life, as if he can step back through the mirror and whisper to his younger self that here rides a demon into your life. There's a voice tells him he can repel any foe, that he's greater than a thousand of my boys – and why?' Albie stalked the chamber's low walls, his boys scuttling to make way wherever his feet might fall. When he reached the doorway, he paused, looked back. 'You think your people are greater than mine because they have families and husbands and wives – because they say they're in love. Well, old man, I told your daughter I loved her. I told her it so I could fuck her, and then I told her it again, so she'd shut up and go to sleep. She doesn't trouble me like that any more.'

Albie threw the door behind him. In the hallway, he stopped. On one side, the darknesses of the stairwell beckoned him on. On the other, the halls were impassable. He turned and marched.

Footsteps rising at his back told him that somebody had followed him from the room. At first, he did not look back.

He palmed along the walls, retracing exactly the path along which Abraham had dragged him, as if undoing the terror of those moments. Then, stumbling upon a stretch of passage where light spilled in through frosted glass, he knew at last that he was finished, that he had erased his grovelling, his cowardice, the apologies for things he had not done.

He heard one of the planes thundering above.

'Shepherd,' he began, pausing on the threshold of the cell where the Whisperer slumped. 'I'll tell you when I need your comfort,' he went on.

'You've never needed comfort in your whole life,' Shepherd softly replied. 'Didn't even want your mother to suckle you at her teat. At least,' he went on, hesitating briefly, 'that's how you want it, isn't it? But I remember the way you were with Elsa Matthews. Tell yourself what you want, now – but you liked that girl. Doesn't matter how many times you say it – you're not an island.'

'A man might be forgiven for thinking you a little besotted with me, Shepherd. The time you've put into narrating the nuances of my character . . .'

Together, they walked on. In places, it seemed that rents in the walls had already been shorn up, bricks crudely chipped and crammed into place. When, at last, they came to the entrance hall, they stood together in the doorway and watched the cowering city. There were shapes shifting out there, but they were only phantoms spirited up out of dirt and dust, shadowmen without any real form. One of them seemed to rise and twist away, as if ducking out of sight.

'We'll lead the boys away,' Shepherd began. 'Put the night behind us.'

Albie shook his head slowly. 'There's nobody knows where he is,' he began, retreating to the relative warmth within. 'Not even that old bastard Wilbur, if I'm right.'

'You're not thinking straight, Crowe. There are a hundred people know where he was bringing you tonight. He let you think he was making a secret of it – but there wasn't any secret to be kept . . .'

When Albie turned, the world seemed to turn with him.

'Didn't I tell you I wasn't asking for your counsel?' he breathed.

'You've got to think about this. Albie, don't presume the boys would follow you on it . . . Murder Abraham Matthews?'

Albie stood, moved around Shepherd in half-frenzied circles, palming at the crumbling walls.

'You're telling me you've got a taste for it. Is that it? But this isn't like Monmouth. He isn't one of yours. And if you string him up, it won't go ignored. The constabulary isn't in your pocket any more. Doesn't that bastard Whisperer sitting soaked in his own bile back there tell you anything? Abraham purged the constabulary. If you string him up now, there isn't a single card you can play. It's back to you building a turret so they build a catapult, you raising a drawbridge so they start building battering rams. You steal from them, so they steal from you; you kill Captain Matthews, and they'll paint the streets with our blood. There won't be a gang any more, Albie. There won't be a damn thing – and all because you got angry.'

Albie fell suddenly still.

'He brought me here to kill me, Shepherd.'

'He didn't bring you here to string you up at all!' Shepherd did not cry the words. 'He's had a dozen chances. He could have let those old men take you from the factory floor. He could have dangled you from the rafters here and been gone, out into the night, carrying your scalp for his wife to see what he did.' He stopped, tried to read Albie's thoughts in those piercing eyes. 'There's something else,' he breathed.

From the folds of his overcoat, Shepherd produced the bundle of black feathers and flesh that was the fallen raven. When he held it aloft, it did not look a remarkable thing, just any old bird fallen to cats or the wheels of some passing lorry. Then, he drew the bloody paper from the crook of its stiffening wing.

'Read it, Albie.'

Shepherd saw Albie tense, as if this was some barbed insult being thrown his way, as if Shepherd was unveiling photographs of him standing, barely a boy, between mother and father with stepsisters holding each hand.

'*Stalwarts,*' Albie began, struggling with the words. '*The siege is tonight.*'

Albie's fingers formed a fist around the crumpled message.

'What's a Stalwart?' he mouthed.

For only a moment, Shepherd was still.

'A man dressed in a grey cowl?' he ventured.

They took their turns with him, after Albie was gone. Some among them were reticent to lash out, but with their elders crowing on their shoulders, it was not long before even the youngest, most nervous of the Young Bloods learnt what it was to make a man whimper.

One of the boys had a knife, a jagged thing stolen from his mother's kitchen and meant for carving bread. It was useless as a dagger, but perfect for goring Abraham's leg.

The doors flew open, bundling Young Bloods out of the way. From the corridor, Shepherd was the first to appear.

'Browning,' Shepherd began. 'Take your brother. A string of the little ones as well. You're to split into three groups, set out from the station along each of the main roads. Keep to the shadows of the bombed-out buildings . . . If there are people out there, I want to know it.'

From the crowd, the elder Browning cast a glance at Albie, as if in wonder at Shepherd's command.

'Get out of here, Browning,' Shepherd hissed. 'This comes from Albie, not from me, right? Or do you want to be back in the black cells?'

The silence lingered. Then, slowly, the boys started to move.

The rest of the horde shifted uneasily. At first they were not certain who they ought to be facing: was it Shepherd, or was it Albie Crowe? Both boys strode into the throng, but it was Albie who spoke first. He lifted aloft a bundle of black feathers and flesh. In the corner of the room, Drew moved as if to voice his protest, but if he was going to cry out, he was wise enough to stifle it fast.

'The bird belongs to you?' Albie Crowe asked, thrusting it at the Captain.

Abraham reeled. Though the pain was ebbing, he remembered well what came next: the sense that you were not quite in the same body, the nausea, the pounding heart. He shuffled in his shackles to the raven's corpse and kicked it aside.

'There were a dozen more birds,' he conceded. 'One fallen raven doesn't mean a thing. Trust me when I tell you, the message still got through.'

The paper was still in Albie Crowe's hand. He uncrumpled it, as if he did not already know the words.

'Stalwarts . . .' he repeated. When he turned the word on his tongue, it did not seem real. He mouthed it again, as if to grow accustomed to the sound. 'You know what this means?'

Through the clamouring boys, Abraham caught Edmund's eye. He held the gaze for a moment, then relented.

'He's got men out there, Albie, hiding in the long grass,' Shepherd interjected. 'That's why he tolled the bells. That was their summons, not ours . . . He sent ravens so they'd know it was tonight . . .'

181

'Ezra's men?'

'Not Ezra's men . . .' When Abraham spat, blood trailed from his lips.

Shepherd lifted his eyes. 'He meant for us to come here, from the first.'

'Your boy's not bad,' Abraham began. It did not matter if they knew any longer; they were already too late. 'Shepherd, you should be pounding the beat instead of prowling the streets.'

There was stampeding in the passageway. When Albie Crowe turned, it was the Browning boy that he saw flailing from the shadows. Footfalls still sounded when the boy stopped, the gang of little ones stumbling in his wake.

Before Shepherd could speak, Albie cut him off.

'Watchmen?' he demanded.

'In hides out in the rubble – shelters of brick where the houses once stood.' The Browning boy was labouring for breath, but perhaps that was due to the cigarette that still smoked in his fingers, rather than any real exertion. 'There's an Anderson shelter still standing south of here. Might be they crawled out of that. But Albie, they aren't watchmen out there. Not watchmen or ARP or Home Guard.'

'Did you really think I was giving you to the Watch?' Abraham slurred, venturing a smile. 'The Watch you tainted? The Watch you sundered? Is that what you thought was waiting at the end of Meanwood Road?'

Albie wheeled on Shepherd, the scrap of bloody paper still in his hands. 'Stalwarts . . .' he murmured. 'Who in hell are they, Shepherd? Where did these Stalwarts even come from?'

'I made them up!' Abraham thundered. 'I made them up and I gave them a name and I made them real – and they're coming here now, they're coming here to finish every last one of you, you pathetic *little boys* . . .' Abraham strained to take each breath. Young Bloods and Whisperers and Stalwarts. If

Albie Crowe could warp the streets around him, spirit up armies with well-chosen words, well, so could Abraham Matthews. 'I wasn't going to kill you tonight!' he roared. 'I'm going to kill the very idea of you!'

* * *

It was Wilbur who came for him. Wilbur who pitched up at the station and stood in the doorway of the little room where Abraham was filling reams of paper with the details of his beat. He knew, when he looked up, what his old friend was here to say. It had been hanging over him for the months since Elsa went to Albie Crowe, and now the wall crumbled away.

They went to the mortuary together, neither one of them speaking. The mortician was a friend, and when Abraham came through the doors, he put a hand on his shoulder and murmured how sorry he was. Abraham brushed him aside. He did not mean to do it so fiercely, but the mortician sprawled backwards, and Wilbur strained to heave him up. By then, Abraham had already stalked ahead.

It was a room Abraham had walked in a thousand times before. Against one wall, the slabs where dead men were drawn and cut; against the other, charts of bodies inscrutable to all but the morticians who worked them.

On the third slab, there she lay, cold and white in a dress he had never seen.

There was no mistaking his daughter. The months had flown between them, but she was still his. She had always been similar to his wife, but now the similarities were striking. Perhaps this was the way Ada had looked when the night-walkers pulled her out of the canal, all those years ago, her brown hair pulled back, her skin pale and mottled in death. Somebody had closed her mouth, but she had died with it open.

Abraham went to her side. When he looked at her, he might have been looking from a hundred yards above: she on the floor of some icy ravine, he perched upon a precipice where the stone met the sky.

'Who was it?' he asked.

'Some weatherwoman in Armley. We sent men to bring her in, but by the time they got there, the whole house had been abandoned. You know these people, Abraham. She went to ground at the first sign of a drop of untoward blood.'

Abraham did not want to know anything further, but something compelled him to go on.

'How far along was she?'

'Jesus, Abraham . . .' breathed the mortician.

Abraham's eyes flared.

'Too far for needles,' the mortician cursed. 'Too far for fucking around with knives inside her. Don't you get it, Abraham? Do you really want to know what they did?'

Abraham kneaded at the cadaver's arms, drew his hands away quickly when he saw that he was tearing her skin.

'I've seen worse,' he went on, pawing the hair out of her eyes. 'I've fished them out of the canal, bloated and half-rotten. I've ridden out to wrecks on the highway to make notes of the way they smeared themselves against the stone. I put my thumbs in a German boy's eyes, for Christ's sake, I ripped out his throat while he was crying for his mum . . .'

The mortician was still for only a moment.

'She's your daughter, Abraham . . .' he tried to say.

'And what was it? The thing inside her?'

'It was a boy,' the mortician admitted, his voice scarcely a whisper. 'It was your grandson.'

Elsa was Abraham Matthews' first-born child. The first-borns in his legacy had traditionally been sons, and it was with some modicum of surprise that he was admitted, at last, to the birthing chamber, and told that the nursery would have to be repainted. Ada was lying in sweat-soaked sheets on the bed beneath the bay, and she took his hand in hers when he sat at her side. They named her Elsa, and slept that night – when they slept at all – with the baby curled between them.

She became their world. 1923. 1924. They measured the years in how she grew and changed. 1925. 1926. When a brother joined her, Abraham understood, at last, how a world might heal itself after the scarring of its youth. A decade before, and his whole family had disappeared together; now, the last of his line, he found himself part of another brood.

He came from his reverie to find Wilbur at his side.

'Get out . . .' he hissed.

'Abraham?'

'Please, Wilbur. Fuck off, please . . .'

And then it was that first night again, and he was saying hello to Ada before he even knew that was what she was called, leaving her there in the darkness with the warehouses looming. He was walking on, and she was sinking in the brine, and the man who meant to kill her was ghosting away, with only a satchel and a brooch to show for his crime. Perhaps he had scarred himself that night, taken a knife to his chest just as Albie Crowe did, something by which he could remember every girl he drowned or tore down. Whatever he had done, it did not matter; it was what Abraham Matthews had not done that would haunt him now.

'What now, Abraham?' asked Wilbur, a voice distant in the haze.

Abraham shouldered past him, bearing the cadaver aloft.

'I'm going home,' he murmured.

Wilbur waited until he was gone. 'That isn't what I meant,' he breathed. 'Abraham, please, you know what I meant . . .'

Edmund was waiting at the corner of the Moor. There were men at work behind him, raising the first walls of the constructions *that would shelter them when the Germans flew over, and he perched atop his bicycle like some prehistoric ranger upon his horse. When he saw Abraham, he took flight, freewheeling down the hill.*

'Dad,' he said, 'is it her?'

'You must have known.'

'I knew what she was going to do . . . After she made her mind up, Albie wouldn't let any of us near.'

'All that's finished with now. Some witch in Armley took to her with knitting needles and knives.'

They came down the hill, two abreast, with the dead girl in between. There must have been eyes watching them from the shadows between buildings. No doubt the word was already flitting its way back to Albie Crowe – but that did not matter to Abraham, now. If they had been waging a war at all, it was Elsa, caught between trenches, who had lost.

Back at the old house, the doors had been locked. There was a time, not long past, when the doors up and down this terrace might never have been locked; now, even Ada had taken to dropping the bolt when she was alone at night. Edmund went into the halls first. Only when he had returned to report that his mother was not there did Abraham bear his daughter over the threshold.

He had known she would come home, one day. If there had been doubts along the way, some faith in him had always remained. Here was the chamber where she had been born, and here the room where she took her first steps; here was the bed in which he had nursed her through measles, and here the chair in which she sat to tell him she had fallen in love. He wanted to feel the rush of memories on her face, imagined the months and years cascading out of her eyes. He put his first foot on the stairs and began to rise, one step after another, a man suddenly grown old and weak beneath his burden.

On the fifth step, he paused, shifted his weight so that her head would not loll.

'I can take her, Dad.'

'Just get the doors, son.'

Abraham cradled her to the top of the stairs. He had been cradling her all of his life, he supposed – and the moment he was brave enough to let her go, she came back to him cold. He set her down on her bed, the stuffed animals of her childhood gathered about in mourning, and opened her eyes. He had not been able to stomach knowing they were closed for ever, but now that only milky orbs peered back, he wished he had resisted. His daughter – Ada's daughter – was gone from her body for all time.

'We could have him for this, Dad. Make him bleed.'

'It wasn't him who tore her inside,' Abraham whispered, uselessly rearranging the rabbits and bears at her side. 'He won't hang for this one.' He stopped. He did not want to look at Edmund – not once had he cried in front of his children – but he found himself turning that way now, unable to see clearly for the tears that he shed. 'Why wouldn't he keep it?' he asked. 'A boy like Albie Crowe, without a family of his own – why wouldn't he want a child?'

'I think he just couldn't bear it – that Elsa might be nurturing this thing they made, that there was something to tie them together for ever, that he might have to love it . . . There's boys in the Young Bloods who see him for what he is, now. Monmouth's let it be known he wants out. He'd have gone already if there was any shred of family left to run to.' He paused. Abraham was kneeling at the cadaver, straining at the cuffs of her blouse, anointing her with the perfume Ada had saved and saved to buy, watching through the window for any sign of his beautifully oblivious wife. 'What now, Dad? What would you have me do?'

'Go back to him,' breathed Abraham. 'He'll suspect this time, if he's got any sense left. He'll want to know why you're there, now there's no Elsa to look over. And tell him . . .' Abraham hesitated, as if preparing himself for the thought. 'Tell him you can't stand the sight of me. Tell him you're ashamed to be my son, that you couldn't bear to turn out like me, that I'm of the past, and the Young Bloods, they're the future. Tell him you've come back because that's where Elsa would have wanted you . . .' Again, he paused. 'And, Edmund, let him carve you this time.'

It was Edmund's turn to be sobbing, now. When his tears broke, Abraham saw him for the little boy he still was, fourteen years old and already ranged against all the darknesses of the world. He stood aside, let his son gaze upon the sister he would never see again.

'It isn't true, Dad. You aren't the past. I'm not ashamed.'

'I mean to end the Young Bloods for ever,' Abraham began, 'but I can't do it alone. I need to raise my knights, put them to siege. And I need a raven whispering me secrets from their camp. I'm sorry, Edmund.'

'Stop it, Dad. Stop saying you're sorry. It's all you ever do.'

There was a place on the Moor, beyond the barrage balloons, where boys went to brawl. Some of the Young Bloods knew each other from that secret haunt between the trees, and it was alongside the older Browning that Edmund had first been admitted to the circle and felt the first fists of his life. Some of the boys there had been full of scorn for this timid, gentle creature that yearned, like a sycophant, to walk among them. They wielded words like 'nice' and 'decent' and 'straight' as if they were the oaths forbidden in Edmund's household – until, one night, by some miracle of chance he sent a boy sprawling before an ill-thought-out right hook, and the boys deigned to share with him their cider. It was a strange fellowship that Edmund had felt that night and, to his later regret, one that he realised his yearning for was not merely acting.

He passed that way that night, lingering between the trees before he stepped out to throw himself into the fray. He picked on the smallest and weakest boy he could find, tried himself against that piece of gristle and bone, fought him into the banks of thorns that lined the clearing and laid him down there. He fought on, taking each boy in turn, until there was one too quick and too strong. Then, bloodied and nursing a blackened eye, he loped back through the ranks of watching boys, listening to the catcalls as he came.

Down in the rubble, boys were drifting back into the boarding house, and he slipped easily among them, as if he too had been taking inventories of warehouses waiting to be plundered. He did not see Albie Crowe, but there was nothing unusual in that; the Crowe had kept different hours to the rest of the boys since the day Elsa announced she was carrying his child. At the foot of one of the staircases, where the banisters had long since fallen away, Monmouth sat alone, trying in vain to roll a cigarette. It was an art for which Edmund had never had a use, but he took the papers from Monmouth all the same and handed him back a cigarette at least half-fit to smoke. The boy's hands had been trembling, and he murmured his thanks.

'I'm leaving,' Monmouth began. Only half of the words could be heard, for already he was chewing on the end of the paper.

'You've said it before,' said Edmund, stepping over the boy to ascend the stair.

'I don't know how you can stay,' Monmouth quaked. 'You of all people, Edmund. She was your sister.'

Half-way up the stair, Edmund stopped.

'Keep out of it, Monmouth. I'll put my fist through your face.'

He meant it, too. Even if he did not have a thirst for it, there were some moments, he had to concede, when a carefully thrown punch was more appropriate than a considered conversation. It was a thing he had not dreamt of six scant months ago.

'Come with me?'

Monmouth turned, over his shoulder – and, for the first time, Edmund saw the terror he was trying to hide.

'Come where?'

'Anywhere but here.'

Edmund relented, took another step on the stair. 'She was my sister, Monmouth, and still I'm staying.' Inwardly, he cursed, for he realised it was not a horror to breathe the words. Perhaps he was more Young Blood than he had reckoned. 'Elsa doesn't lie dead on Albie's account. Did you see him scar his chest that night?' Edmund waited, but he had never expected a response. 'Get some rest, Monmouth. Draw a line. Go through a mirror. You'll feel a different man.'

Upstairs, he found an empty bunk and fell into the dog-eared sheets. Before he had closed his eyes, a glut of other Young Bloods, Shepherd among them, descended on the room with a crate of pilfered beer. Almost absently, Edmund took one in his hand.

'What did you say to him, Edmund?'

Edmund looked around. Shepherd's face was level with his own. He had been bruised in the night, but the colouring would not be hard.

'Who?'

'Monmouth,' Shepherd replied. 'He's about set to sob. Took one look at us coming back in and off he ran, out into the night.'

'He wants to leave,' Edmund breathed. He looked into the faces of the boys around him, but not one of them looked back. 'He just wants it back the way it was.'

* * *

The Brownings heaved chests along the passageway, one after another, while ahead of them a clutch of little ones scurried to collect fallen masonry and pieces of rock. In an old theatre where criminals had once been tried, two boys tore books from shelves and smashed pews apart. There was only one route into the station, and they did not mean to let the Stalwarts stride in.

A single hall ran from the barricaded entrance, down through the gutted station to the collapsed wing at the rear. Some of the boys had unearthed a cache of candles from a larder, and brackets along the walls now flickered with light. The rooms along the way were being torn apart as Shepherd stalked by. Behind the furthest door, Albie Crowe and Abraham continued their dance – but Shepherd passed on without a whisper. At the landslide of brick and timber, a staircase rose into inky blackness above.

'Did anyone venture up?' he asked, snatching at the sleeve of a boy as he scuttled past, arms laden with iron bars prised from some obliterated cell.

'I don't know, Shepherd. They couldn't get in from above, could they?'

Shepherd remembered advancing upon the station. The windows in the upper layers of the station were shattered and gone, empty holes staring out as blankly as Elsa Matthews' eyes.

'Not unless they started building scaling ladders,' he admitted, as much to himself as the boy who scurried on. 'Towers to go with their battering rams . . .'

There was movement on the stair.

Shepherd started. There was an iron bar, no doubt salvaged from one of the cells, propped against the wall, and he took it in his hand as he mounted the first step.

'Who is it?' he cried. 'Who's up there?'

He took the first few steps at a run, paused there, between levels, with the railing brandished high. Craning his neck upward, he tried to track the movement. There were different textures in the blackness, but he was not yet certain from which direction the breathing came.

Movement again. He rubbed his eye raw, tightened his grip on the iron rail.

'You better come where I can see you . . .' he called, vaulting to the next stair. It had been long months since Shepherd had last gone to brawl on the Moor, and he was not certain he had the stomach for it any longer.

'I'm sorry, Shepherd,' whispered a voice. 'I didn't mean nothin' by it . . .'

Shepherd cast the railing against the stone, where it spun uncontrolled and clattered from ground to wall.

'Drew!' he cried. 'I might have put that thing through your face.'

'I'm sorry, Shepherd. It's just – Shepherd, you ought to see this.'

Shepherd followed Drew into the darkness of the stairwell. By the time they had reached the second landing, where passageways plunged in three directions, the firelight was gone from below. Along the length of the passageway, floorboards had buckled and erupted. Through a rent in the boards he saw a gaggle of little ones piling bricks together; if the Stalwarts broke through, there was going to be a fight.

They rounded a corner, and the world opened up.

They stood on a precipice where there had once been halls. Below them, the remnants of the station sat, heaped high and never to be rebuilt. Along its fringes, they could see where the foundations once ran. Fires had pitted the rubble below, but they had long since been doused, and ditches of dirty water ran stagnant along dams of timbers and stone. Out there, the shadows of hooded men walked the periphery.

Drew kneaded at Shepherd's shoulder, forcing him to turn around. On the very edge of the devastation, there sat a room, one wall open to the world like some crude set in a theatre.

In the middle of what had once been an office, there lay a long table, bedecked with great bowls of salads and fruit, pitchers with the dregs of dark ale and joints of meat only half-cut from the bone. At the heart of the banquet there sat the carcass of some bird, picked at until only the skeleton was left, and on the plates around the table's edge there lay the remnants of crackers and cheese. A dozen and more seats crowded the table, with more stacked up along the walls.

Drew reached out and palmed a hunk of gammon into his mouth. Satisfied, he started to chew.

Shepherd ventured in. If he faced in one direction, he might even have tricked himself that the station had not been shelled. Behind him, flurries of wind arose.

'So the watchmen had themselves a little feast,' said Shepherd. 'So what? Better that than have them snooping about the taproom or out on the street, hunting for us . . .'

'The coffee's still warm, Shepherd.'

Shepherd pressed his palms to the pot. 'Oh, shit . . .' he breathed. 'Did you see anyone?'

'Not a soul, Shepherd. Honest I didn't. But they've been here tonight. And . . .' Drew paused, as if uncertain how to use the word. 'It wasn't watchmen, was it, Shepherd? It was Stalwarts.'

There was more. Between the carcass of the chicken and a jug of fresh cream, flecked with strands of stray meat, a dozen leather-bound books were piled. They were old ledgerbooks, the sort grocers and butchers used to tally their trade, but when he opened the first, Shepherd saw that the pages were filled, not with measurements and costs, but with long, scrawled passages instead. At the head of the first page the legend read 'Francis and James Browning'.

'There's pages about all of us here,' Shepherd said, scrabbling with each ledger. 'This is the Captain's hand, I shouldn't wonder.' He stopped. 'Look, Drew, here's yours . . .'

Drew had already begun to drain the dregs of ale left behind. He looked up from the chair he had taken, drawing the back of his hand across his lips.

'The Captain knows about me?' he asked, not bothering to mask his nerves.

'"Andrew Greene",' Shepherd read. '"Born 19 April 1924. 'Drew' came to the Young Bloods through John Shepherd, drawing on an alliance forged in the winter of 1935, when the two boys were kept in the same cell at the watchhouse of Harehills Heights."' Shepherd paused. 'He has a copy of your arrest report here, Drew. That boy you put in the infirmary . . .'

Drew stood. 'Shut up, Shepherd! We're not to talk about it! We haven't talked about it in years!'

'"Drew is illiterate and perhaps the most unwilling of the Young Bloods, too oblivious to engage in the Crowe's romance. When the hour comes, he will surrender without a fight – on the understanding that no harm is meted out to his close friend and protector, John Shepherd."'

Shepherd shuffled through the other ledgers. 'How old did Browning tell you he was? The Captain's got a birth certificate here. Looks like he's been telling lies . . . They've been saying they're from Chapeltown all this time – but, look, they were born in Rusholme. *Manchester* . . .'

The Captain had compiled ledgerbooks to tell every one of their stories. There were things written here that not even Shepherd remembered: the circumstances of his first schoolyard fight, the date and time of the train his father had taken when he finally left his mother. Later, every crime and transgression was related in scholarly detail. Even the little ones had pages in a ledger of their own – names and birthdays and familial histories, the things no Young Blood ever cared to mention.

'Does this say "Crowe"?' marvelled Drew, lifting up the final tome.

'You keep that bastard thing closed,' Shepherd said. 'Albie would as soon see you dead as have you trawling through that. You know what he's like when you ask him about his past. There was only one person he wouldn't cut down for even suggesting he might have been a boy once.'

Drew held the ledger close to his breast. 'But wouldn't you like to know?' he asked.

Shepherd paused.

'He wasn't a Young Blood all his life. He must have had something before. We've been followin' him for such a long time, Shepherd – we'd follow him into hell. We followed him here, tonight! There's not one of us even knows what he's like.'

Shepherd reached out and took the ledger from Drew. When he opened the first page, Drew looked up again, a smile creeping across his face.

'Albert George Crowe,' he read. 'Born on 2 April in 1921, the fifth of eight children to Victoria Brook. Severed ties with friends and family on 26 August 1938 . . .'

In the chamber, Abraham still stood, shackled to the pillar of stone.

'She said she was sorry when she told me, you know. That she ought to have taken care of it. That there were teas she ought to have been drinking. But, do you know,' Albie Crowe went on, 'I don't believe she meant a word of it. You can't hide a thing like happiness. It lives in the eyes.'

Albie had not often thought about that final journey on which he walked with Elsa Matthews. There were times when his thoughts strayed as far as the moment she told him she was carrying his child, but he was disciplined enough to drop the portcullis, then, and never let his waking self ride through. It was only when he slept that he lived it again. It was the little things that he remembered: the way she had brushed his hand as she climbed down from the carriage, her head bowing as the weatherwoman took her into the terrace, the taste of the cigarette he had been smoking as he prowled the untended hedgerows and counted the hours. He might have been able to eradicate the memory of Elsa Matthews, had her father not hunted him through the terraces, but perhaps he would never have obliterated those small moments for ever.

'I found your father, you understand.'

Not even Albie Crowe, strutting on the stage of his own creation, could mask the discomfort that passed over his face.

'Which one?' he countered.

Abraham had to concede it was a good response. The boy's mother had had a dozen or more men.

'The one who called himself Crowe.'

It was not an idle boast. Abraham had been diligent in his work, seeking the right counter-magic to undo these spells of Young Bloods and Whisperers – but he had come to the father three years too late. He lay, now, in a country cemetery outside Settle, where flowers grew wild over his grave.

He had dreamt of how it might have been, were he to find the old man alive and well and languishing at some lathe – or, more likely still, squatting in some prison cell while, outside, the world went to hell. He had imagined walking through these streets, Albie's father at his side, cornering the Crowe one night and revealing that the grey-cowled spectre who stalked him had never been Captain Abraham Matthews – but his father and his brothers and his sisters and his mother, all of the things from his past that did not belong in this fiction he was making the city live. In his blackest, most satisfying moments, Abraham had imagined standing there, flanked by the figures of Albie Crowe's past – and watching as the boy's world crumbled.

'How often do you think about it?' Abraham asked.

Albie had not anticipated the question.

'About it, or about him?' he returned.

The sound of footsteps pounding through the passageways grew louder. Through the masonry, somebody was calling Albie's name.

'Albie,' said Edmund as he came into the chamber. 'They're gathering at the stockade . . .'

In silence, Albie Crowe went to Abraham's side, taking care as he shackled the old man to his wrist. As they shouldered past Edmund, Abraham's eyes locked with his son's. They held the gaze.

'How many Young Bloods made it here tonight?' Albie demanded, wrenching the Captain into the corridor. Behind them, the landslide arose, half-obscuring the stairs that climbed to the shell above.

'Not all of the little ones made it,' Edmund began. 'They'll be cooped up in the Anderson shelters. Some of the boys in the blitz scouts found a way through.'

'If there are stragglers left,' Abraham interjected, 'they're not Young Bloods any more. They're just little boys.'

They came to the station's face, where the final levels of the barricade were being hauled into place. A gaggle of little ones were still ferrying bricks from the landslide, while the Brownings hauled cabinets against the windows. Opposite the barricade, a locked gateway led to the cells beneath Meanwood Road. Many of the boys toiling here had been locked in those cells that night of Abraham's ambush, and a pair of the youngest Bloods pried at the grille with a crowbar, eager to unearth whatever treasures were hidden beyond. When, finally, the locks sheared, a small cry of triumph went up. One of the boys, the elder Browning, turned around, grappling at Albie Crowe's arm as he pushed past.

'Albie,' he ventured. 'That night the Captain ambushed us, when he locked us down there – there were racks there, weapons under the lock of the turnkeys. Remember?'

Albie seized the moment. 'If I'd have been so careless to have ended up in a watchman's cell, I might have known it for myself. As it is,' he went on, 'we need everything we can, if we're going to drive them back. And if you remember the way?'

Abraham noticed the momentary furrowing of the Browning boy's brow, and remembered starkly the night he had staked them in the blackness down there; while the other boys bawled fury at the men who gaped on the other side of the bars, the elder Browning had not breathed a word.

'Send a boy with me,' Browning ventured.

In the corner of the room, Edmund stood banked in shadow.

'You've never seen these cells, have you, Edmund?' Browning murmured.

'I saw them when I was a boy.'

Abraham supposed he should have been shocked, for his son had grown to be a convincing liar. There were some fathers among the constabulary who would lead their sons on gleeful tours of the deepest cells beneath Meanwood Road, but Abraham had never been one of them.

'Then you'll know to lead the way.'

Abraham tried to brush his son's hand as he passed, but too many boys clamoured between them, and he could not grope out. With the grille pulled back, it was Edmund who disappeared first into the blackness, the elder Browning on his back. As he faded from sight he did not steal a glance back at his father. Abraham did not linger long in watching him go, but turned back to Albie instead.

The Crowe cut a swathe through the huddled boys and pressed his eye against a rent in the barricade.

'Where did they come from, Captain?' he asked.

'The same place as your Young Bloods,' Abraham sniped, lifting their chained hands and fingering the side of his head, playing the puppeteer with Albie to make him do the same.

'You remember the night you told me about the Grey Cowled Stranger, Albie?'

'What of it?'

'God help me,' breathed Abraham, 'but it gave me an idea . . . The streets that produced Young Bloods, they could throw up Stalwarts as well.'

Abraham had never told Ada of the men with whom he ran when he made war – though, perhaps, if she ever deigned to see him again, he would tell her it all. It had been long years since their faces last invaded his thoughts. After the years of his roaming, he had stopped reading the letters they sent, stopped writing his own to them, slowly worked a magic that only Albie Crowe would understand – and carved for ever their faces from his recollections. But his soldier friends stood here tonight, shoulder to shoulder, while Young Bloods bayed within the station walls.

In the rising dust, each man wore his grey cowl drawn tightly around his shoulders. The light of a cigarillo flared and, for an instant, Abraham was crouched in some dugout with the stars showering down.

It had not been easy to bring them together. Twenty years carved chasms between men, and Abraham himself had been deepening the crevasse since last they met. But, alone in the city, with Ada gone to the hills and Edmund running with Albie Crowe, Abraham had set to work. He followed a trail of paper and broken memories, knocked at doors to ask questions, pored through the letters piled in Wilbur's attic – and, slowly, he came to know of the farms to which they had retreated after their killing was done. There was one among them he could remember so vividly that, in spite of all his years of studied neglect, he could feel again the texture of his skin, the stink he left in his wake: Jacob, a rag of a boy from the Sheepscar streets, whose dearest friend deserted on the day they went over the top. Perhaps he had drifted back into Leeds once the fighting was finished, but he had not lingered there long. He lived, now, as a man of the hills.

The look on his face when Abraham walked the trail to his farm was not something he could easily describe. At the end of the lane they made their mute hellos, and then they wandered within to meet the wife and children with whom he had spent the last twenty years. It was only when the first drinks were done and the night was drawing in that Abraham made his plea. He had not spoken more than three sentences before his friend looked up and swore that he was with him, the first of his Stalwarts to ride against Albie Crowe.

After that, he made other treks. He walked to a remote homestead high in the Lakes. He turned up at a small taproom in Penrith. On a lonesome night, he rapped at the door of some lowly night-watchman in the Manchester backstreets.

'It's a lesson I learnt this year,' he admitted. 'You can't live your life in the company of ghosts, pretending the past didn't happen – so I brought them back, tonight, to show you how it ought to be done . . .'

'They're not Stalwarts,' Albie spat, rearing from the barricade. 'They're just old men.'

Abraham grinned as he saw a rag of the little ones gazing up at their hero.

'Now you're getting the idea,' he smiled.

Through the archway of stone, the passage was black.

'Fetch a light,' murmured Browning, stooping to go under the points of the first portcullis. There was a stench here he was familiar with from the night he was led, bound by his hands, along these same halls; the memory roiled in him, but it was not the first time he had been in a cell, raging at the falling of a bolt, and he doubted it would be the last.

Edmund lifted a candle from its bracket on the wall. There were matches in one of the chests in the fallen brick, and he struck one against the stone to hold to the wick. When the candle rose to life, shadows swirled in the sloping passage.

Edmund, too, remembered the night the boys in the Bloods had been led, each shackled to another, into the deep cells beneath Meanwood Road. He had been alone, pacing the halls of the ruined schoolhouse, when he saw Albie Crowe stealing, unharmed and untouched, back into his kingdom – and, as Albie's eyes lifted to his, as the thief turned to the chamber where his sister lay waiting, Edmund believed he understood: Albie Crowe had not slipped through the snares of the constabulary; Albie Crowe had bewitched even his father.

'Stay up until dawn,' Albie had instructed as he mounted the first stair.

The next night, a lone candle flickered in Abraham's window.

Edmund held back, let the Browning boy go first through the narrow archways of stone. At first, Browning was resistant, as if to go first into the blackness might invite some strange horror upon him; then, at last, bravado got the better of fear. The tunnels from here on grew more narrow, and they moved in low light to the catacombs below.

Around a crook in the passageway they came, stumbling upon each other as they reached the head of a narrow stair. A storeroom was open on their left, but it had been pillaged long ago.

'There's still some boys number you with your father,' Browning began, looking back for the first time.

Edmund thought it apt that he was whispering, when surely there was no need. It might have been the darkness, the way the narrowing walls made a boy feel he himself was growing smaller, but there was something else here, too. It was only bricks and mortar around them, but Browning was no doubt imagining his descent to the underworld, just as he had done on the night he was captured.

He was starting to think like Abraham.

'I can't stop being my father's son,' answered Edmund, half under his breath. 'I'm not Albie Crowe,' he might have added.

They descended the stair, where the uneven stones at their feet felt as if they might slide suddenly away. Palming the walls, Edmund sensed Browning's pace slow until, at the foot of the stairs, he stalled.

And here lay the cells in which the Young Bloods had once been staked. No turnkeys kept watch tonight, no lanterns lit the grid of narrow halls in which the hollows squatted. There was only a cold darkness before them, the open cells gaping on either side of the passage.

Where the last of the candle's thin light spilled, Edmund could see racks of weapons sitting against the stone.

'Browning?' murmured Edmund.

'Let's just get the guns and be done with this.'

Browning was the first to reach the rack of weapons. At the end of the tunnel, he set the candle down and, standing in that sullen halo, measured each barrel in his hands, palming them back to Edmund when he was done.

'Muskets,' Browning swore. 'What did they think they were playing at? They put these weapons on us that night they arrested us, and we needn't have felt a thing . . .'

In reply, there was only stony silence.

'Don't you get it? These guns are no use to anybody. A show of force, that's all it is – when, if we had any guts, we'd be painting the stones with your father and his . . .' Browning hesitated. 'What does he call them?' he asked.

When there was no answer, Browning froze. He turned, a bundle of the weapons still piled in his arms, and saw only a barren tunnel before him.

'Edmund?' he began, pitching the word into the cells that flanked the passage. 'Edmund?'

Browning pushed the shotguns back into their racks and thrust the candle in front of him as he reared around. So quickly did he move that, for a second, the flame dimmed, caught in the gust that ripped around him. He froze, the blackness closing in, willed the candle back into life. He had seen boys blowing upon embers before, but he did not dare coax the flame in that manner. There were things that country boys knew that he had never suffered to learn – and, in his ignorance, he waited.

The flame flickered back into life – and, in the new light, there loomed a face.

Albie dragged Abraham back through the crowd. As they reached the back of the hall, cries went up on the other side of the barricade. Abraham turned to see the commotion. Then, the Crowe pitched him into the passageway.

'You'd abandon them?' began Abraham. 'You told those boys you'd get them out of the station tonight . . .'

'I told them they were Young Bloods as well, remember . . . But you and I know, now – they're just little lost boys.'

There was movement on the stair. Snapping his head around, Albie saw Shepherd and Drew descending out of the darkness.

'It's started, hasn't it?' Shepherd began.

'Upstairs with your catamite, Shepherd, while the boys are slaving down here?' Albie began. 'They need you at the barricade.'

Shepherd descended the last stair. At the end of the corridor, boys screamed. There was a lull, a second of silence – and then the boys heaved again. The barricade was being attacked.

Shepherd stood back, while Drew moved along the passage toward the barricade. For the first time, Albie saw that

Shepherd's hands were not empty. He was holding on to a ledgerbook. The name on the front read "John Shepherd"; even Albie Crowe could recognise the words.

'He knows everything,' said Shepherd. Shackled to Albie's side, Abraham allowed himself to believe there was a barb in those words. 'That's what he was doing. He wasn't just ferreting in our yards. He was ferreting in our lives. He wrote down everything about me. About Drew. About the Brownings and the rest, information he could feed these Stalwarts of his . . .'

Another cry went up at the barricade. A glut of little ones, panicked as hares, darted down the passageway, holding to each other so as not to cry. When they saw Albie Crowe staring back, they froze, turned on their heels, dredged up the courage to return to the barricade.

'Ledgerbooks about all of us?' Albie breathed.

'Every little thing we've done,' said Shepherd, turning to follow the little ones. 'Don't you understand, Albie? The Stalwarts – they're already in the station . . .'

Browning lunged forward. It was an old instinct, and it served him well. The man dropped, instant and unconscious, into his waiting arms. Together, they sank gently into the stone.

As they fell, the Browning boy lost his grasp on the candle. Darkness had descended before the candle hit the floor. For a moment, he was paralysed. He opened his mouth to cry out for Edmund, but some fearful instinct reined him in. Trapped momentarily beneath the body, he imagined that there were things in the darkness, old men slithering toward him.

There was still a heart beating in the bastard's breast. Browning pushed him aside and climbed to his feet.

He took one step at a time, walking as uneasily as some foal just dropped from its mother to land in the grass. The walls, where he touched them, were dripping with some effluent whose stench he was only now starting to sense. Awkwardly, he reached the first cell, palmed his way past the entrance, clinging to the wall as if treading the edge of a precipice without end.

The first voice was only a whisper, but still Browning stopped. He looked back along the passage, cocked his head to hear if the fallen stranger had risen at last – but he could not see, nor sense, any movement in the dark. Perhaps it was only Edmund, the Captain's son, playing some crude trick on him from the other side of the stone. Browning would finish him for this. Whether Albie Crowe sanctioned it or not, Browning would push him back into his quiet, closeted world and make sure he never crossed the chasm again.

Half-way along the passageway, he stalled. He knew he was meant to hear the voices. He was not certain, yet, from which direction they came. It might have been that the stones were speaking to him, for whispers seemed to flurry and fly from every hollow along the row.

'This one's the son,' a low voice insisted. There was gravity in that tone, and Browning imagined a face, pitted and hollowed with age. For a moment, it appeared before him, etched in lines in the stone. 'But no son of mine would ever be found running with those fuckers.'

'Now isn't the time,' another voice returned, this one lighter, more feathery. 'Abraham's word is what matters, and he swore his son was a Stalwart too.'

'He looks like his father used to look.'

At first, Browning thought it was the first voice again – but, when that voice chimed its assent, he understood that there were more men hunkered in the shadows than he had reckoned. He shuffled along the wall, but the voices rose louder, and he dared not go on.

'He's as quiet as his father. Why don't you say something, boy?'

'There is another,' Edmund began. 'A Young Blood in the tunnels. One of the Browning boys.'

Browning permitted himself a smile. The boy was a turncoat, after all. Albie would send him the same way as Monmouth for this, after the night was finished.

'We know all about Mr Browning,' the first voice returned. 'We've all read Abraham's ledgers. And I shouldn't think a boy who calls Lancashire his home will prove himself much trouble.'

'We've got to go,' said Edmund.

A soft chorus rose. 'Not you, son. That wasn't your father's orders. We're to get you out of here before it starts . . .'

Edmund's voice quaked. 'Get me where?' he demanded.

'Back to your mother. Back into the real world.'

Instinct drew Browning's eyes to the black roof above. He pushed forward a little, careful not to let his shadow step into the lantern light spilling from the cell. For a second, the voices were hushed, and he drew back, as if betrayed. Then, they rose again, readying to move out. Browning retreated into the darkness, treading on the fallen man's arm as he came. The cold stone reared at his back, and he froze.

There had only ever been one way to the surface. He had known that from the day Abraham Matthews first staked him in a cell down here, and told him he was going to rot. They would come after him – but they would come in single file.

Browning took flight, vaulting the pools of stagnant light as he flew. Before he had reached the first stair, he could hear the tumult rearing at his hind. He plunged on – but the blackness ahead was absolute, and the only light rose behind him, in the hands of the advancing men.

He clawed on, reached a new set of stairs rising into the blackness. The footfalls of the men behind him echoed from every surface, so that it seemed as if the walls themselves crawled. He could no longer see the light that chased him, but that meant only little – the Stalwarts were surely around the last crook in the passageway, Edmund among them, spilling every secret the Young Bloods ever shared.

He took another step, smashed his face against iron bars, cried out involuntarily as he slumped to the stone.

'Mr Browning . . .'

The first ray of light groped around the corner, and he braced himself with fists clenched at his side.

The outline of a man stepped into the encroaching light. At first, Browning could see nothing beyond a stark silhouette; the advancing man was ringed in the fire of lanterns, but he wore no features tonight.

'Who are you?' Browning demanded, suddenly straightening his back.

'We're the Stalwarts,' the silhouette shrugged, as if it was the most natural thing in the world. 'Why? What are you?'

Browning straightened – but he held the posture for such a slight second that even he must have thought it pathetic. 'I'm a Young Blood,' he ventured. Then, slowly, his face fell. 'I'm just some boy,' he finally said.

'We were hoping you'd say that,' grinned the stranger.

Albie watched Shepherd bustle along the passage, to where the Stalwarts clamoured at the gates.

He turned to the stair. At the first landing, the blackness seemed absolute. He dragged Abraham half-way up, the Captain too weak to resist, and paused there as if to let the darkness envelop him. Then he was gone.

Through ruptured floorboards, Albie caught glimpses of the little ones as they scrambled in the entrance hall, piling against each other every time the Stalwarts rained at the gates. Ahead, through a gaping maw, he could see swathes of the city, pitted with fire. The boards were fragmented here and he unshackled himself from the Captain, locking the old man's arms together and forcing him along the naked rafters. Near the precipice, the maw widened. On their left, a commander's office was bedecked with Christmas tinsels, open to the world.

'Beautiful, isn't it, Captain?' Albie began, marvelling at the glowing roofs.

There were planes dancing in the distance. One tore through a low bank of smoke, pirouetting as it reappeared.

Abraham looked down. On the edge of the yards, he saw Stalwarts preparing their wagons. A thunderous cry went up – and a raft of men stepped back from the walls, regrouping to charge again.

'Call them off,' Albie hissed.

The Stalwarts charged again, and Albie Crowe flinched. 'No,' Abraham softly replied. 'Because, after tonight, Albie, the fantasy is finished. The boys you bewitched, they'll fall back into real life – jobs and schools and shirking their duties at home – not quite believing they used to go out on midnight missions with you. The comatose princes and princesses, they'll all wake up and wonder what they were thinking. There won't be any Young Bloods. There won't be Whisperers collecting up secrets and asking for your coin.' Abraham gave a bloody smile. 'There won't even be any Stalwarts, after tonight. There'll be streets and there'll be houses, births, marriages and deaths. And people will start scoffing about those pathetic little boys who called themselves Bloods and met up on the Moor. Do you remember what their king was called? they'll say. Called himself the Crowe, they'll smirk. Drank down in the Packhorse taproom and said it was his empire. And now where is he? Shackled up and sent off to war . . .'

Albie hauled Abraham away from the precipice. Before him, the banqueting hall sat, its table still set like some ship suddenly abandoned at sea.

'You had a last supper, did you?' Albie began.

'A man needs to fortify himself before a hard night's work,' Abraham replied.

It was not the food in which Albie Crowe was interested. In the centre of the table, there lay the pile of ledgers. He approached them sheepishly, as if expecting some trap to be sprung. He lifted the first, and opened the covers. And if ever there was a perfect moment in the life of Abraham Matthews, here it was: Albie Crowe reading the details of his life, the history he could never change, no matter how carefully plotted his fantasies – and his face blanching as he soaked up the words.

Albie closed the book, drew it high, tensed his arms for the swing.

'Captain,' he said as he delivered the blow. 'You've got me all wrong.'

Blackness. There was cold, endless blackness.

They rose from the cells, stair by stair. Always, there was a paw at Browning's back; always, a voice telling him to move on, to put one foot after another, to keep his head held high. At last, they came to the final grate, swung shut but still limp on its hinges.

Peering through it, now, Browning saw Shepherd bustling a horde of boys back to the barricade, bawling out commands. Each time a rag tried to break away to hide in one of the obliterated rooms, he hauled them back into place. Albie Crowe was nowhere to be seen.

'Brace the barricade!' Shepherd hollered.

Against each of the windows, the shadows of Stalwarts shifted. A rock pitched at one of the panes, and when the glass

209

exploded inwards, Shepherd caught, fleetingly, the visage of one of the men underneath his cowl. He froze, as if uncertain of what he was seeing, and then a boy reared from beneath the window, thrusting a length of timber into the portal to drive the invader back.

Hands grappled out, snatched the boy through shards of shattered glass. Too late, Shepherd clawed out, felt the boy's boot beneath his fingertips as the Stalwart turned to flee. Feebly, the boy's little legs wheeled and kicked – but, like an infant in the arms of some story-book ogre, his struggles were to no avail. The boy and his captor disappeared.

Shepherd braved the shattered glass, peered out with a hand cupped around his eyes. He could not see the men gathered at the barricade, but he saw others, dotted around the obliterated yards. They had stirred cauldrons of fire in pits in the ground, and on a rise beyond the ruined outer walls, a string of Young Bloods plucked from windows were already piled into the back of a wagon. One of the Stalwarts had the audacity to be sitting, content, upon a boulder of fallen brick, tossing scraps of sandwich to a hound waiting at his heel.

A tremor took the barricade, and the boys screamed out as the Stalwarts ran a second charge. Thrust back, one of the little ones landed, winded, against the stone at Shepherd's feet. He lay there, frozen, for only an instant, before groping hands heaved him back upright.

The boy's lip quivered, as if he was being scolded by his mother. 'What happened to Albie?' he asked.

'Forget about Crowe,' Shepherd said. 'The Crowe will look after himself. He always has.'

Shepherd joined the throng at the barricade. Crammed there with boys at either side, he strained to keep his footing. A thundering of arms and legs – and then the Stalwarts drove forth. Shepherd readied himself for the blow – and sprawled backwards when the old men threw themselves at the doors. Outside, a cry of triumph went up.

A gang of little ones struggled to heave the upturned cabinets back into place.

'On your feet!' Shepherd bawled.

Drew was at his side. Together, they raced back to their stations.

'We can't hold it for ever,' Drew began, putting his shoulder to the wood.

'We've got youth on our side,' mocked Shepherd.

A moment of stillness, and around them the boys tensed. On the other side of the wood, the Stalwarts too must have been sharing urgent looks, the young and the old charging together on different sides of the glass.

A final heave. Caught off guard, the boys still at the barricade stumbled back, sprawling into the boys piled behind. Wood splintered and came apart. Too late, Shepherd hauled a gaggle of Young Bloods back to their feet. Drew threw himself forward – but wind was already whipping within, and in the break in the barricade a strange face loomed.

Shepherd turned, flailing out to stop boys pouring back into the station. The little ones who had fled were all frozen.

'I believe you're the one they call John Shepherd,' an old man smiled.

Around the gate that led to the catacombs underneath the station, the Stalwarts were ranged: six men in dark grey cowls, with Edmund standing behind. Even as the boards at the barricade splintered, the Stalwarts who spilled from the portcullis were whispering commands to the little ones, ordering them to submit. They moved slowly, without alarm, their only expressions those of the mildest curiosity: that a night of bombs and fire, the death of Abraham's daughter, might have come down to this, a gaggle of boys playing at being bandits.

In front of them, the elder Browning boy stood with his head bowed, his hands tethered behind his back. 'I'm sorry, Shepherd,' he whispered, the Stalwart above him lifting a finger to command him to hush.

All was still in the station.

'Jacob!' the first Stalwart through the barricade called to his cohort coming through the grate. 'Abraham was right. They're all just boys.'

Shepherd watched the Stalwarts drifting in from both within and without. He had wanted to see weathered faces and evil, hooded eyes, mottled scalps with lank hair drawn back, fingers wrapped around muskets and blunderbusses – but, as they came, emerging slowly as if stepping through a veil, he saw only aged men in long trench coats and cowls. Something inside him sagged – for, in that second, he realised that something of Albie Crowe must have tainted him after all, set him on seeing fantastic apparitions where there were none. A band of men too old to wage war assembled on the far side of the cavern – and suddenly, the Young Bloods around him were just little boys, building forts and sobbing when they grazed their knees.

One of the old men to rise from the black cells broke away from the rest. With the air of a schoolteacher addressing his class, he started to speak.

'You boys,' the Stalwart began, 'are in a spot of bother. Which one of you is Albie Crowe?'

In the crowd, the little ones were trembling. Some boy darted forward, as if he might snake through the Stalwarts' legs, but one of the scarecrows stalled him and, with a gentle tap on the shoulder, sent him back to join his kin.

'You're too late!' somebody started. 'He isn't here!'

Shepherd's eyes drifted to the rafters above. He thought he saw shadows moving over the ruptured boards.

The Stalwarts moved forward, until they were close enough to touch – real men of flesh and blood, not spectres spirited up by bricks and mortar. The eldest one gazed into each of the boys in turn, and not one of them dared peer back. He drifted on, looking for a face he might have known, searching for something he must have seen on the endless pages of Abraham's books.

'What have you boys done with Captain Matthews?' he breathed.

The sky swirled with ash, fragments flying wild, rising and falling as if buoyed by a bonfire. Through squinted eyes, Albie Crowe gazed out from the banqueting hall, high in the ruined station. The vaults above the city were still streaked with the trails of planes, the horizon still pitted with cauldrons of flame – but the streets around the station lay as stagnant as they had done twenty years before, when the terraces last sat empty, waiting for the dead to return.

'Come on, Captain. There's no need to be afraid.'

The Captain did not respond. He slumped, eyes closed, on Albie Crowe's shoulder, his nose bloody where the ledgerbook had caught him.

Albie Crowe settled beside him. With the wind frenzying around them, they might have been cocooned from the world.

'You want some leftovers?' Albie asked, offering up handfuls of food.

Far below, the Stalwarts started to emerge from the station, marching, just as they had done in the days of their own youth, the Young Bloods trailing behind them on lengths of rope. At the head came Shepherd, head held ridiculously high, as if there was something pathetic to be proven in the posture; then, if Albie was not mistaken, the Brownings, strung to each other like infants still on reins. In pairs, they were piled into the waiting wagons.

'Look at them, Captain. They've got a new quest now. They'll hunt us through the terrace. Your Stalwarts were never quite like my Young Bloods. They wouldn't leave you behind, would they?'

One after another, the wagons rolled away. Behind them, some of the Stalwarts set out on foot, breaking into pairs as they took the tributaries of snickets and streets, still crying out his name. Among them, Edmund too set off at a run, his tiny legs stirring a storm of ash as he went.

'You were right, Captain,' said Albie, chewing on a strand of meat, 'we picked one hell of a night for this.'

* * *

He came to in darkness, thinking of the mortuary slab.

Even before his eyes grew accustomed to the gloom, Abraham knew he was no longer in Meanwood Road. The curtains hanging in the blacked-out windows were threadbare, only a single armchair remained, and even the carpet had been ripped back. Across the floorboards, there lay the rags of what had once been a covering of straw. It was a simple touch, and one of which Albie Crowe would have been tremendously proud: the boy had crafted, here, his very own dungeon. Like everything else in the boy's life, it was made out of smoke and thin air.

The sirens had stopped. Abraham peered at the curtains, but only pale pre-dawn light shone through. It might have been less than an hour since the storming of Meanwood Road, since the crusade became nothing but an evening stroll. Soon enough, the sun would rise – and then the rest of the city would begin to forget.

He shuffled so that he could prop himself against the wall. The handcuffs around his ankles were threaded with chain and locked to a fireplace grille – the flaking metal was cold to the touch, and the room was chill. On the other side of the chamber, beneath bay windows with blackout blinds peeling back, there was heaped a pile of blankets and rags.

Abraham did not try and draw himself up when the door slowly opened, for he knew, now, that this thing would not be done with flying fists and teeth bloody and bared. The lantern light from beyond was so bright that instinctively he averted his eyes.

A man of shadow entered, long and lean as some condemned man hoisted on a cross.

'They're still hunting for you, no doubt,' the familiar voice began. 'Off they ran, into the streets, crying your name. That turncloak son of yours stirring up dust as he scurried away. And do you know, Captain – as I watched them, I could almost see them waver. Like something you see in the corner of your eye – you turn, and suddenly it's gone. And that's Stalwarts and Whisperers and Young Bloods, isn't it, Captain? You got your wish in the end.' He paused. 'They evaporated,' he said.

Abraham strained so that he could see the silhouette as it advanced.

'Where are we?' he asked.

The shadowman circled. 'Have you really no idea?'

Abraham peered into the fringes of the room. On the mantel there stood a set of frames – but the photographs had long since been shredded.

'This is your home . . .' he began. 'You came back to your home? But you hate this place – you've shed all that . . .'

Abraham imagined he could hear the cries and catcalls of children as they tumbled through the halls. In his mind, a dozen children came – brothers and sisters and step and half-siblings, all of them crying out in incomprehensible tongues – and, in the middle of the maelstrom, there stood the lost little boy. When the horde was nearly upon him, he opened his palms – and suddenly he was no longer there, but hidden in some dark crevice instead. In his hollow, he wrapped his arms around his knees, shrank until he could hardly be seen, and with whispered words started to sing: *'Don't fall asleep . . . don't fall asleep . . . don't let them catch you . . .'* Hours later, still murmuring the words, he came to from his reverie to find that they were gone, his prayers answered for the first time in his short life.

'You're using the wrong word. *My* home?' the viper hissed. 'That little boy's name might have been Albie Crowe, but what's in a name? You proved that tonight. The Young Bloods are little boys, the Stalwarts are old men – and that little boy scampering around these rooms, it wasn't *me*.' When he spoke again, it was with a new ferocity. 'Don't you understand this yet, Captain? I can tread these halls as freely as I can walk the streets where that boy grew up. I could sit at the table with the old bitch who birthed him and make small talk over supper – but it doesn't have to bother me. I don't have to think about them, all the things that they did, all the things I was when they used to drag me around. She wasn't my mother, and he wasn't my father, and they weren't my brothers and sisters – not any more.'

When the breath came from Abraham's lips it was mangled in laughter.

'The world has a record of everything you say and do. Ledgerbooks it's writing every day. Just because you say it wasn't you, that doesn't change a thing . . .'

Even as Abraham said the words, he felt himself faltering.

'You and your ledgers . . .'

Albie stepped forward, into the pale light, and for the first time Abraham saw the book in his hands. His fingers strained at the cover, but Abraham knew, without looking, what tome he was carrying. The name on the front was Albie's own.

'You thought that because you wrote it down, that made it true?' Albie Crowe turned to the first page, where his name was written in tall, ornate lettering. He was still slow with the written word, but he read aloud the names of his mother and father, the date of his birth, the bastard brother born ten months later to take his place in the crib. 'Do you still think it has any bearing on me, the day they found me crying in a cupboard? That I was a little boy, frightened of the dark? Do you think I even remember going cold that winter my mother wasn't bedding some new tinker?' He paused, brandishing the ledgerbook like it was a weapon. 'This isn't *me*, Captain. You got it all wrong. You don't *make* me by putting me in your book. That was some little bastard who just happened to share the same name. *I* make me now.'

Albie ripped the first page from the ledger – then the second, then the third. The first he scattered in shreds across the room; the next he crumpled in his hand and tossed into the grate; the last he clutched as he dropped to his knee and palmed it into Abraham's mouth.

'It doesn't matter that you write it down. It doesn't matter what other people say. Not when I *know* it isn't true. You can be anything you want to be, Abraham, if you just let yourself. Of all the people in this bastard city, I thought *you'd* understand . . .'

Abraham rose, hawking the mangled paper from his throat. 'You're a boy. Just a stupid, sorry boy . . . You can't unlive the things you've lived, you can't not have thought the things you've thought, not without a bullet in your head.' Abraham stopped, still labouring for breath. 'I'll do it, if that's what you want. I'll put that bullet in your head. Just get me a gun.'

Albie Crowe's face contorted. Perhaps it was only the wan light, but Abraham was certain it was a smile he had not seen the boy wearing before, some new expression he was trying out for size.

'It's too late, Abraham. The old Albie Crowe, he wasn't the sort of boy who could do the things I've done. He wasn't the sort who would have boys clamouring to bunk in his den or drink at his side in the taproom, the sort who tempts your daughter out of her petty, cloistered world and makes her fall in love. There's no more truth in this ledger of yours than in some simpering fairy tale. That boy is gone. Don't you know what it is that I've done?'

Albie stepped over Abraham and bent low over the pile of rags in the bay. When he drew the blankets back, Abraham saw the boy who lay there, cold and pale. A dark scent rose. Though he had long breathed his last breath, the dead boy's lips were parted in what might have been a smile. To be finished, he seemed to be saying, was a relief.

'Oh, Albie, you sorry bastard, what have you . . .'

It was not like looking at Elsa, that day in the mortuary. Somebody had kept the boy fresh, but his death had been longer in working its magic. He had faded out of life, just as the blood had faded from his skin, and his open eyes were glazed and reptilian.

'His name was Monmouth,' Albie Crowe began. He stood on the other side of the corpse, and when he fixed his eyes on Abraham it seemed that he was peering from one world into the next. 'You've heard the name, of course? You, with your Whisperer inside my ranks . . .'

'He's the one tried to leave the Young Bloods,' breathed Abraham, recalling Edmund's words when they last met, high on the Moor. 'Why, Albie?'

Even before he said it, Abraham knew how useless was the question.

'You know the answer to that one, Captain . . .'

Abraham began to speak, rasping out his worthless words of wisdom, but Albie heard not a word. Instead, he reached out and lifted the corpse.

Seven days and seven nights. Was that really all it had been? Albie had seen the boy piling books into a bag before sloping out the back door, and had known, as he watched from his hiding, that Monmouth did not mean to return to the Young Bloods that night.

He caught up with him, at last, under the shadows of the Moor's surging trees, where the barrage balloons were flying high. At the call of his name, Monmouth started and drew to a halt.

'I'll walk with you,' Albie said.

'You don't have to,' Monmouth began. 'I need the air.'

Albie's arm curled around Monmouth's shoulder. 'But I want to,' he replied. 'I've been thinking. Elsa's in my head too much, Monmouth. Just like she's in yours. You and I, we're so very alike.'

When he set out, he had not known he was leading the boy to the old house. It must have been his feet that remembered the way, for it was certainly not his head, nor his heart; he had worked hard at erasing that route, and surely it was long forgotten.

Looking up at the boarded windows, he realised that his family, too, had fled the bombardment. Pleased with himself that he had not known they were gone, he shepherded Monmouth on, through the doors and empty rooms. A mercenary army of memories rampaged toward him, but one after another he repelled their advances. There were tricks he had learnt since the day he threw two crooked fingers at this place, and with the dismissal of each old feeling, another one of the scars on his chest started to sear.

He left Monmouth in a living room that had once doubled as a den for half-brothers, and rose to the attic room that the younger Albie Crowe had once called home. The memories were fiercest here, but he braced himself and weathered the attack. His name was being called in the hallways below, the thunderous voice of the stepfather whose name had been hardest to erase, and he slid slowly into a cavity between the walls, murmuring to himself as he came. 'Don't fall asleep . . . Don't fall asleep . . . Don't let them catch you . . .' Beneath him, the footsteps rose on the stair. Then, as if pushed back by his prayer, they disappeared.

Every last scar was singing, now.

When he was ready, he ventured back into the living room. A dark stain was already pooling around Monmouth's boots.

'You've come a long way, Albie,' said Monmouth.

'Not far enough,' said Albie. 'But I'm going to go further.'

He had seen boys brawling before, watched them from afar as they scrapped over nothings on the Moor, but it would not be like that tonight. He curled a fist to fell the boy – but, after that, it was only hands wrapped around the sorry bastard's throat. In the end, it was an easy thing. It was not long before his limbs stopped flailing.

Monmouth would leave the Young Bloods tonight, if that was what he wanted – but Albie Crowe would leave something behind as well.

He looked down at the lifeless body – and, for a long time after, he did not leave the house, but prowled the hallways instead, running his hands over every wall, every door frame, every ledge. For the first time, he could not recollect a shred of what it had been like to grow up here. He tried to recall the sound of his mother's voice, and there was only silence. He tried to summon up the smells and squalls and childhood lessons, but nothing would come. Over and again, he tried – but the emptiness was vast.

Back in the living room, he looked at Monmouth and whispered his thanks. He had made it through the mirror, at last.

In the darkness, Abraham's eyes flickered from Albie to the fallen boy.

'The deepest scar you carved on your breast. It was never meant for Elsa . . .'

'I didn't kill Elsa.' Albie said it quietly, as if some silent understanding was at last being reached.

Abraham closed his eyes. 'I strangled my first boy as well,' he ventured.

He had expected Albie to turn away, but instead the boy's eyes opened by fractions, tempting him to go on. There was a time in which he believed all of that was the work of some former Abraham Matthews whose skin had long ago been shed. But men from his old company had risen again tonight, and with them came every bullet he fired and dagger he drew. It was not only the Stalwarts who flocked to his banner in the ruined station, but ghosts from every moment of his life.

'There was a raid gone wrong and he was trapped in our dug-out.' He said it nonchalantly, teasing a length of straw between finger and thumb. 'He had a knife. I only had fingers and thumbs. I just held him until he stopped moving. It was the cleanest I ever did it. Maybe he wept a little. Maybe he pissed all down my legs. But there wasn't any blood. I got good at killing them without any blood.' He stopped. 'I didn't like to change my shirt,' he quipped.

It wasn't just Monmouth that the Crowe had slain that night, Abraham realised. Just as surely as he'd put his hands around Monmouth's throat, so too had he choked to death the little boy who once roamed in those halls – the other Albie Crowe.

He had found his rite at last.

'And afterwards?' asked Albie. 'It felt different after that, didn't it, Abraham? *You* were different.'

Abraham looked up, eyes aglow. 'Oh, I was different, Albie . . .'

Slowly, the boy nodded.

'I spent three years roaming, trying to undo it,' said Abraham. 'Back-pedalling and scrabbling, as if a man could ever stop the world from turning. I thought I could pay it back, that I didn't have to be the same man I'd been in those holes in the ground.' He hesitated. 'When I came back to England, I thought I was clean – but twenty years have gone, and, damn it, Albie, I've never been clean. I cut myself off from my company, I wiped out the way I marched whenever I walked, every little tic I'd picked up from the boys in the brigade.' He paused. He would have spun the whole fable for Albie Crowe, if only the boy would have listened: every soldier he slew, every step he trod as he tried in vain to forget. 'Does any of this sound familiar yet, son? Because it doesn't matter how strong you are, how cleverly you craft it, what stories you trick everybody else into believing . . .' He lifted up the shreds of the ledgerbook with which the boy had choked him. 'You can't get away from it. In the end, you're every little thing you ever did . . .'

Without reply, Albie sank to the floor at Abraham's side. With the first light of dawn falling upon him through filthy glass, Abraham did not flinch, nor put up any protestation. He lay still as Albie fumbled to loosen his ties.

'It doesn't have to be that way, Captain. I'm alive – and I won't feel guilty for it.' He paused. 'I thought I was bringing you here to kill you,' he admitted. 'But I was never going to kill you, Captain – just like you were never going to kill me.' He looked back at Monmouth, tempting Abraham to look that way too. 'I just wanted you to know. I found my way out . . .'

Albie stood, took a step back. There would have to be a new name now, he decided, new faces and friends and adversaries to attack. 'Abraham,' he whispered as he stole toward the door.

'There's a whole world out there. It's like I said to your daughter – you can sit back and accept your lot in life, or you can strike out and take somebody else's.' They looked at each other across Monmouth's sprawled corpse. 'What do you want, Abraham?'

It was the same question that Ada had asked. He blanched.

'I want to stop pretending. I want to live in the real world. I want ...' He wanted to breathe his daughter's name, but something stopped him. 'I want you to understand ...'

In the doorway, Albie stopped. 'That the world has a record of everything I say and do?' he said, as if musing on the Captain's old words. 'That, twenty years from now, I'll be just like you, realising I couldn't start again, crying for all that wasted time, desperate to go back to the beginning?' Albie looked down at Abraham – and, if ever there had been a shred of pity between the two, now it was gone. 'I'm sorry,' he said, as he slipped away, 'but I'm stronger than you, Captain. I write my own ledger now.'

The sirens would wail again tonight – but, before that, there was work to do. As he ventured forth, the terraces were already alive with men pouring out of their bunkers. Smoke still poured from the southernmost stacks and, through a gang of men riding the Kirkstall lane, Abraham spied Ezra and his band surveying the wreckage of a fire house obliterated by some falling bomb. There would be bodies in the ruin this morning, morticians to stalk the houses, undertakers to dance wildly in the smouldering pyres. They would find another body to list among the dead before the day was done, some poor bastard felled not by bombs but by hands around his throat.

Young boys were scouring the rubble already, tussling over the trinkets they unearthed. At a snarl in the streets, Abraham stopped to watch them. Perhaps they had seen him, wild and matted with the blood of the night, for at once they took off, darting like rats into their dens. He was still standing there, alone, when he heard a familiar voice crying out. Edmund appeared from the smoke as if he walked from one world into the next.

'Dad!'

Edmund rushed along the road. Five paces away, he stalled.

'Is it finished?' Abraham asked.

'They took them away, rode off to the stations at Harehills Heights and Burley Park, just like you said. The Stalwarts and the Young Bloods . . .'

'Don't call them that,' breathed Abraham. He inched closer to Edmund.

'. . . they're gone now.'

Tentatively, Abraham put an arm around his son's shoulder. He put one foot in front of another, and in that way they slowly started to walk.

The boys who had once called themselves Bloods would be chained up, already, listening to the lists of charges levelled against them, hearing of the cells to which they might be sent and the sentences they faced. Some of them would fall into the cracks, of that Abraham was certain – but, for most, there would be a way out, a path back into the normal world of births and marriages and deaths. There were battalions waiting for boys like that. The transports might already be wheeling into place.

Along the fringes of the Moor, into the shelter of the first redbrick rows – and there, sitting on the crossroads with its curtains flying, sat the Violets tearoom. From a distance, it was only bricks and mortar – and as they grew near, that was all it was too: four walls and tables and chairs and the clattering of crockery through the doors. For the first time since the breaking of day, Abraham felt the burning in his shoulder, looked down to see the patterns of red that still stained his hands. Through the tearoom windows, some of the girls were considering him curiously, straining to put a name to the half-familiar face.

'Come on, Dad,' said Edmund, a hand in the small of his back. 'Let's get you cleaned up.'

It would take some scrubbing, but the dirt of this night would surely come clean; there was another sort of magic in that – but not one that Albie Crowe would ever understand.

Edmund pushed through the doors and slowly drifted to a seat. At first, Abraham did not recognise who it was who greeted his son. He faltered. And then, as if drawn without warning into another of Albie Crowe's enchantments, Abraham Matthews was twenty years away, standing alone with his feet square against the same doors, a creature who was neither a man nor a boy, but some strange blank slate of his own creation. He could see, through the glass, that she was busy clearing tables, that she had worked hard through the day and stained her dress with yellow and red and brown. There was a smell of summer in the air, and when he lifted his hand to straighten his hair, a sudden compulsion to turn away came upon him. There was a place for him, already ordained – *you'll put a thousand bad men in their mausoleums before you're through* – and there could be honour in that, a life of which he might even be proud; he did not have to wait for ever, looking in on the good life he knew he was fated never to find, watching everybody else live lives while he just slumbered. He could walk away from her, choose something else.

Yet something in him refused to be moved. All he had to do was step through the door, tell her his name, become the Abraham Matthews on the other side of the glass. Surely it was not such a difficult thing to take exactly what you wanted from life. He'd done some bad, he'd done some good, and now there was just life left to be lived. He pressed his hands to the glass, spectred himself there, cursed himself that his courage had been crushed in those foreign fields, that he had doused for ever the fire in his gut.

A voice broke the enchantment, and Abraham found that the door was open.

'There's a train leaves here in the morning,' said Ada.

'I'll take the window seat,' said Abraham, and took her hand in his own as she led him through the doors.

Three Days Later

The sky was streaked, but it was only with stars; no flares nor fires marred this long night. On the horizon sat the gaslights of Leeds – and, before that, the little clusters of orange that were the city's outlying hamlets and towns. It might have been that they were a stone's throw away, but it was only a trick of the night; that city sat in a different world, and surely the portal was closed.

At the edge of the rails, the boy stood with only a sack upon his shoulder. Thin drizzle had been falling for more than an hour. There was a string of little lean-tos set back from the rails, and in them there huddled other wearied passengers, waiting for the engines to lumber through. The station keeper had disappeared an hour before, leaving them with the promise that, come sleet or snow, the train would make it through. He had not made mention of wet leaves left lying on the tracks.

The boy moved to the shelter of an overhanging willow, and set his sack on a boulder nestled in its roots. The rain had not properly broken yet, but still he was drenched to the skin, his shirt clinging closely to the contours of his body and illuminating the lattice of scars that he wore at his breast. He produced a small torch from his pack and, twisting it until the light flared, set it in the roots. Then, he began to ferret in the treasures he had stowed away, removing from the bundle a new shirt, freshly laundered, and a jacket, slightly too large, that had seen better days.

Running a hand through his hair, palming his skull as if only now growing familiar to the shape and cut, he started to unbutton the shirt. After fumbling awkwardly with the first two buttons, he paused before tearing the shirt away; he would not need it again. Finally squirming from the sodden arms, he screwed it up and cast it aside. In the torchlight, he waited for the rain to run from his shoulders and then moved to don the new shirt.

He tightened the drawstrings of his sack and hoisted it, again, to his shoulder, before starting to walk. The boots he was wearing were new, and they would take some breaking in; whenever you stepped into something different, it took time to mould your body to its shape.

He saw the lights approaching, the sound of the whistles carried high on the wind. In the little lean-tos, passengers started to scrabble their packs together. The tall boy was content to let them board the train first, and even found something to amuse himself in the way they tore at the opening doors – as if some malign conductor might suddenly turn them away and condemn them to another pitiful hour on the platform. When, at last, he boarded the carriage, an old ticket collector was looking on, eager to take the few crumpled notes he had left in the lining of his pocket. In the end, there was only a single torn note left, the last fragment of a life all but erased. He teased the note between thumb and forefinger so that the conductor's eyes lit up.

'You want help with your packs?'

The tall boy nodded.

'You got to do some good in this world.'

The conductor folded the last note into his own jacket, and bent low to lift the boy's pack. The train's pistons were grinding now and, sluggishly, it started to move.

'Sure is heavy, lad. What the devil have you got in there?'

'Just books,' the boy answered, with a fleeting smile. 'I'm a big reader. Couldn't stand to go anywhere without my books tagging along.'

'Never had much of a head for writing, haven't I.'

'I've known people like it – but I've read everything I could find ever since I was a lad.'

The boy stowed his baggage away and fell, sharply, into a seat beside three old men playing cards. Although they murmured their disgruntlement, they did not ask him to move on.

'City boy . . .' cursed one of the huddle.

The boy's eyes widened at that. He lifted his head to face them, and as he turned he caught sight of himself in the glass, mirrored there against the rushing night. The hair was shorter than he would have liked, but there had been sense in that. He had never worn a beard before, but he had to admit that the thickening stubble suited him. The clothes, of course, were an aberration – but it would not be long before his body had shifted to suit them.

'You got me all wrong,' he began. 'I was country born and bred. I'm only now going to the city. A boy can't stay green for ever.'

'Where you bound, son?'

The boy looked, again, at his reflection in the glass. If he held his head slightly crookedly, it seemed to change completely the features of his face. He experimented with a lower lip pouting, a left eye squinting slightly beside the right. If he held the pose properly, at last it would set; it had happened before.

'London,' he decided. 'I reckon I can make a thing of myself in a place like that.'

The old men might have smirked at that. 'Yeah,' one of them said, dealing another hand of cards. 'You and a thousand others, boy.'

THE END

Acknowledgements

Among too many to thank: everyone at Faber, and especially
Walter Donohue and Helen Francis; Susan Armstrong, Lex
McNicoll, Elliott Hall, Amy Fletcher, and my parents.

Also, many thanks to Simon Kerr at the archives in Leeds,
and to Martin France for his recollections of wartime
West Yorkshire.